THE FRAY THEORY 1
RESONANCE

A NOVEL BY
NELOU KERAMATI

COPYRIGHT

To our collective consciousness.

ACKNOWLEDGEMENTS

With words as my instruments, time and time again I fail to compose a melody worthy of my loved ones.

My incredible mom and dad, I love you more than words could ever express. Thank you for keeping the world big for me. And my lovely friends, Penny and Salma, without your relentless love and support, this novel would've remained an obscure idea at best and a faded memory at worst. I am beyond grateful that the thread of my life crossed paths with yours.

CONTENTS

TITLE PAGE
COPYRIGHT
DEDICATION
ACKNOWLEDGEMENTS
CONTENTS
TITLE
PROLOGUE

0 - THE ANVIL	1
1 - LANGUOR	12
2 - ENCORE	24
3 - THE HARBINGER	34
4 - HAPPENSTANCE	42
5 - THE KINETIC	51
6 - EXHIBITION	59
7 - CALAMITY	66
8 - DOUBT	76
9 - SOLACE	84
10 - GALEN	95
11 - RETROSPECT	109
12 - GRAVE CIRCUMSTANCES	119
13 - PROPHECY	126
14 - REDEMPTION	138
15 - PRELUDE	151
16 - THE FRAY THEORY	163
17 - THE REQUEST	175
18 - RESONANCE	182
19 - QUANDARY	194

20 - Hollow	202
21 - Asunder	209
22 - Leeway	222
23 - Full Circle	228
24 - Entropy	235
25 - Caprice	242
26 - Aftermath	253
27 - Enigma	265
28 - Rendezvous	278
29 - Limbo	291
30 - The Glitch	298
31 - The Cage	306
32 - Inquiry	317
33 - Trigger	322
34 - The Reaper	333

Preview of Book 2 – Amalgam

Letter to Readers

Author Bio

THE FRAY THEORY 1
RESONANCE

"Dreams are devoid of logic. They neither begin, nor end. In dreams, we do not question reality. We bend the laws of physics, and defy gravity. And I know it's hard to believe, but you are not dreaming."

THE ANVIL

NEVE OPENS HER EYES TO A BLEAK SKY. To a canopy of dark clouds with slender silver linings. They are so ripe with rain that their weight is dragging them down through the atmosphere.

The sky is falling.

Neve's focus trickles back down to earth. Down to where she finds herself enveloped by vibrant colors and gleaming lights. It's as though she is the subject of a living painting. But whether this painting is of a miracle or a massacre, she is yet to know.

Her body heat is slowly seeping into the ground.

She tries to rise, but even the smallest movement feels like a huge undertaking. Not only does her body feel heavier than a boulder, she can barely feel her limbs.

Am I dying?

With that thought, her flickering eyelids fall shut, sweeping the world away, and all that remains is a rippling echo: *'I know it's hard to believe, but you are not dreaming,'* she hears in her mind over and over again. She hears it in her own voice, but those are not her words.

And then, a warm gust of wind trounces the mild scent of freshly-cut grass, bringing with it the stench of something synthetic.

Burnt plastic?

When Neve opens her eyes, she detects lights of a police vehicle oscillating between pink and blue on a nearby building. And with a short burst of static, she becomes aware of radio dialogue in the distance.

Voices of strangers are emerging from obscurity, but they're far too dissonant to make sense of. If the occasional gasp is any indication, however, what's happened here was no ordinary incident.

The distant wailing of an ambulance disrupts her thoughts, and with what little energy she can muster, she turns her head towards her salvation.

Instead, her focus closes in on a horribly mangled SUV with its snout completely caved in.

Neve stares at the locus of damage, incapable of making sense of what she sees. It looks like the front of the car is wrapped around an invisible column.

Is she imagining this?

And confusion paves the way for panic.

An accident...

Clicks of doors and hurried footsteps drown out the growl of the idling ambulance. And right on cue, a middle-aged paramedic emerges from behind the decimated vehicle.

At the sight of Neve, his speed begins to dwindle. And then he's simply standing there, suspended in as much disbelief as the spectators behind him.

Snapping out of his stupor, he quickly bridges the gap. But even once he has kneeled by Neve's side, he does not engage her.

As his bewildered gaze soars over her body, Neve tries her best to read him. But the deeper the crease between his brows become, the more terrified she is to ask him what he sees.

Is the damage to her body that catastrophic? Is that why she can barely feel a thing?

Summoning the courage, "how bad?" she manages to ask with a tattered voice.

"You're, um—I don't see any blood," he says as his eyes dart about Neve's frail frame. He keeps blinking as though expecting what's before him to change.

To make sense.

"Do you remember what happened?" he carefully pulls a lock of Neve's black hair from her face.

"N-no," she stammers, welling up.

"Okay, it's okay. We've got you, sweetheart."

The corners of his eyes wrinkle as he attempts a comforting smile, and Neve feels a rush of warmth in her right hand.

He must be holding it.

σ

Paving the way for his team, the paramedic rushes to the driver's side of the disfigured SUV.

He peers in with anticipation of horror. Of blood and broken bones. Of lives lost and those hanging by a thread. But instead, he finds nothing.

No one.

Through the windshield's frame, he looks further up the street to where the driver would have been thrown upon impact. But once again he finds himself at a complete loss.

He returns his focus back to the vehicle, searching the cavities for survivors. But not only does he fail to uncover even the smallest speck of blood, he realizes there are no keys in the ignition.

With a frown tainting his puzzled expression, he backs away from the vehicle and stares at the wreck in its entirety. It's like looking at an empty can of pop that's been crushed against a pole.

The hood is crinkled, and the front bumper and engine have been pushed back into the front seats. But the question is, upon impact with *what*?

The paramedic's eyes are drawn to the unscathed crash victim as she's placed onto the stretcher.

She is rather small, and probably weighs no more than a hundred and twenty pounds. There's no way a girl her size could withstand a collision like this and live to tell the tale.

Things aren't adding up.

"How's she doing?" a police officer approaches.

"Well, she's got no visible injuries," the paramedic licks his lips and glances at his team. "There's always a chance of internal bleeding, though. So we won't know for sure till we get her back to the hospital," he delivers his usual spiel, but given the circumstances at hand, it feels especially contrived.

In truth, he has no idea *what* to think. And time is fast running out if he is to quench his curiosity. "So what exactly happened here?" he looks to the officer who puffs his cheeks as he exhales.

"Honestly, never seen anything like it," he glances over his shoulder at the SUV. "Got a whole bunch of witnesses swearing they saw the car crash into her." He squeezes out a chuckle. "I mean, I keep thinking it's a prank or something..? But the skid marks, and the scraped pavement—" he points out the trail of damage behind the mangled SUV. "I honestly don't know what to tell ya."

"What about the driver?" the paramedic's inquiry falls on deaf ears as the officer marches back into the crowd. Towards a young man in a dark leather jacket weaving through the onlookers.

σ

The lone wolf detects the ensuing threat, and with his Husky blue eyes, sizes up the officer marching up to him: middle-aged, balding, and quite thick around the waist. Judging by his pompous grin and labored swagger, he must have been a pretty big deal some thirty pounds ago. Definitely not the type who'd let you off the hook with a warning.

The young man tucks his blonde locks behind his ears, wincing as a sharp pain shoots through his left shoulder. And with his chin lowered, he takes a whiff of his damp shirt.

"*Shit,*" he curses under his breath.

The smell of alcohol is overwhelming, and it's not something he would be able to explain. At least not without raising more questions.

Should he make a run for it? Is it worth the risk in his condition? Should he even be considering it with his track-record?

Doesn't matter. His small window of opportunity has already come to a close.

"Don't I know you..?" the officer bridges the gap and stands fortified between the young man and his objective.

"You're asking me if *you* know *me*?"

And without warning, the cop's inquisitive squint broadens, brightening his expression.

"You're that kid," he says with a self-satisfied grin, "Romer Anthony. I was the one who processed you a few years back, remember?"

The ambulance is taking off.

"Is there something I can help you with? Or are you just brushing up on your solo good cop/bad cop routine?"

With that remark, the cop's face darkens slightly, but he masks it as though it's second nature. "Fancy running into you here," he grins from ear to ear, his tone loaded with subtext. "You wouldn't happen to know anything about this, would'ja?"

"Nope," Romer crosses his arms. "Just a regular, impartial bystander."

"That right?" the officer takes a half-step forward, standing far too close for comfort. "Then why the hell are you so nervous?"

σ

Inside the racing ambulance, the paramedic ends a phone call with an anxious frown on his face. He glances down at Neve, then turns away and whispers something to the EMT.

There's something unnerving about the secrecy of their exchange, but Neve's mind is too foggy to figure out what it is.

She doesn't feel any pain, but her stiff neck-brace is making it a big challenge to keep her head raised. So she quits eavesdropping and relaxes back down.

Judging by the short glance she took at her body, it doesn't seem like she's suffered any fatal injuries. With luck, maybe the hospital will release her after a quick check up.

Then again, they will most likely insist on keeping her until at least some of her memory returns.

Exhaling a weak sigh, Neve's gaze soars up to the overhead lights. They run the length of the ceiling in pairs, sort of like a row of headlights on a busy street at night.

Oh my God...

Her heart skips a beat as the horrible memory of the incident comes crashing back.

Color drains from her face.

Adrenaline floods her veins.

What is she going to—

"What's your name?" the paramedic's voice snaps her out of her downward spiral. His tone is friendlier than before. Almost alarmingly so.

"I can't remember," Neve lies.

She needs to get out of here ASAP. The ambulance won't be stopping for traffic lights, but it *will* have to slow down to take a turn. And when it does, she just might be able to jump out and make a run for it.

And time is running out.

Neve raises her upper body as high as she can to sneak a better look at the back doors.

Is there some sort of locking mechanism? Can she just burst through?

"Lie down, please," the EMT presses down on her breastbone and forces her onto her back.

Wide-eyed, Neve stares up at him as the twinge of his prodding seeps in deep.

This is *not* how you treat a crash victim. She was right. These men aren't who they seem.

"I don't need to go to the hospital," she says, but neither acknowledges her. "Seriously, I'm okay."

"You're *okay* once the doctor clears you," the EMT says with his back to her. He then holds up a syringe containing a faint blue serum.

Neve's brows furrow. "I don't need that."

"Don't worry. It's just antibiotics," the EMT flicks the tube twice, getting the air bubbles out.

"I said I don't need it."

"Just lie back and relax. You're in good hands," the paramedic smiles, but there's something in his eyes that speaks another truth—a concoction of guilt and fear, which frankly shakes Neve to the core.

Her heart is pounding in her ears. Her breaths are shallower than a film of dust. Her anxiety is flaring, and her entire body is atremble.

"Relax your arm, please," the EMT grabs a hold of Neve's wrist, but she yanks it out of his grasp. "Okay, I'm going to need you to cooperate now," he warns with a steely voice, then makes another attempt.

Neve swats the syringe out of his hand and tries to rise, but the men swiftly pin her back down.

"LET ME GO!" she screams. "ROMER! DYLAN!"

The EMT throws a strap over Neve's floundering frame. The paramedic grabs and clasps it in, securing Neve's midsection.

Oblivious to Neve's pleading, they work their way down her body, applying additional reinforcements until she can't lift a finger.

"Oh no no, please—help—" Neve gasps for air, but the sensation of drowning floods her lungs instead.

No oxygen-mask descends upon her dry lips, and no compassion rains from the men's vacant eyes.

Is this it? Is this how I'm going to die?

She shuts her eyes as the promise of unremitting peace seduces her resolve.

It's too tempting to surrender. To just let go, and sink into the depths of darkness.

'I know it's hard to believe...
But you are not dreaming.'

The EMT grabs the syringe off the floor and rises to his feet. But he drops it not a second later at the sight of Neve's eyes igniting to a ravishing shade of scarlet.

The stretcher starts to squeal, and then collapses under Neve's weight with a blaring bang!

The speeding ambulance starts to sink as though being weighed down by a massive anvil. And when the wheels abandon the deforming axels, it DROPS to the ground, its momentum propelling it onwards.

An ear-splitting screech saturates the atmosphere as the vehicle's base grinds against the asphalt. And the whole world holds its breath until the ambulance lurches to a staggering stop.

In an utter state of shock, the paramedic and EMT surrender their authorities and seek refuge in the far corners of their confinement. They watch as Neve effortlessly liberates herself from her restraints, and ascends like a phoenix rising from the ashes.

With her glowing gaze glued to her assailants, she steps off the deformed stretcher, sinking the vehicle by another few inches.

And then all that lingers in the air, is fear.

"Move."

CHAPTER 1

LANGUOR

~Two Weeks Ago~

The lecture hall is filled to capacity. The air is thick with tension, and the silence is all-consuming. And in the backmost row, Neve slouches in her uncomfortable aisle seat, inspecting her multiple choice sheet for what feels like the hundredth time.

Her weary gaze soars over her colleagues to the front of the hall, where the proctor is slowly pacing the platform.

His piercing glare is beyond incriminating, akin to how a detective would stare at his prime suspect in an interrogation room.

Not that Neve can blame him.

If any student were to ever cheat on any exam, this right here would be it. And at this very moment, morality feels more like a burden than a virtue.

Neve waits for him to turn his back to her section, and then she sneaks a glance at her colleague's exam.

Poor bastard, she thinks at the sight of the messy markings on his exam package. Looks like he's trying to use the process of elimination to weed out all the wrong answers.

She feels for him. She'd probably do the same. But unfortunately, deductive reasoning is of no use when the exam has been formulated by Marcus Holt.

A frazzled breath escapes her. She pulls her hair back behind her ears, and makes one final attempt at giving a rat's ass:

> **24.** *Phantom Limb is an example of:*
> **a.** *sensitization of cutaneous pain endings due to injury*
> **b.** *sensory projection*
> **c.** *referred pain*
> **d.** *psychological hallucination*
> **e.** *pain modulation*

'f. this.' Neve scribbles under 'pain modulation', a triumphant grin tugging at the corner of her lip.

Oh, how she wishes she could just leave it. She might as well. The odds of anyone passing this exam are slim to none, even without antagonizing Holt. At least this way she can revel in her own small victory.

Eager to throw in the towel, Neve looks up at the hideous mass-produced clock above the east exit.

Still 3:53 pm!?

She slides down in her seat. It feels like time itself is stuck in limbo.

She *could* just take off... It's not like if she keeps sitting here, the correct answers are going to leap off the page at her.

But then, if she fails—which she probably will—a part of her will always wonder whether it's because she didn't give this damn test her all.

And it's much easier to blame Holt than to blame herself. So she begrudgingly stays put, and endures another seven or so eternities.

The moment the proctor announces the end of the exam, Neve springs out of her seat and strides down the steps towards the front of the hall.

Tight-lipped, she drops her insipid burden on the desk, avoiding eye-contact with the proctor.

The urge to flip him off is simply too real.

She exhales the tension she's been bottling up and turns to scan the crowd for a string-bean in hipster clothing.

Failing to spot her best friend, Elliot, she makes her way out of the nearest exit onto green university grounds.

The timid Vancouver sun is peeking through the pillowy clouds. Generous stretches of emerald grass carpet the landscape. But prettiest of all would have to be the cherry blossom trees, their plush canopies flush with pastel pinks.

Springtime in Vancouver is absolutely enchanting, especially at the University of British Columbia, or UBC as everyone affectionately calls it. And although the stress of final exams is weighing down on nearly everyone, today's gorgeous weather makes it almost impossible not to smile.

Neve walks over to the nearest bench and takes a seat, the sunbathed panels toasty-warm beneath her thighs. It's such a far cry from the sodden surfaces she's long become accustomed to, so she closes her eyes and pretends to be somewhere else.

Somewhere different.

σ

Like a broken line of ants, Neve's colleagues slowly trickle out of the building. It's beginning to feel like she's been dawdling out here for hours, so she grabs her phone and texts Elliot.

<Dude where are you? Thought we were grabbing soosh…>

A few minutes go by, and nothing. Neve is starting to seriously wonder about what's taking him so long.

She rises from the bench to go back and fetch him, but just then, she receives a text from a number she can't quite place.

<I need to talk to you>

Is it from Elli? Did he lose his phone?

Neve sighs and plops back down on the bench.

<Sorry, who is this?>

Her text is immediately marked as 'read', but no response pops onto her screen.

After a drawn-out minute of waiting, she gives up on the prospect and rises once more. As she throws her purse over her shoulder, she receives another text from the same number.

<It's Dylan>

Neve's blood freezes. Feeling dazed, she stumbles back onto the bench.

'It's Dylan?' She stares into space. 'Hey Neve, how's it going?' 'Oh hey, Dylan, what have you been up to?' 'Oh you know, just locked up in a cell for the last three years, or I would've totally dropped you a line.' 'Oh, ha ha, you're so funny, D. You smart good.'

Neve shoves her phone into her jacket pocket and begins to tap her foot maniacally. She's not going to respond. She owes him nothing.

A few more minutes drag by with no sign of Elliot, so Neve surrenders to her compulsion and pulls up the text again.

This time, it hits her.

It's *Dylan*.

σ

"What!?" Elliot's door flies open from under Neve's pounding fist.

She stares at him deadpan, and then marches into his dorm room and plops down on his couch.

Elliot swings the door shut and walks over to his bed. He collapses onto it, making his comforter puff up around him like a loaf of bread rising in the oven.

His room smells like stale junk food, and there are far too many empty cans of beer lying around. But at least she can hear the peaceful sound of ocean waves through the crack in his window.

Or is it the swoosh of all the cars speeding along the coastal road? It's hard to tell.

"I waited for you," Neve breaks the silence.

With his face still buried, he draws a deep breath and exhales it back into his comforter. "Sorry."

Neve's gaze loses focus as her mind starts to drift off again. "Dylan texted me."

"*Confuse me*!?" Elliot's wide and hostile eyes peek from behind his sheets. "Are you *kidding* me?"

"He wants to talk."

"It's been *three years*!"

"And two months."

"Jesus Christ," Elliot props himself onto his elbow, staring at Neve with equal parts anger and unease.

It's coming: another one of his anti-Dylan tirades.

"I don't even..." Elliot mutters and sits up.

He runs his fingers through his mousy hair, which is in desperate need of a good wash. And his eyes are bloodshot. *And* he seems spindlier than usual.

"Are you okay?" Neve asks. "How'd you do on the final?"

Elliot's posture wilts. "I didn't go."

"Uh... please be kidding."

He shuts his eyes and squares his shoulders.

"Elli—did you actually skip the final?"

"Yessss," he groans.

Neve continues to stare. "Why?"

"Because who cares? That's why."

She turns her head slightly, eyes still glued to him. "Did you at least call in sick, or something?"

Nothing. He doesn't even acknowledge her.

"Elli—it's *Marcus Holt* we're talking about. He's not going to cut you any slack just because you're at the top of his class."

Elliot remains stoic, staring into space as though she's not even there.

Failing to inspire a sense of urgency, Neve rises from the couch and sits down next to him on the bed.

Still nothing.

"Elli," she takes his hand, "I know it's hard. I can't even imagine how hard, but you gotta push through these episodes."

"Neve—" he grimaces, "don't shrink me. Please."

"I'm just trying to help."

"Well, don't," he lies back down, his hand sliding from Neve's gentle grasp. "It is what it is."

Neve bites down on her lower lip. "Look—I know this is probably the last thing you want to hear, but I really think it's time you see a professional."

Elliot frowns. "Were you counting the ceiling tiles in Ethics class?"

"I think I might've been fluffing my pillow."

"Every shrink's first priority is to cover his own ass. They don't give a shit about their patients."

"They're not *all* like that. You just need to find one you click with."

"Thanks, *mom*. Are you going to tell me to wait at least an hour before I go swimming?"

"You know—you can be a real chore sometimes."

"Then why don't you go hang out with your other bestie? *Ohhh*, you can't." He crosses his arms behind his head, challenging Neve with raised brows.

"I would if it didn't cost me a flight to Paris."

"Yeah. I'm sure little 'Miss Croissant' is just dying to hear about your epic adventures in *Neuroscience*."

And for a moment, Neve wonders if Elliot's got a point. That it's naïve of her to cling onto a childhood friendship strained by a five-thousand-mile gap.

"You're still here," Elliot grumbles.

"Elli—" Neve lies down next to him. "It is not easy being friends with someone who has depression. *Not* because it's a burden, but because you *love* them. So their pain becomes your own." She rests her hand on his chest. "You really expect me to just sit by and do nothing?"

"You're the one to talk."

"Anxiety is different."

"No, it's not. Shut up."

"It is," she chuckles, smoothing out the wrinkles in his shirt. "When I have a panic attack, I just want to ride it out without someone suffocating me."

"That whole 'suffocating' thing goes both ways."

"Except my attacks come and go, and last a couple of minutes, tops. Some of your episodes have lasted for *months*. You can't keep brushing this off."

Elliot shuts his eyes and exhales through his nose.

"Look—I can start looking for a psychiatrist—"

"It's all *bullshit*! They all sit there, looking at you like you're damaged. They nod at everything you say, but what they're *really* doing is making mental notes of what *not* to say to you, just in case you decide to go and off yourself."

And suddenly Neve is six years old again, tightly clutching her mother's hand.

The waiting room is well-lit, but its aura is darker than the night itself. The woman sitting behind the front desk is beautiful, yet there is something unnerving behind her glossy smile.

Like a poisoned candy apple.

Elliot stares at the ceiling with vacant eyes.

His defeated expression is practically a portrait of Neve's childhood. She was too young to know how to write, so she would draw. She would awaken from a dream and dive straight for her little notepad.

And just draw.

So that once her dream came true, she'd be able to prove to everyone that she wasn't making it all up.

But instead of being applauded for her initiative, she was chastised. Her enthusiasm was extinguished, time and time again, until she became just another rehabilitated child.

A statistic.

"Elli," she props herself onto her elbow, "It's easy to look at other people and feel like you're alone in this. But just because we all pretend to be fine," she shakes her head, "doesn't mean we are."

Elliot's chest deflates. "I guess."

"Just hang in there while I look into some options for you, okay? And summer's just around the corner! We can go to the night market, bike the seawall—"

"Ugh, activities."

"Alright, *fine*. We can have one of those sarcastic movie review marathons you like so damn much."

Elliot smiles in spite of himself. The first smile she has seen on him in a while. And it's a good one.

"I can't believe Dillweed had the balls to call you."

"Texted."

"You didn't text back, right?"

"No!" Neve says, sounding offended. "Not yet."

"*Yet*? Do we need to go over this again?"

"I just want to hear him out."

"*Why*? Why give him the satisfaction?"

"*What* satisfaction?"

"Even responding is going to come off desperate. Like you've been sitting around, waiting for him to reach out. Which isn't *that* far from the truth..."

"Look—I know, okay?" she lies back down. "I do. But this could be my chance to finally find out what the hell happened."

"Neve. You were a mess."

"I know."

"*No*... I really don't think you do. When we first met I thought you didn't even have a personality."

Chuckling, Neve swats him on the belly with the back of her hand. Not that he's wrong. It's just hard for Neve to remember how it felt... being numb.

"And besides, you got way too much to do before tomorrow," Elliot adds.

"I know. I'm heading to the gallery right now," she says, then faces him. "You *do* know if you skip it, I'm going to kill you, right?"

"Sssss, yeah... I was hoping to get my haircut..?"

"Like—hunt you down, and kill you dead."

Elliot laughs. "So, are you selling at a fixed price? Or doing a silent auction?"

"Auction," Neve sits up and scoots to the edge of the bed. "I figured it's a good way to test the waters... see what people think of my work."

"Make sure you have a Reserve Price."

"What's that?"

"Like a minimum bidding amount?" Elliot's brows soar, creasing his forehead. "The last thing you want is for someone to bid three bucks on a painting you spent five months working on."

Oh God... Mom was right, what am I doing?

"Yeah, no, I will. I *have*." Neve rises from the bed, feeling completely disoriented. "Um—make sure you schedule a make-up exam before it's too late," she throws her purse over her shoulder. "I mean it, Elli. Call them today."

"Go away already," he pushes her toward the door with his foot, but she lingers.

"Are you absolutely sure I can't text him back? It's been three years."

"And two months."

CHAPTER 2

ENCORE

On the green outskirts of the university, Neve enters a quaint little café. The rich aroma of freshly-ground coffee tickles her senses, enveloping her in memories of a not too distant past. It takes her back to when she and Dylan would rendezvous here at all hours of the day, almost every day. Back to when she thought of change as adventure, and not loss.

She looks about the space, taking in the changes.

The espresso brick walls have been painted ivory, and the stainless steel counter has been retrofitted with a thick slab of reclaimed wood.

But they've kept the marble mini-tables and the black metal chairs. So that's something.

With the baristas engaged in idle chit chat, Neve bypasses the semi-obligatory purchase and wanders towards the back of the café. Towards the industrial chandelier that put this place on the map. Back then, she just couldn't understand why Dylan was so crazy about it. To her, it was just a thick, square block of wood with mismatched light bulbs dangling from it.

But today, the mere sight of it makes her want to burst into tears.

Beneath the chandelier, a pair of worn-out leather armchairs bracket an old coffee table. All three look like they've taken quite a beating since her last visit.

She sits down in the armchair facing the fireplace. In the same seat she always took whenever she and Dylan were lucky enough to grab this corner spot.

It was always such a treat. So warm and cozy.

With their books sprawled in front of them, they'd sit here for hours on end, sipping their drinks at a glacial pace while chatting about nothing.

And that was by far the most precious thing this place gave them.

Time.

Neve nestles herself in the cushy comfort of her chair, reminiscing about the obnoxious stories they dreamt up for their fellow caffeine devotees. Dylan would pick someone at random and come up with an elaborate conspiracy theory. And Neve could never resist a forbidden love affair between the unlikeliest pair in the café.

But today, their favorite setting is nothing more than a refuge for the lonesome.

Neve reaches into her purse and pulls out her old diary. The one she reads more often than she cares to admit. The one she has long stopped writing in.

Ever since Dylan disappeared without a trace, her collection of memories slowly morphed into a safe. A secure asylum where she locked away her entangled thoughts and unruly emotions.

It's easy for Elliot to dismiss Dylan's text.

With each passing moment, Neve's decision to not respond is feeling more and more like a tragedy in the making. So with hopes of stumbling upon some hidden wisdom, she runs her nail along the edge of her diary and opens it to a random page:

> *And sometime next week, I will run into you at a café. And I will hate myself for not having bothered with makeup that day. And you will kick yourself for not taking the time to shave, even though you had plenty of time.*
>
> *We will both make and break unintentional eye-contact, trying desperately to conceal our inner thoughts.*
>
> *Mine, of missing you.*
>
> *Yours, of wanting me.*
>
> *You will strike an overzealous conversation with the barista, pretending to not have seen me at all.*

And I'll burn a hole in the chalkboard menu with my concentration, then pretend to text someone who cares about me.

We will each put on an act of just how well we're doing.

Standing feet away, yet miles apart.

And then, we will strategically part ways to avoid confrontation, and once home, sink into the nook of our comfort zones, feeling lonely, rejected, and maybe even heartbroken.

Neve caresses the black ink that's bled deep into the paper. She was so sure of her imminent run-in with Dylan. So certain it would be a matter of days.

She flips to another page further in her diary:

To tell you the truth, I don't want to move on. I don't want time to heal my wounds and wash away my feelings for you into nothing but faded memories. I don't want to become jaded, skeptical of love, and go on to question everything because I now know the pain of loss.

It breaks me to think that I will never see you again. That I'll never have the chance to tell you what I thought the first time I ever saw you: that I've never seen anything greener than your eyes.

The words on the page blur beyond a veil of tears.

They made plans. They were going to backpack through Europe after graduation, slumming it from hostel to hostel on their own dime, as if neither came from a wealthy family. They wanted to venture into the unknown with nothing but a map to guide them.

Instead, Neve is sitting alone in a place which no longer feels like home, wondering how none of it turned out the way she thought.

"Neve," a familiar voice nears.

Neve quickly collects her amassing tears with her sleeve, and then looks up at the silhouette towering before her.

Oh my God...

Her heart drops like a heavy apple snapping off its branch. Darkness frames her field of vision, and her bones befall a deep ache.

Dylan...

He steps into Neve's memory of his face as though walking into a mask.

His features are far more defined than they used to be. His blood-red locks are longer, fuller, and set ablaze by the sun's warm gleam. And his hauntingly beautiful eyes are even greener than she remembers.

What is he doing here? What are the odds?

He sinks into the chair across from her, the fabric of his dark and stylish clothes tugging at his muscles. He's really come into his own these past few years.

"It's—" Neve goes to speak, but her voice is much smaller than she expected it to be.

"I know," he exhales a shaky breath. "*Long* time."

Act normal. Act normal. "How've you been?"

"Good," Dylan nods. "Good, you?"

"Good, yeah."

"Me too," he says in a way that reminds Neve of the night he confessed his love to her. And she knew it was true, because his smile lingered in his eyes.

Like now.

When Dylan sneaks a glance towards the front of the café, their broken eye-contact alerts Neve of the silence between them. It is barely filled with the hiss of the espresso machine breathing warmth into milk.

"So, how have—" Neve clears her throat, realizing she has already asked this question. "What have you been up to?"

"Just got back into town," Dylan says.

Silence.

Off Neve's blank stare, "military school," he adds.

"Oh..." she stammers. "*Here?*"

"West Point. It's in New York."

New York!? You just upped and took off to New York!? "Wow, that's—" *really unlike you.* "Guess your dad finally talked you into it, huh," she squeezes out a chuckle.

Dylan presses his lips together and forces a smile. "Yeah, well—" he drops his head and starts playing with his jacket's zipper, "leave it to him to show love with discipline."

Discipline, Neve wonders? What could Dylan have possibly done that would warrant being shipped off to military school? "Don't they make you shave your head?" Neve asks, her eyes narrowing.

"Not if it's long enough to tie back."

She nods, unsure of how else to react.

"So, how about you?" Dylan asks.

And it hits Neve like a late-night hunger pang: the compulsion to embellish the non-happenings of her mundane life. But it's *Dylan*... It's *them*.

"Same soup, reheated," Neve indicates Vancouver in its entirety. "But at least I'm graduating this term."

"That's great," Dylan nods with raised brows.

"Yeah. I mean—I would've graduated already, but I ended up switching my major twice, so..."

"What are you planning on doing now?" he asks.

And suddenly, it feels cloudy outside.

"Med school, I guess."

"You guess?" Dylan arches a brow.

"Yeah. I mean—*yeah*. That's the plan."

"That's awesome," he says, but it's rather obvious he doesn't really mean it.

"Thanks..." Neve looks down, feeling as though all topics of discussion have already been exhausted.

All but the one they're both tiptoeing around.

"So what exactly—" Neve looks up to find Dylan's attention misplaced.

"Hmm?" he quickly flings his gaze back onto her.

"Everything okay?"

"Mmm hmm. Be right back," he rises and makes his way over to the front counter.

And without warning, a tormented frown weighs down on Neve's brows. A murky concoction of hurt and disappointment is welling up inside. Did he just waltz back into her life like it's nothing?

Like she meant *nothing*?

And she suddenly realizes that this is it: the long-awaited run-in that she, for three years, thought was just around the corner!

Feeling completely out of her element, Neve pulls out her phone and starts to text Elliot: <Call in 3 min with fake emergency! Code red! Redhead ex alert!>

She sends the text and looks up just as Dylan rests two large mugs on the table.

"Here you go," he gently slides the latte with the prettier leaf art towards Neve, and then retakes his seat across from her.

Though this gesture is probably meant to remind her of what the two of them once shared, Neve can't help but think of it as an apology. An inconsequential apology for the *nightmare* he put her through.

Dylan licks his lips and lowers his head. "You're still mad at me, aren't you?"

Mad? Neve's heartstrings tighten enough to snap.

"I'm sorry—" she slips her diary into her purse. "I have to go,"

"Neve, come on."

"Look—Dylan, it was great seeing you and all. I mean, at least now I know you're not *dead*. But this whole pretending like everything's fine?" she shakes her head as she rises from her seat, and then heads straight for the front door.

Don't cry. Don't you dare be that girl.

Dylan springs out of his seat and falls on her trail. "You have *every* right to hate me..." he follows Neve out of the café. "Just give me a chance to explain."

"No need," Neve says in full stride away from him, "got your message loud and clear."

"I'm so sorry if I hurt you."

And Neve suddenly finds herself pinned in place.

"*If?*" she turns to him, her strangled voice barely escaping her aching throat. "*If* you hurt me?"

Dylan drops his head and slides his hands into his pockets.

"You just *left*! You could have been lying dead in a ditch somewhere, for all I knew," she leans back onto the balls of her feet, and yet can't seem to rip herself away. "*God*—I had to hear from your *classmates* that you'd moved away! Not *moving* away, *moved* away! They all just stared at me like I was some psycho ex, showing up at your class, looking for you!"

Dylan parts his lips to speak, but at the sight of something in the distance, his face goes slack.

Thrown off by his sudden shift in demeanor, Neve glances over her shoulder, but there's nothing worth noticing as far as she can tell.

Just a dilute crowd of haggard students.

"I'm sorry," Dylan says as he makes his way past her. "I have to go."

"What—" Neve practically whispers, the shock of his departure shielding her from fully registering her reality—from accepting that he is in fact abandoning her for the second time.

So she stands there as Dylan becomes smaller and smaller, until she can no longer tell him apart from the crowd. And despite the pain brewing inside, she stands her ground and fights gravity's resolve to bring her to her knees.

CHAPTER 3

THE HARBINGER

One tormented step at a time, the space between Dylan and Neve stretches. And although he can practically feel her pain he can't rip his gaze from his target up ahead—from a gentleman in a gray suit and charcoal fedora, carrying a dark, vintage briefcase.

It's him... Dylan's pace accelerates. *Has to be.* And then he finds himself running with little regard to his surroundings. The students he zooms past blur into swatches of color, but his focus never wavers. At full speed, he segues off the sidewalk and cuts through traffic with an absurd level of confidence, ignoring the upheaval of loud honks and angry shouts from drivers.

With his eyes glued to his target, Dylan dashes up the green landscape towards UBC's pharmaceutical building: a modern monstrosity composed of darkly-tinted glass cubes.

But his chase comes to a staggering stop when he notices a security guard manning the entrance.

The man in gray swipes his key-card, exchanges a terse nod with the guard, and makes his way into the building.

Dylan retracts a bit, clenching his jaw. Even if his student ID hadn't expired, it's still highly unlikely it would grant him access into this particular building.

With his window of opportunity fast coming to a close, he retrieves his phone from his back pocket and pulls up his Contact List.

And he finds himself hesitating. It *has* been three years of nearly zero communication between them.

But what if this is a sign? What better excuse than a spontaneous run-in for Dylan to reach out?

Just do it, he banishes his doubts and dials 'Alex'.

He slaps the phone to his ear and flings his focus back onto the man in gray.

Through tinted windows, Dylan watches him stop, pass his briefcase to his left hand, and pull out his phone from his jacket's pocket.

A wave of optimism brightens Dylan's expression. But his smile melts off his lips when Alex puts his phone back into his pocket and resumes his walk.

One... two... three... Alex's steps down the stairs synchronize with Dylan's heartbeat until he vanishes from sight entirely.

σ

Dylan enters his apartment like a soldier returning home from battle. He applies the door's bolt-locks, takes a step back, and then slams his palm against the cold, hard steel. The door quivers in its frame, its wavering groan awakening the stale air.

Chasing after Alex was stupid. Today wasn't about him. It was about making things right with Neve, and now he might never get another opportunity.

Feeling lightheaded from his jetlag, he walks wide of his luggage crowding the entry and makes his way into the living space. Standing there, he finds himself taking in the subtleties he was forced to entrust to memory. Like the oaky smell of his furniture. Or the muffled noise of street traffic from down below. And especially, how shadows dance along the hardwood as the night chases the sun across the sky.

With a somber smile, he extends his hand into a golden sheet of sunlight, soaking up the remnants of the day.

Warmth: the most comforting of all comforts. And all too soon, it's gone.

Dylan withdraws from the living space and heads towards his bedroom. And although the last thing he wants to do is sleep, he's nearly passing out.

He takes off his jacket and throws it onto his bed, but its weight drags it down onto the floor.

Swooping down to pick it up, he detects a subtle pattern at the foot of the bed. He crouches down for a better look and realizes he's looking at shoeprints stamped onto an otherwise undisturbed film of dust.

And they seem fresh.

Dylan's eyes dart about his room. Nothing seems tossed or missing, at least as far as he can tell. Could these prints belong to his father? That would make sense. Someone would have had to check up on the place in Dylan's absence.

So why can't he shake the eerie vibe crawling up his back?

And his heart drops the instant he realizes what's wrong with this picture: the prints are in an isolated cluster. No trail leads to, *or* stems from them.

Thoroughly alarmed at this point, Dylan pulls his switchblade from his ankle sheath, and rises.

It's going to be fine. He has trained for this sort of thing. All he has to do is keep his fear at bay—make sure it doesn't compromise his judgment.

Wielding his blade, he makes his way through the apartment, inspecting it for disturbances that could lead him to the intruder.

His search quickly yields more shoeprints in the ensuite bathroom, pantry, laundry, and the kitchen. In fact, there is a cluster of prints in practically every isolated section of his home.

By the time Dylan returns to the living space, he's more or less confident the intruder has already left.

After scanning his vicinity once more, he drops down onto his white couch, sending a flurry of dust motes into a stray shaft of light.

And then all he can think about is *her*, and how she'd be diving for her camera to capture this golden ribbon draping across the room.

With the thought of Neve, his place is set ablaze with vivid color. And then she is everywhere, like a tuxedo kitten curled up in every corner of his heart. Leaning against the windowsill, snapping a photo of a raspberry sunset. Down on all fours with her hair up in a messy bun, wiping the red wine she spilled tripping over nothing. Lying on the couch across him with tears in her eyes, begging him to stop making her laugh so she can get a few minutes of shuteye.

And a deep ache in his chest rips through the rosy veil, and he is back in the gray prison of his doubts.

It frightens him to think that the memories he has of her, may be all he ever will...

♃

The darkness is all-encompassing, and Dylan has no idea where he is. If the breeze tugging at his clothes and the mild scent of pine trees are any indication, however, he is somewhere outside, facing the northern mountains.

From far below, he can hear the splashing of waves onto rocks. And just then, he becomes aware of the rough, metallic texture beneath his bare feet.

A weak source of light beckons his attention from behind. He looks over his shoulder to find the glimmering towers of downtown wedged between the dark soil and the mulberry sky.

In light of his vantage point, he realizes there is only one place he could be standing: up on the southern apex of Lions Gate Bridge.

With this revelation, the teal titan reveals itself beneath him.

But something feels off.

The bridge seems weathered. And the white lights that make it resemble a wide 'M' from far in the distance are snuffed.

With no cars driving on the bridge deck, it feels like looking down at a desolate future.

A swatch of black grabs Dylan's attention, and he looks up to find a young man mirroring him on the northern apex of the bridge.

He is ghostly-pale, and cloaked in a black trench-coat. His dark, shoulder-length hair is swaying in the wind, and although his mouth is concealed beneath the flap of his collar, his tiger-wild eyes are fashioning a sinister smile.

Despite his calm exterior, his presence feels menacing.

Lethal.

Dylan's heart starts to pound madly inside his ribcage, like a wild animal trying to break free. He can feel the drumming in his temple, fingertips, even the balls of his feet.

Because he knows this man.

And he knows exactly what comes next.

"HELP!" Dylan shouts, but little more than a gasp escapes him. He tries to move, but fear has pinned him in place.

A roaring rumble beckons his gaze up to the clouds. There is a distant crackling sound, and then he's being showered with glistening chunks of hail.

The soft patter becomes progressively more aggressive until it starts to puncture his flesh. And there is nothing he can do but to stand still and tolerate the pain.

And so he does, until riddled with icy bullets and drenched in blood, his legs give way, and he plummets down towards an endless abyss.

Dylan kicks awake on his couch, shaking from the bone-splitting pain that followed him back to reality.

Though his flesh isn't ruptured, he can't seem to rid himself of the sense-memory of bullets lodged in his skin. So he recoils in utter misery, waiting for the pain to subside... to knock him out... to kill him.

He'd settle for anything at this point.

'All pain is a state of mind.'

With his switchblade firmly gripped, he struggles to his feet, straightens his back, and tries to will the pain into submission.

But all too soon, a distant crackling sound sets his teeth on edge, and he turns towards the window and stares with contempt as hail showers from the coral sky.

The icy specks sparkle in the sun's golden gleam, taunting him with their timely arrival.

Through the arrhythmic melody of the downpour, Dylan detects a creaking sound. And not a moment later he has spun around, his arm extended along the trajectory of his aim.

Across him, on the opposite end of the apartment, his blade is lodged between the eyes of the portrait Neve painted of him over three years ago.

He approaches with caution, and directly beneath the painting, discovers a small cluster of shoeprints identical to the ones he found earlier—exactly where his portrait's feet would be, if it had a body.

And Dylan doesn't know whether he missed these prints the first time around, or whether the intruder he'd thought was long gone is still in the apartment.

Skeptical of his own shadow, he slowly reaches up and yanks his blade from his portrait.

He turns his back to the wall.

And waits...

CHAPTER 4

HAPPENSTANCE

It's been roughly an hour since Dylan left her behind. An hour consisting of an absentminded drive, followed by sitting in her parked car and reliving the encounter in her head. Though she feels like she's got every right to be furious, she can't seem to quite get there.

It *has* been years, and Dylan may very well have changed. But the boy she used to know did not have a single strand of selfishness in him.

So why would he take off like that? Did he just not want to deal with her? Did she push him away?

Neve exhales a frustrated sigh and gets out of her car. Still weighed down by melancholy, she feeds the meter, and then walks to the intersection.

Beyond the threshold lies Gastown: Vancouver's historic district, and one of Neve's favorite places to pass the time. Quirky cafés, avant-garde galleries, and souvenir shops enliven rows of brick and mortar buildings, and the sinewy trees that run along the cobblestone road are adorned in champagne lights, year-round.

Gastown's magic stems from authenticity. History. And not once has it failed to ground Neve in an ever-changing world dominated by steel and glass.

As the pedestrian light is illuminated, Neve steps off the pavement and ventures into the heart of the district.

The coral sky is slowly yielding to cooler hues, so she waits with great anticipation for the moment the street's Victorian lamps ignite.

Instead, something tiny bounces off her shoulder.

She tries to see what it was and where it landed, but her curiosity is quenched as hail starts to shower from the sky.

Awe and laughter saturate the air as people seek refuge under awnings. Grinning Patio-dwellers cover their meals with whatever's within reach, and little children cup their paws as the tiny chunks of ice patter kisses on their chubby cheeks.

And then, as though orchestrated by magic itself, the rows of street lamps are kindled, making it seem like glistening diamonds are pouring from the sky.

The world somehow feels much bigger than it did a minute ago.

What a lovely intermission to life.

Arriving at her destination, Neve sneaks a glance into the dimly-lit gallery. Squinting, she brackets her eyes with her hands in order to block out the glare from street lamps and headlights.

WHAT!?

Bolting towards the entry, she winds up slipping on a chunk of ice. She grabs the door handle just in time, and dangles from it like a banana peel.

Sexy.

She pulls herself up and escapes into the gallery.

Oh, no no no, her eyes feverishly scan the vicinity. The place looks like a hurricane aftermath. Tools and supplies are splayed haphazardly, and there's a thick layer of sawdust on everything.

A loud CLINK from the back space startles her. It sounded like someone just dropped a tool.

Ready to unleash hell, Neve marches towards the source of the noise, ducks under a hanging sheet of semi-transparent plastic, and enters the significantly dimmer staging area.

There is a young man up on the ladder before her, wearing a white tank-top and washed-out jeans. And he's about to hammer a nail into a wooden beam.

Neve looks to the light switch on the wall next to her, shakes her head microscopically, and flicks it on.

A 400-watt bulb turns on an inch from the young carpenter's head. Startled by it, he loses his footing and falls off the ladder onto his back.

"Oh my God!" Neve dives to his aid. "I'm so sorry! Are you okay!?"

Groaning, "the hell's your problem!?" he rolls onto his side and starts rubbing his back.

"I am so, *so* sorry! Your head was blocking it," she indicates the light bulb.

"Oh—so it's *my* fault now?" he blows his hair off his face and struggles to his feet.

"Yes. Yes it is," she jokes to lighten the mood, but instead of taking the bait, the young man walks back out into the main space.

Okay. I deserved that.

Neve follows him out of the staging area, bracing herself to grovel. But it's proving harder and harder as time drags on, especially with his back to her.

Waiting for a window of opportunity, she watches him comb through his wavy hair with his fingers, his honey roots contrasting the platinum locks they fade into. With his bare forearm, he wipes the sweat from his temple, and then starts to brush off the sawdust clinging to the back of his jeans.

He finally turns to face her, and the moment their eyes meet, she's thirteen again. His eyes are like the clear blues of the Maldives, and as deep as Mariana Trench.

He's the kind of guy who walks into a room, and everyone takes notice. The kind who has a never-ending string of girls pining after him.

But much to her surprise, he is reciprocating her shameless stare. She can't quite tell what's behind it, but it doesn't feel flirtatious. If anything, it's making her a bit nervous.

"So, how much longer do you think it'll be?"

He continues to stare as if he didn't even hear her question.

"A rough estimate would be fine," Neve nudges.

"What's your name?" he squints.

"Oh—" she extends her hand. "I'm Neve."

And a faint, knowing smile softens his expression. But instead of taking Neve's hand, he pulls an elastic band from his wrist, and starts to tie his hair back into a half-pony.

Neve retracts her hand as he walks away from her again. She'd be offended, but with his hair no longer framing his face, he's starting to look really familiar.

"I'm sorry, do I know you?" she asks.

"You seriously need to expand your vocabulary," he drags a block of timber onto the table, and slides it to the middle.

Neve's eyes dart to the corner of the room as she tries to figure out what the hell he's talking about.

"*Or* you could stop apologizing every five seconds. Both'll do."

Or I could switch to bitch-mode and start raining sass on your ass.

She crosses her arms. "What happened to the guy that was taking off the shelves a few days ago?"

"Filling in for him," he measures the timber and makes a small mark with his pencil.

Neve looks about, trying to gauge the progress.

It looks like the previous exhibition has been fully taken down, so that's good. But none of the dozens of easels she needs for her paintings seem to have been assembled yet.

"Um—how much longer is it going to be, again?"

"Couldn't tell ya."

"Cause I'm opening tomorrow evening and—"

"Yeah, not going to happen," he laughs.

Neve's heart drops. "Why not?"

"Time. Plain and simple."

Neve gawks at the block of wood he's measuring. Is *that* what the easels are to be made of!? "No. *No.* I gave you guys a *week.* I even paid extra to make sure everything would be done on time."

"Listen, Bev—"

"Neve."

"Whatever," he throws his pencil down. "I've been working fourteen-hour days for the past five weeks, and if I didn't need the money, there's no way in hell I'd be standing here, taking crap from *you.* So kindly hop off my ass, and let me do my job, okay?"

He turns his attention back to the timber.

Neve's eyes narrow. There's just something about his mini-tantrum that makes her certain she knows him from somewhere.

"Do you have a brother by any chance?" she asks. "Named Romer?"

He sighs dispassionately. "You're looking at him."

Neve's brows shoot up.

Although his hair is considerably longer than she remembers, it's how much older he now looks that made him so difficult to recognize. Compared to the obnoxious boy she remembers, he seems so... *worn.*

"What?" he looks at her sideways.

"God—you just look so... *different,*" Neve indicates his hair. "Do you remember me? I'm Dylan's—um..." *Dylan's what? Ex-girlfriend? Abandonee?* "We've met a bunch of times, actually. Really brief, though."

Romer stares at her with as much emotion as you would register on a wall.

"Okay, how about that Halloween party four years ago? I was the white jellyfish with LED lights in my umbrella..? You said I should've won first prize..?"

"Wow. Way to cling onto a compliment four years after the fact," he bends down to grab his saw from under the table.

It takes a moment for Neve to register the blow. "I'm not clinging to anything."

"*Ohokay,*" he mocks.

"I'm just reminding you of what *you* said. It's kind of how memory works."

"Actually, memory is selective."

"What are you even saying?" she grimaces.

Visibly fed up, he rests the saw down on the table and starts to rub his temples. "You want me to finish in time, or not?"

"Okay, I'm sorry—do you have a problem with me or something?"

"Course not. I'm a masochist," he rubs his back.

48

"I turned the light on to *help* you," she says as he resumes his work. "Who hammers in the dark?"

"Someone who needs to hammer a nail two inches below the bulb, sugar."

Oh.

"Look, I'm sorry. I've already apologized multiple times, as you so graciously pointed out. Can you at least not be a prick about it?"

Romer says nothing. He doesn't even look up.

Feeling exposed and vulnerable, Neve wraps her cardigan around her frame.

This is really bad. Things are already way behind schedule without him dragging his feet.

If she wants out of this mess, she's going to have to swallow her pride. "Is there anything I can do to help things along? I can grab you a cup of coffee."

Romer looks up at her with crinkled brows, and yet there's a ghost of a smile on his lips.

He seems... *offended*?

"What, are you allergic to coffee, or something?"

"You think I don't know he put you up to this?" He holds Neve's gaze for a moment, and then turns his attention back to the task at hand.

His wide eyes are unblinking as he saws through the timber, and his strokes become more and more aggressive until the end-piece falls to the floor.

"Okay, *what* are you talking about?" Neve asks.

"Look—just... don't," he frowns. "I know you guys had a thing, but don't sink to his level."

With that, a wave of relief washes over Neve, and she suspects that Romer's abrasiveness may actually have nothing to do with her.

She makes her way around the table and stands in front of him, but once again, he does not look up.

"Were you at UBC today?" she asks.

"Nope."

"Yeah you were," she nods. "That's why he left."

"How about we *don't* play the pronoun game?"

Neve puts her hands on her hips. "Dylan."

Romer's pencil hovers over the timber as though he's forgotten what he was just about to do.

"He was at UBC?" he asks. "Today?"

"Yeah..?"

After a short lull, Romer licks his lips and goes to resume his work. But he seems to have lost his place entirely, so he slides his ruler back and measures the timber again.

Neve turns her head slightly with her gaze glued to him. But before she can ask what the big deal is, he drops his pencil down and leans onto the edge of the table.

"When was this?"

CHAPTER 5

THE KINETIC

Romer enters his workshop and shuts the door behind him. Without bothering with the lights, he grabs a padlock off a rusty nail and secures the entry. The smell of burnt walnut reminds him of a commission, but in light of his amassing fatigue, he couldn't care less.

It's way past midnight, and he's exhausted. But at least the exhibition setup is done.

One less thing to worry about.

Making his way towards the back of the shop, he looks out the murky windows. And for what feels like the thousandth time, he marvels at the stunning panorama stretching beyond.

To anybody else, it's just an industrial harbor—a blue inlet adorned with gigantic cranes and colorful cargo containers.

But to him, it's much more than that.

There is just something about the soft breeze and the careless ruckus of seagulls that gets him every time. It's a quality he can't quite put into words, but in simplest terms... it's freedom.

He arrives at the far end of the shop and begins to strip down to his boxers. He throws his clothes onto a pile already burdening a flimsy chair, and collapses onto his dingy mattress.

The stiff, squeaky springs push up against him like iron fists. He yanks his leaf-thin pillow from under his head and flings it away, then rolls onto his side and nestles his head into his folded arm.

Despite promising himself to kick the habit, his fingers seek the scars on his torso. Scars which have long healed. Faded into tight, silver engravings. Scars that should no longer hurt, but ache whenever he is reminded of what they represent. Scars that pulsate every time his veins flood with rage.

A loud screech makes him jump out of his skin.

He grabs the flashlight by his mattress and shines it towards the source of the noise. His wide eyes stare with sheer terror as the indented blade of his table-saw gains momentum into a blurred disk.

At the onset of another power-tool, he leaps out of bed and bolts towards the front of the workshop. He flicks on the overhead lights and turns to find the sandblaster, drill, and other power machinery follow the initiative of the table-saw.

A choked sound escapes his throat.

Let me go.

σ

~Three Years Ago~

A patchy field of green fortified with walls, weapons, and prying eyes. A cage reeking of bitterness, regret, and resentment. This will be home for the next one thousand and ninety-five days: a place where threats are locked in, instead of out.

Hiding in plain sight, Romer sits on a bench in the prison yard, watching the flow of orange specs in the distance. Black, white, yellow and brown: all reduced to the color of hazard.

"Hey fish!" a coarse voice snaps him to attention, and he swings his head towards a forty-something year-old felon boasting more ink than the first draft of a manuscript.

Isaac: the only convict amongst them with a triple life-sentence. The only man within the establishment who has pled guilty to all counts of murder. A killer so proud of his own brutality that he has a string of skull tattoos running down the length of his spine.

And Romer can't help wondering whether in due time, he too shall be reduced to ink on Isaac's flesh.

"Heard you turned down my offer," Isaac lingers a few feet shy of Romer, brandishing a sly grin. "Guess you ain't got a taste of how dangerous things can get around here."

"I don't need protection," Romer says. A flagrant lie, but what Isaac is offering comes at a price he is not willing to pay.

Isaac takes another step forward, his playfulness dimmed down considerably. He leans in and puts his hand on Romer's shoulder like a father giving his son a pep talk. "Listen, kid—you obviously got some shit luck getting tossed in here with the real thugs. So it's a good thing you're pretty enough to secure yourself a spot in my corner," he licks his lips, "you feel me?"

Before Romer can come up with a safe response, Isaac takes a lock of his hair and leans in to smell it. Cringing, Romer slips away, sliding to the opposite end of the bench.

"You gonna make me work for it?"

"I said I'm not interested," Romer asserts slightly louder, desperately hoping Isaac can't hear the fear in his voice.

"Do I look like I give a shit?" he crosses his arms as his crew closes in.

Romer's gaze darts up to the watch towers, but the blinding glare from the overcast sky is making it impossible to find peace of mind.

"It ain't like me to give second chances," Isaac starts, "but you look like a smart kid. You're *not*, but you look like one."

The men burst into a roaring laughter.

"So, what do you say?"

The darkness framing Romer's vision is closing in. Is he about to faint? He can't. They prey on the weak.

"TODAY!" Isaac startles him, and then his laughter weaves into the uproar.

Beyond the hollering fence of felons, Romer takes notice of a C.O. in the near distance and leaps off the bench towards him. But a few steps in, Isaac's small army drapes off his only glimmer of hope. And when he feels a firm grip on his shoulder, he swings back, unwittingly elbowing Isaac in the face.

The thunderous roar of the crowd wanes into awe and anticipation. But instead of unleashing hell Isaac grins from ear to ear, flashing his blood-glazed teeth. "I misjudged you," he wipes his mouth on his sleeve. "You got more balls than half of *these* fuckers."

Romer stares, having no clue whether his blunder has made things better for him, or worse.

"Now, get outta here," Isaac dismisses Romer like a toy he's done playing with. "AIGHT! SHOW'S OVER! Get back to your nine to fives!"

Romer slowly backs out of his cage, adamant not to re-label himself as prey. He almost can't believe it. With Isaac on his side, he just might be able to—

The thought flees from his head as multiple hands grab him from behind, and throw him to the ground.

He reaches up to his aching head, but Isaac's crew grab his limbs and firmly pin him down. He looks up just as Isaac leaps onto him like a wild cat, and he instantly knows his seconds are numbered.

"HELP—" Romer begins to shout, but Isaac's hook against his jaw knocks his consciousness elsewhere.

'*Bludgeoned to death*', Romer hears the voice of a news reporter in his head. He braces himself, but no second swing comes his way. Instead his focus closes in on a small, rusty blade in Isaac's hand—a weapon made from scraps gathered from the crevices of the establishment.

"Help—" Romer's second outcry is barely louder than a thought. And not a moment later, his ears are ringing from a scream he doesn't initially recognize as his own.

Isaac twists the blade he plunged into his victim's shoulder, savoring his anguish. He yanks it out like a savage, and marvels at Romer's blood gushing from the slit in his flesh.

At the sight of the spectacle, the convicts explode into a roaring cheer, and all Romer can see are their silhouettes against the silver sky. *I don't deserve this.* He chokes on the pain as Isaac stabs him in the ribs. *Not this.*

Another stab in the gut, and Romer's cries weave into the uproar. Liquid warmth creeps up inside his chest, and overflows from the corner of his mouth.

"Slice his throat!" someone screams.

"No, cut out his heart!" shouts another.

Isaac's grin keeps shifting in and out of focus. He leans in and dangles his blade over Romer's eyes.

"How about I add a little red to your baby blues?"

Pain. Just dirty, debilitating pain.

A drop of blood drips from the tip of Isaac's blade. It splats onto Romer's cheek, flooding his mind with images of his mutilated face.

Terrifying, dying without a face.

And suddenly, the clamor starts to sound distant, and Isaac's speech becomes slurred as if he's saying multiple things at once. And then, all Romer can hear is his own voice, filling the void in his mind.

Help.

With the prospect of his imminent end, Romer's pupils constrict to a pin-prick. The gold flecks in his eyes flicker and his blue irises radiate a silver glow. Suddenly, an invisible force rips Isaac's weapon from his grasp and flings it up towards his head.

The rusty blade punctures his throat and vanishes into his skull, leaving nothing but a slit from which blood fountains all over Romer.

Did I do this? *How*?

Choking on his own blood, Romer stares at Isaac's convulsing body as it rains crimson, drenching him. It runs down Romer's face and pools in his ears, but he can still detect the muffled shouts of the C.O.s flooding the grounds.

As Isaac's listless body topples over, his startled crew release Romer and begin to disperse.

Drowning in warm crimson, Romer shudders next to Isaac's corpse.

His mind wants to shut down. To stop feeling this excruciating anguish. But he clings onto every breath and fights the darkness closing in, by counting the precious seconds ticking by.

σ

Stop... Romer pleads with whatever God there is, but the shop's machinery continue to groan, growl, and shriek, demanding to be heard.

Demanding that Romer remembers, always, who he is, and what he's done.

"Stop," he demands, but his voice is barely audible over the cacophony. "I said stop," he asserts louder, "Stop! STOOOOP!"

BLACKOUT.

Romer stares into darkness as the noise from the machinery tapers off. But even after silence has once again befallen his dwelling, chaos continues to wreak havoc inside him. Because it doesn't matter whether he accepts or denies his circumstances.

He'd have to be mad to do either.

CHAPTER 6

EXHIBITION

Twilight. Cool hues of navy and blue drape over the city, complimenting the warmth of nightlife. And nowhere in Vancouver is livelier than Gastown when the day paves the way for its darker side.

At the heart of the neighborhood, a bright gallery lures the curious with the promise of novelty. And inside, friends and strangers alike weave through one another like colorful fish in an aquarium.

Suffocating in her scarlet dress, Neve navigates through the crowd with a tray in her hand. A smile, a wider smile, a '*heeeeey*, thanks for coming!' and she crosses the threshold into the dingy staging area.

She plops onto a wooden crate, cursing the entire family tree of whoever invented high heels. But then again, she should've known better than to wear five inch stilettos on a night like this.

Stretching out her legs, she pulls her phone from her waist-belt, and scrolls through a string of texts from people who won't be able to make it.

No big deal. The place is already packed. But what she can't get over is that—despite being shamelessly late—Elliot hasn't even bothered to reach out.

With her lips tightly pressed together, she shakes her head and dials him. It's one thing to leave her hanging when she needed a fake emergency call at the café... but missing the event she's been beaming about for *months*?

Voicemail.

"Elli! You better be stuck in traffic, you jackass. You were supposed to be here *two hours ago*. I had to serve everything without crackers."

Leaning over to sneak a peek at the refreshments table, her gaze lands onto Romer, looking deliciously dashing with his hair slicked back, donning a black leather jacket and a powder-blue shirt.

Neve watches him scan the dwindling selection of edibles, shrug, and then pop a cube of cheese into his mouth. And it isn't till someone blocks him from her view that Neve remembers still being on the phone.

"Elli—I know this is the last thing you want to do right now. I get it. But it's just me, and I really *really* need you. So just come, okay?"

Her hopes of Elliot actually showing up perish the instant she ends the call. But maybe it's for the best. He'd probably be miserable, anyway.

She glances in Romer's direction, then with an act of sheer will, rises back onto her throbbing feet. She runs her fingers through her wavy hair, takes a deep breath, and then ventures back into the main space.

Where'd he go? She scans the gallery, but Romer is nowhere to be seen.

Eager to stage a run-in before it's too late, Neve heads straight for the entrance. But with her focus misplaced, she winds up bumping into someone. A very strong and sturdy someone who ends up saving her from a humiliating tumble.

"Whoa—you alright?" he asks.

"Oh God—I'm so sorry about that," Neve forces a laugh to mask her embarrassment. "Thank you."

"Not a problem," he dashes a charming smile.

She takes him in: early thirties, build of a rugby-player, crew haircut, and thick, expressive brows. In his slick bomber, white shirt, and dark jeans, he is the 'everybody's type' kind of handsome.

"Are you a friend of Elliot's?" Neve asks to fill the silence, and immediately imagines him responding with: '*Yeah, I use him as a toothbrush*'.

"No, I was just walking by and noticed the line up. Thought I'd check it out," he shrugs and looks about the gallery. "Are these all yours?" he spins his index finger in the air.

Neve's face lights up. "They sure are."

He nods impressively. "Well done."

"Thanks," her smile broadens as she pulls her hair behind her ear. "I'm Neve, by the way," she extends her hand for a shake.

He reaches out and takes Neve's hand, but his face suddenly goes blank. "I'm—" his pauses, staring at Neve as though he's trying to remember something important. "Victor," he says. "Victor Young."

His grip is too firm all of a sudden, and what little emotion is registered on his face feels... *hostile*?

"It's very nice to meet you, Victor," Neve smiles, trying to conceal her unease over his sudden shift in demeanor. "Well, I'm going to make a round—" she indicates the gallery, then looks down at her hand.

Realizing he's still firmly gripping it, he lets go.

"Right," he nods, and then wanders back into the heart of the gallery.

Neve's brows knit, having no idea what to think. He seemed so personable at first. What happened?

"Macking on the commoners, I see," Romer's voice by her ear snaps her to attention.

He's still here... Neve feels a fluttering in her chest. "Done gorging on cheese, I see," she crosses her arms and turns to face him.

"Been watching me, have you?" he sips from his plastic cup and leans against the column.

His playfulness feels so out of character. This is, after all, the same guy who just yesterday made Neve feel as sexy as a dustpan.

"Yeah, well—it's on me to make sure everything runs smoothly."

"Oh *please*... I saw you eyeing me from your little hideout in the back."

What! *When*? *Shit*!

"Well—it's not my fault you stick out like a sore thumb. A powder-blue shirt? I mean, we get it, you have blue eyes."

She waits for him to retort with a witty comeback. But instead, he just looks at her, taking in the details of her face—like the freckle on the rim of her upper lip. "And I wasn't *macking*. I was introducing myself."

"Mmm hmm. And I'm sure 'bumping into him' was totally unintentional," Romer takes another sip from his drink with a lingering smirk on his lips.

Is he flirting with her? Was his hostility yesterday just an isolated incident?

"Don't tell me you're jealous," she counters.

With a gulp of his drink still in his mouth, his lips form into an even tighter smirk. He shakes his head and swallows. "Jealousy's not my color."

Blue, Neve thinks, and realizes she's staring again. "So, um—thank you. The setup looks amazing."

Romer looks down and swirls the drink in his cup. "Is Dylan coming tonight?"

His question jars her. "I don't, um—" she tries to play it cool. "No, I don't think so."

"Busy?"

"I didn't invite him," she looks away, scanning the crowd for a boy she knows she will not find.

"How come?"

And Neve finds herself tongue-tied. She can't tell whether Romer is trying to put her on the spot, or if he actually doesn't know.

"You're mad at him," he squints, then nods with a knowing smile. "It's all over your face."

Neve scoffs, tongue in cheek. "What about you?"

"What *about* me?"

"Why don't you just call him if you want to see him so bad?"

"Who says I want to see him?"

"It's all over your face."

His smile broadens. He goes to say something, but instead just glides his tongue over his lower teeth.

Gotcha. Neve flicks up her brows.

"So..?" she coaxes, but Romer just shrugs it off and averts his gaze. "What?"

"It's a long story," he shakes his head and downs the remainder of his drink. "Thanks for the brew," he crushes his cup and starts looking around at knee-level. He spots the bin next to the refreshments table and makes his way over.

"Are you taking off?" Neve follows.

"Been a long day," he throws the cup into the bin.

"Why don't you just call him?" she asks.

"I don't have his new number."

"It's the same number," Neve says, knowing damn well his excuse is bullshit.

"I got an early day tomorrow," he tries to squeeze past her. "Good luck with everything."

"Okay, hang on—" she rests her hand on his arm, and to her surprise, he actually stops—like he wants to be talked into talking.

"I just..." Neve struggles to finesse what she really wants to ask him. "I'm just a little confused."

"About?"

About why you're acting like Dylan is a complete stranger? "Well—aren't you guys best friends?"

"No," he says firmly. Terminally. "We're definitely not that."

CHAPTER 7

CALAMITY

H*ome sweet hole.* Neve collapses onto her bed, her arm and leg dangling over the side like a starfish. With her face buried in her sheets, she kicks off her shoes and relishes the soothing sensation of cool air on her aching feet. Her entire body is so sore that it feels like she's fallen down a flight of stairs.

Months of tedious planning, thirty-six paintings, stress, sweat, and tears, and she barely managed to break even with her expenses. Elliot never showed. Her mom's brief visit was really more of a critique of Neve's life choices than actual support. And chatting with Romer just wound up raising more questions.

For some reason, she keeps thinking back to four Christmases ago. Back to that gloomy afternoon she was waiting for Dylan by the escalators of the movie theater, holding two cups of hot chocolate.

A matinee on a snowy day. *Perfection.*

She remembers spotting Dylan as he walked past the windows of the lobby, his rosy cheeks peeking from beneath his navy scarf. And although his mouth was concealed, she remembers him smiling.

It must've been in his eyes.

And she remembers how as Dylan reached for the door, a boy suddenly appeared from behind the wall, running towards him at full speed. And how when he leaped onto Dylan's back, his momentum propelled them both onto a pile of snow.

And she remembers beaming with envy as 'Ro'— the boy she often heard of, but rarely saw—shoved handfuls of snow into Dylan's mouth, their laughter audible even through the thick windows.

It was little more than a moment in time, and yet it instantly became one of Neve's favorite memories. Because that was the kind of friendship she'd kill for.

Neve finds herself inside the university's Aquatic Centre, standing on the higher of two diving boards. The water beneath her is as still as glass. The humidity is suffocating, and the smell of chlorine is strong enough to be tasted.

Scanning the vast open space, she tries to pinpoint the source of dripping water. There's an eeriness creeping about, but it eludes her with much finesse.

I thought I was afraid of heights…

She looks down to find herself fully clothed. But what's even more peculiar is that she is clutching a heavy steel anchor.

Makes sense, *she thinks.* Without it I would float right back up.

With that thought, Neve steps off the board and plummets towards her reflection.

Like missing the final step going down the stairs, Neve kicks awake in her bed. Her heart is pounding, and her skin is glazed with a thin layer of cold sweat.

She can't seem to shake the sensation of falling, so she just lies there and waits for her nerves to calm.

It's still dark outside, so she slips her hand under her pillow, grabs her phone, and checks the time.

6:12 a.m.

She groans. It feels blasphemous to be up so early on a Sunday.

With the exhibition now behind her, Neve realizes she's made no concrete plans for the summer—none besides hanging out with Elliot. And with most of her exhaustion now stripped away, she's starting to feel really raw about him.

He didn't even bother to send her a quick text. At least then Neve wouldn't have spent the whole night alternating between checking her phone and staring out the gallery's windows.

But worse than being mad at Elliot is how badly Neve wishes she could just call Dylan to talk about it. About anything, really. And to be fair, she still hasn't heard Dylan's side of things. So reaching out to him wouldn't be pathetic... right? It'd be the mature thing to do.

She huffs a sharp breath and pulls up his number.

She stares at it, expecting to come to her senses. But for the first time in a long while, her mind and heart don't seem to be at odds. So she swallows the tension in her throat, licks her lips, breathes in the courage she desperately needs, and calls him.

It rings, and rings, and rings, and rings, and, "Hey, you've reached—"

She hangs up.

σ

Neve wipes the bathroom mirror with her towel, and steps out of the steamy cocoon wearing a white tank top and black and white striped pajama shorts. She grabs her phone off the bed and checks it, saddened to not have a single text, notification, or missed call.

Well, I did call him at the crack of dawn...

She drops her phone back down and walks over to her mini-fridge. Minus a few condiments, it's more or less empty. With finals and the exhibition keeping her occupied, she's been surviving on frozen dinners and instant noodles.

Mulling over her limited options, a faint dial-tone reaches her ears.

Neve looks towards her phone and sees that the screen is lit up. She walks over and grabs it, realizing it's making an outgoing call to Elliot.

Thinking she dialed him by mistake, she taps and ends the call. And then her eyes widen at the sight of a string of outgoing calls—all to Elliot—and all of which were made while Neve was in the shower.

She stares with knitted brows.

Software bug?

Without being prompted, her phone begins to dial Elliot again. This time, Neve finds herself starting at it, not wanting to end the call.

She might have always been a bit of a malfunction magnet, but this feels different. Darker. The kind of feeling you get when you're watching a horror movie all by yourself.

An incoming call makes her jump out of her skin.

It's from a blocked number.

With zero guesses as to whom it could be, Neve clears her throat and receives the call. "Hello?"

"Is this Miss Knightly?" an unfamiliar voice asks.

σ

Neve's damp locks lash against her skin as she bursts into the hospital's emergency ward. And right before a fresh onslaught of panic cripples her, she notices a young girl behind a small reception desk.

There is a 'VOLUNTEER' tag clipped to her shirt.

"Can I help you with something?" she chirps with an excessively chipper voice.

Neve goes to speak, but a police officer at the end of the hall beckons her attention.

Is he the one who called her?

Neve swallows the tension in her throat, and with gravity clawing at her feet, sets out in his direction.

Her steps become smaller and smaller, and then she is just standing still, waiting for him to meet her halfway.

"Miss Knightly?" he approaches.

"How is he?" Neve asks with a whisper-soft voice.

"Can I see your ID, please?"

"Oh. Yes." With her eyes struggling to focus, Neve rummages through her bag until she finds her wallet. She pulls out her driver's licence and hands it to him. "I'm not family," she says as the officer checks her ID. "His family lives in Toronto."

"We're in the process of getting a hold of them as well. We called you because you're listed as his local emergency contact."

Neve nods, barely registering his words. "So, what happened?"

"I'm afraid I haven't been updated on his status. But the doctor should be out soon."

"Okay, but what *happened*? You said you would explain once I got here."

"Well—" he drops his gaze and rubs his stubble. "I don't want to jump to conclusions, but so far it looks like attempted suicide."

Suicide.

She's underwater. She can no longer hear a word he's saying. The world is fading to black, and all she sees is Elliot dangling from a rope in his dorm room. Or lying in a pool of his own blood with slit wrists resting face up on the rim of his bathtub.

"Did you have any knowledge of this?" the officer asks, redrawing Neve's wavering focus.

Her frown deepens, and she shakes her head, 'no'.

"Because we found eighteen missed calls from the same number we reached you at."

The calls, Neve's heart drops.

"My phone was—um... I was supposed to see him last night, but he didn't show," she starts to well up.

"I'm sure he's going to be fine."

"How did he—" Neve chokes on the words, hoping he'll spare her the gruesome details.

"It looks like he was trying to drown himself."

Confusion taints Neve's expression. "What..?"

"Apparently, the custodian kept hearing a phone ring, and figured someone had lost it. And when he turned the corner, he saw Mr. Wilder jump, and dove in after him."

Dove? Custodian?

Off Neve's expression, "into the pool," the officer clarifies. "At UBC's Aquatic Center."

She can't breathe. She can't think. The heavy pain in her gut is threatening to drop her to her knees.

"Real lucky timing too. If it wasn't for your calls," he shakes his head, his lips pressed together.

"But, Elli's a world-class swimmer," she says. "He even used to compete."

With that, palpable unease overcomes the officer and he drops his gaze. "When we got to the scene, we found a fifty-pound disc-weight and a metal chain in the deep end of the pool." He scratches his temple. "It was apparently quite the struggle to pry them off of Mr. Wilder."

An anchor...

Neve's vacant gaze sinks through the air, and she stares through the floor at where the pool's surface would be, if she was back up on that diving board.

"I really can't imagine how hard this must be," the officer says, "but try not to worry. The doctor should be out soon."

"Well what's he doing in there anyway?" she looks up, body atremble. "You either drown, or you don't."

σ

Neve leans forward on her elbows, and buries her face in the palms of her hands.

It has been forty four minutes since she arrived at the hospital. She almost wishes there was someone else in the waiting room. Someone she could sneak glances at, wonder about, distract herself with. She'd settle for a screaming child at this point. Anything would be better than to sit here in silence while the officer's account of the incident replays in her mind. And what's worse, she can't seem to make sense of any of it. Of the timing of her outgoing calls to Elli. Of the similarities between her dream and how he tried to—

Her fingertips rake into her hairline. She grips her aching head, trying to piece her fragmented thoughts together. But they keep being drowned by the sound of her heart, pounding. Counting.

What the hell is taking so long?

At the sound of approaching footsteps, Neve leans back in her seat with her eyes glued to the door.

An older man with gray hair and matching scrubs emerges from the hallway, and his eyes immediately land on the only other person in the waiting room.

"Are you waiting for Mr. Wilder?" he asks.

"Elliot Wilder. Yes." Neve slowly rises to her feet. "How is he?"

The doctor looks down at his clipboard, but he's not actually reading what's on it. His lips are parted as though the words are on the tip of his tongue. "I'm afraid we were unable to resuscitate him."

Neve watches him readjust his glasses.

"I'm guessing you've been briefed with regards to the pool, but the official cause of death is overdose."

Cause of death, Neve thinks, robbed of all hope.

"Phenobarbital," the doctor elaborates when Neve fails to acknowledge his revelation. "He had almost ten times the recommended dosage in his blood."

"Overdose..." Neve lags behind.

"I'm terribly sorry for your loss," he heads for the door, but hesitates. "If it's any consolation," he turns to Neve, "Phenobarbital is a sedative. It's unlikely he felt any pain."

And all Neve can do is stare, devoid of language.

With a terse nod, the doctor makes his way back out into the hallway, and vanishes from sight.

But not from memory.

And eventually Neve finds herself wandering back towards the entrance, the flogging of her flip-flops echoing through the hallways. She walks through the sliding doors and heads towards the parking lot. She walks in anticipation of her emotions catching up to her. Of becoming completely undone.

But with each step, she feels even less.

CHAPTER 8

DOUBT

I vory clouds hang low in the cerulean sky. The gentle breeze is so bashful Neve can barely hear its whispers. Lying on a plush blanket of moss, she closes her eyes and gently caresses the delicate texture. It's spongy and slightly cool to the touch. Soft and soothing. She could lie here forever.

Minutes meander by with nothing on her mind but peace. And then a gentle breeze lifts the heat off her cheeks, prompting her to open her eyes.

She sits up and marvels at an enchanting field of grass. A serene meadow sprinkled with thousands of white daisies.

Straight ahead, the meadow meets the sky as though it is overlooking a cliff. Neve follows the rim until it dawns on her that it spans the entire perimeter.

She's atop a secluded summit.

And she's not alone.

Right next to her stands a boy—she looks up—with scarlet hair.

A gust of wind swooshes past and Dylan's tousled locks ascend to bid it farewell.

Neve waits for him to look down, but he keeps staring into distance.

"Hey," she rises to her feet and faces him.

He remains oblivious.

"What are you doing here?"

With Neve's inquiry, the clouds above begin to blush a deep shade of pink.

Captivating, yet frightful, somehow.

All of a sudden, the sun seems to be diving towards the horizon as if trying to escape the night. Sheets of light pour down like water as darkness wrings out the sky.

"Dylan?" Neve reaches out and touches his arm. "Oh my God, you're freezing!" She weaves into him, but his arms remain dangling.

She closes her eyes and starts to rub Dylan's back, but his body remains ice-cold. And in that moment, with her cheek pressed onto his neck, Neve realizes he doesn't have a pulse.

"Do pink clouds rain blood?" Dylan speaks in a voice far steelier than his own. And when Neve opens her eyes, her vision is draped off by longer, darker strands of hair swaying gently in the breeze.

Neve's heart skips a beat, and she pulls back, only to be struck by the familiar features of a complete stranger. A young, androgynous man with wild eyes, blade-like brows, and dark hair draping over his shoulders.

There's a soullessness to him that's hard to put into words. His beauty feels toxic.

Lethal, like an exotic serpent.

"Who—" Neve takes a step back, realizing the man is gripping both of her wrists. "Let me go," she demands, but he doesn't even blink.

Neve tries to pull herself free, but the man's grip is firm. Unyielding.

"Do pink clouds rain blood?" he repeats.

A warm drop of rain lands on Neve's chest, and she looks down at a crimson splat seeping into her white shirt.

Her eyes fill with terror. She looks up just as another drop lands onto the stranger's cheek. It hugs the contours of his face as it runs down to his defined jaw.

"Let me go," Neve demands once more, her voice reeking of fear and desperation. "Let me go. Let me go! LET ME GO!" she belts out like a

broken record as the stranger's stare wreaks havoc inside her.

Another crimson drop lands on Neve's bare shoulder, "help—" and another, "help me!" and another, "HELP!" until all she can see is red.

Neve opens her eyes to the white ceiling of her apartment. But the horror of her nightmare—the red filter of the world drenched in blood, lingers.

Through labored breaths, she awaits her return to normalcy. But instead of peace, she finds pain.

It's been six days since Elliot stopped breathing. Since his broken heart stopped beating. Since Neve ate anything larger than a bite, or remained asleep for longer than a few hours. Ever since the incident, she's been plagued by nonsensical nightmares jolting her awake at all hours of the night. By lyrics of songs she has not listened to in ages. Ever since that awful phone call, she has been wavering between hollow denial and heavy anguish. And in just a few hours, she'll be forced to rip off the scab and feel the burn all over again.

σ

Adorned in black, Neve stumbles out onto the stone deck of the country club. Her eyes are bloodshot and her nose and cheeks are rosy thanks to the cheap tissue paper. Her body feels bruised and beaten.

One more tearful outburst, and she fears her skull will crack.

She turns a corner and seeks refuge on the side stairs leading down to the parking lot. Mourning all morning has finally taken its toll.

She can still hear the homemade video of Elliot playing in the ballroom. A lengthy compilation of the milestones in his life, punctuated with random clips of his shenanigans as a child.

Every once in awhile, the tormented laughter of his family and friends roars, and then slowly wanes into somber awe.

This was intended to be his celebration of life, but it's been nothing but a painful replay of all the things she will miss about him. Things she will now have to live without.

But worst of all has been the parallel she keeps drawing between reality, and her vivid nightmare heralding Elliot's untimely demise.

Her tears escape her once again, and she reaches up and collects them with her damp sleeves. Did she somehow *know* this was going to happen? Is the gut-wrenching feeling bending her at the waist really guilt disguised as grief?

Could she have intervened before it was too late?

With that thought, Neve retrieves her phone and dials her mother. By the second ring, she is already bracing herself for the answering machine. But much to her surprise—

"Hi sweetie," her mom picks up.

"Oh—hi," Neve stammers. "Hey, mom."

"How're you doing, honey?"

Neve breathes a silent sigh. "I'm... okay."

"How was the service?"

The service, Neve thinks. It was well-orchestrated. Uncomfortable. Heartbreaking. It was—and still is—all the things it's supposed to be, and none of the things it needs to.

"Mom—" Neve starts, but hesitates.

"Honey, I think you're cutting out," her mom says.

Neve looks over her shoulder. Roughly thirty feet behind her a slender man—*Elli's uncle?*—is lingering by an antique cart filled with red geraniums. Staring into his whiskey glass, he seems far too broken to even notice Neve, let alone care to eavesdrop on her conversation.

"Neve? Can you hear me?"

As Neve turns her back to the grieving man, her obsidian hair drapes off of her shoulder, concealing her face.

"Mom—do you remember how I used to have all these weird dreams. when I was a kid?"

There's a pause. Too long a pause. "Everyone has weird dreams, honey," her mom eventually speaks. "It's normal."

"If it's normal, then why did you take me to see a psychiatrist?"

A soft, yet frustrated sigh. "It wasn't the dreaming itself. You kept riling up all the kids, telling them you can predict the future."

And it's like Neve is six years old again...

...sitting by herself on the seesaw at recess. This autumn is an explosion of yellows, reds and browns. The sky is fog-gray, and the air is comfortably crisp.

All warm and cozy in her rouge parka, Neve watches the boys chase one another on the playground. Her gaze closely follows the boy in the marigold sweater, who seems to be losing steam already.

He waddles into an impasse, his shoulders slacken, and he tilts his head back, breathing puffs of white clouds into the air.

Lazily, he wanders back over to the swings, grabs the chains, and pulls himself up onto the wooden seat.

At the sight of this, Neve rises in quiet anticipation. Her big, brown eyes dart back over to the other boys who are gathered in a small cluster, visibly disappointed.

One of them jolts as though he's just come up with the best idea there ever was.

Mischievous grins blossom on their faces as their new group strategy reinvigorates them.

They giddily run back and gather behind the swings, and each time the marigold boy swings back, they collectively push onto him.

The higher the boy reaches, the louder his pleas for mercy become, but the others seem adamant to swing him all the way around the horizontal bar.

Neve's mittens rise up to cover her mouth, her panting warming her tiny fingers through the thick layers of fabric.

She's wrong. She has to be. Because if not—

The screaming boy reaches the apex and unwittingly releases his grip of the chains.

Neve's mittens swallow her scream as the bar breaks the boy's back in the process of breaking his fall.

That horrific incident was Neve's first damning premonition. One she had hoped would also be her last. But time kept taunting her with more unsettling surprises, some big, and some small. And now with Elliot six feet under, she's once again fallen victim to confusion, doubt, and despair.

And if her mom couldn't empathize with her as a child, there's no reason to assume things would be any different now.

CHAPTER 9

SOLACE

Dylan finds himself inside an empty room. Inside a concrete cube with no door and no windows. He has no idea how he's come to be here, but looking down, he realizes he is strapped to a metal chair bolted to the ground.

He struggles to free himself, but instead his restraints become even tighter, trapping the blood his heart is pumping into his hands.

It feels like the space is getting smaller. As if the walls are closing in on him, inch by inch.

With a loud and echoing blast, a spotlight is cast onto him. It's so bright that it bleaches whatever surface it touches.

And suddenly it starts to glide down Dylan's body, draping over his knees and sliding down his shins. It slips off the tip of his shoes and begins a slow crawl towards the center of the confinement.

Panic rattles Dylan's bones. The spotlight's crawl seems purposeful. But for the life of him, Dylan can't imagine what it intends to reveal.

Suddenly, the bright disc starts to deform, crawling onto what seem to be a child's shoes.

It creeps up the legs and torso, and when it reaches the collar, Dylan gapes at the dark hair resting on the child's shoulders.

With a blaring bang the spotlight is snuffed, and all that remains is an echo, swelling up within the darkness.

Dylan quivers in place.

Not once has he encountered the Reaper in the form of a child. So, what could this mean?

What's going to happen?

The borders of the room reappear as soft light fills the space from no apparent source.

The boy has vanished. And there seem to be no instruments of torture lying around.

Has the cycle been broken?

Is today the exception to the rule?

His hope is extinguished when he notices a dark and veiny pattern forming on the ground, like the growing branches of a dead tree. And he jolts as he realizes what he's witnessing is a crimson liquid oozing from the cracks in the concrete floor.

It spills onto the surface, its borders quickly coalescing. Within seconds, the entire floor is submerged beneath a thick veil of red—in the blink of an eye, Dylan's feet are swallowed by what looks, smells, and feels like blood.

He exerts his full capacity, trying to break free, but his bindings tighten in retaliation. His hands are turning blue, and the only thing he feels in his legs is the warmth of the deluge slowly drowning him.

It's already up to his knees. It's as though time is skipping forward in larger and larger increments.

Dylan stares helplessly as the red threshold swallows his lap. It glides up his torso until it has engulfed his shoulders.

And then, it slows down along Dylan's neck like an unwanted caress, warm and invasive.

As though savoring the kill, it fills the space around Dylan's throat, curves along his jaw, and creeps up to his gaping mouth.

It lingers at the brim of Dylan's lower lip, taunting him with false hope. And then, like a merciless wave, it dives into Dylan's throat and fills his lungs with pain.

Gasping for air, Dylan soars into consciousness in his bed. He clasps his hand onto his throat, heaving wet coughs, but the wretched sensation of drowning refuses abandon.

He feels like such a fool for thinking—even if for the briefest moment—that he would ever see an end to his suffering.

He can't do it anymore. This burden is too heavy for him to keep carrying on his own.

He pulls his phone from his pocket and sits up in his bed. It's desperate, and probably futile, but what has he got to lose at his point?

He clears his dry, aching throat, and dials Alex.

Pick up. Just pick up and—

It goes straight to voicemail, reminding Dylan yet again of how things may never be the same.

"Hey, Alex... Um—I'm sure you're really busy. And it's been forever," he exhales, wishing he'd rehearsed what he was going to say. "Do you think that maybe we could... catch up?"

Catch up? He cringes. *Just cut the shit.*

"Alex, they've gotten worse. Way worse. I'm—"

Drowning.

With nothing else left to say, he ends the call. This was it. He just played his final hand. If after hearing this message Alex still doesn't care to get back to him—like when he screened Dylan's call at UBC—then it really is over.

Suddenly, like a tidal wave of warmth, a peculiar feeling washes over him.

He slides off his bed and heads out into the living space, stopping a few feet shy of the front door with his eyes glued to the buzzer.

σ

Neve waits behind a regal pair of bronze doors—the twin gates to the antique elevator of Dylan's heritage apartment complex.

She barely remembers the drive back from Elliot's celebration of life, or how much she fed the parking meter. She just can't believe she's here, when only a week ago the mere thought of it was stranger than fiction.

The lift comes to lurching stop, its sinewy gates sliding open. It's a welcoming gesture, and yet Neve feels like she's being lured into a cage. 'A birdcage lift' she remembers Dylan calling it.

How fitting.

She steps in and pushes onto the topmost button for Dylan's floor. The instant the doors begin to slide shut, an onslaught of anxiety twists her core, and she knows there is no going back. She peers down at the lobby through the gaps in the lift's ornate skeleton. And then—one by one—the floors are sliding down across her vision, bringing her closer to him.

This was a horrible idea.

What was she thinking, dropping by like this? She should make up some excuse and take off—just ride the lift back down and text Dylan an apology.

But the lift is already coming to a stop.

What the hell is she going to text him? 'Something came up'? What if he asks to reschedule? What if—

And she catches a glimpse of Dylan in the hallway as the lift's doors slide open.

At the sight of him, years of suppressed emotions swell up inside, threatening to spill from her eyes.

"Neve," his brows crease as he steps forward.

"No—" Neve backs away, pressing the button for the lobby. "No, no, no," she keeps pressing it, but the damn doors won't slide shut.

And then, she bursts into tears.

"Babe—" he steps into the lift.

"No, don't you *dare* CALL ME THAT!" she shoves him back.

Dylan staggers out of the confines of the lift, his expression a blend of shock and hurt.

And instead of taking the ride back down, Neve steps out into the hallway and shoves him again, and again, until he is backed up against the wall.

With tears streaming down her burning cheeks, "I loved you," she barely manages to get out, "and you just left... You *left*," she heaves, "*he* left," her anguish bending her at the waist, "everybody leaves..."

Dylan reaches out, but Neve swats his hand away. He goes to pull her into an embrace, but she pushes him away. And then her efforts are too feeble, and he is wrapped around her, warm and strong.

"I'm so mad at you," she sobs into his chest. Her arms are folded, and her fists are too weak to pound onto him. "I am *so* mad at you," she cries, her throat tight and throbbing.

"I'm sorry," Dylan buries his face in her neck. "I'm sorry, Neve. I'm sorry," he repeats over and over, his voice tainted with guilt and regret. And even when Neve's knees give out from under her, his hold keeps her from falling to the floor. So she surrenders to the compulsion, and cries over what feels like a lifetime of heartbreak, longing, and loneliness.

"Come on," Dylan whispers while gently stroking her hair. "Let's go inside," he starts to shift, and like a crutch she needs to keep her from crumbling, Neve lets him lead the way into his apartment.

Once within the confines of his home, Neve pries herself away, adamant to hold her ground.

"Can I get you something?" he asks.

"Don't do that," Neve looks at him, fury encasing her pain. "Don't go acting like everything is okay. It's *not* okay. You don't get to walk back into my life and act like nothing's happened."

Dylan's shoulders slacken, the sorrow in his eyes draining Neve of her intensity. And once again, she's feeling vulnerable and defeated. The same goddamn feeling she's been struggling to suppress all day.

"They all just stared at me like, 'who's *this* bitch'? 'Why is *she* here'?" Neve shakes her head and diverts her gaze. "Just because they didn't know me, it was like I didn't have the right to be upset over *their* loss. Like what I was feeling wasn't qualified."

"People grieve in different ways," Dylan says.

"They were *judging* me, Dylan. It was almost like they were blaming me."

"For what?" concern twists his brows.

"I don't know. Not being a good enough friend? Or maybe they thought I was his psychotic ex-girlfriend. That *I* drove him to it."

Dylan squints, visibly perplexed by what she just said. And in that moment, Neve realizes she never explained in her text to Dylan *how* Elliot died... only that he did.

"He killed himself," she practically whispers.

And silence swallows the room.

Dylan breaks eye-contact and slips his hands into his pockets—what he does when he feels defeated.

"God—I'm sorry," he shakes his head. "I thought it was an accident, or something."

"Oh, it was anything but," Neve walks over to the window and leans against it, gazing out at the urban congestion—at the view she never thought she'd see again, at least not outside of her memories.

"I don't know... Maybe they're right," she mutters as Dylan approaches her from behind. "Maybe it *was* my fault."

"Don't say that," Dylan rests his hand on her back. "I know blaming yourself may seem comforting, but it's just a way for you to feel like you're in control."

"I knew..." she says, oblivious to Dylan's attempts at consoling her. "I *knew*... I *must* have."

"Knew what?" Dylan sits down on the windowsill, looking up at her.

"I had a dream about it. About his death."

"Neve. Hindsight is twenty-twenty. You look back and feel like the answers were right there in front of you, and start blaming yourself for not doing things differently. But you can't think like that. You need to make peace with things that are out of your control."

"What if it was?" Neve whispers as though telling him an ugly secret. "What if it *was* in my control?"

"How do you mean?"

"It wasn't just some random dream. When the cop explained—" Neve's heart skips a beat, "Jesus, it was like he was describing my own dream to me."

Dylan's gaze darts between Neve's eyes as though searching for something. Does he think she's lost it? That she's crumbled under the stress of it all?

"People don't have control over their dreams," he finally speaks. "I *wish* they did, but—"

"Do you remember the nightmare I told you about a few days before you took off?"

He squints. "The one with the red river?"

Neve nods. "I was standing on an old, stony bridge all by myself. And the water running below was this deep, *deep* red. And it felt like everyone in the world was dead, and their blood was tainting the waters."

"Right," he nods. "What about it?"

"A few days later—after you were already gone— I read about a group of Czech artists that had poured gallons of paint in the river to protest animal rights.

Everyone thought it was such a brilliant idea," Neve drops her head. "And *I* was fucking terrified."

Dylan's eyes lose focus, and then his sinking gaze is zigzagging through the air.

"I told you," Neve diverts her focus back out onto the horizon. "It was my fault."

"No," Dylan shakes his head and rises. "It wasn't."

"It *was*, Dylan," she insists. "I *lied*. I didn't want to get locked up in a psych ward, so I told everyone the dreams were all made up!"

She heaves an exasperated sigh and rubs her face. But the tightness of the dry trail of tears remains.

"Maybe I should have just let them lock me up. Maybe if they'd done experiments on me they could have figured out what the hell is wrong with me," she continues in spite of Dylan shaking his head. "I could have helped them. I could have helped prevent horrible shit like this from happening, and Elli—"

Dylan grips the back of her neck and pulls her in. And Neve loses her conviction as his body heat seeps into her. Though he still smells the same—like green apples—he feels infinitely stronger than he used to. So steady and unyielding.

Incredible, what time can do.

"It's so easy to do away with things—or people— that you don't understand," he mutters. "To just cast them aside, so you don't have to deal with them. But just because science can't explain something, doesn't mean it's not real... and it sure as fuck doesn't mean it doesn't hurt."

Welling up, Neve pulls back and looks up at him. And her lids fall shut as he kisses the crease between her brows—just like he used to whenever she was upset. And surely enough, true and time-tested, her frown melts beneath the warmth of his kiss, and her soul is no longer heavy.

But when he pulls her back in, all Neve can think of is how she would dream about him almost every night like nothing's happened. And how when she'd wake up and remember that he's gone, it was like losing him all over again.

"It's been three years for me too, you know," he says, the gravity of his sincerity a complete shock to Neve's system. And before she can wrap her head around what that really means, Dylan's phone rings in his pocket, shattering the moment.

As their bodies part, Dylan rushes to silence the call, but hesitates at the sight of the caller's name. He stares at his phone's screen for a few moments, and then much to Neve's disappointment, picks up.

"Alex, hey…"

Great, Neve thinks. What better excuse for Dylan to keep avoiding the giant elephant in the room.

She starts to pull away with her eyes on the front door, but Dylan's hand clasps around her wrist.

"I'd really like that," he says, "but actually, Alex—I need a favor." He locks eyes with Neve. "And I'm not taking no for an answer."

CHAPTER 10

GALEN

The hidden sun has tinted the clouds a warm shade of gray. And although it's hard to tell the exact time of day, it's far too bright out for no other cars to be on the road. But Neve doesn't mind. It's been a long while since she's had the road all to herself.

She cranes her left hand out the window of her white Fiat, relishing the sensation of cool air weaving through her fingers.

Although she has no idea where she is, or where she's going, she feels perfectly content. Peaceful even. That is until an exit sign from further up the road kindles her curiosity.

She squints to read it, but the letters seem garbled. So she flings her focus onto the exit number instead.

'EXIT 6' she reads as the sign approaches. And the moment it flies past her, Neve notices a young man sitting in her passenger's seat.

He's got a stunning profile: straight nose, high cheekbones, and a chiseled jaw line. And his slicked-back, dark brown hair is resting on his shoulders. He is wearing a loose, charcoal sweater and black fitted jeans. And although Neve can't imagine how, she feels like she has met him before.

"Hi," she says, but the young man doesn't respond. So she directs her gaze back out onto the road.

Another highway sign is fast approaching.

'EXIT 6' she reads again as it swooshes past them. But this time, Neve feels like she has just missed a second opportunity.

"Merge," the stranger's steely voice beckons her attention.

Neve braces herself to apologize for missing their exit—or what she assumes to have been their exit—but the man's indifference shatters her resolve.

This time when she looks out onto the road, she realizes she is speeding up a ramp—one she must have taken without even noticing.

She peeks over at the highway her path is converging into, and her jaw drops at the sight of thousands of white Fiats idling bumper to bumper. It's like staring at a stream of white ladybugs in total gridlock.

"Merge," the man repeats.

"There's no room," Neve feverishly scans the gaps between the vehicles as the two of them continue to speed into peril.

"Merge."

"I can't!" Neve stomps onto her brakes to no avail. "Oh my God—" she tries to pull the car over onto the side-road, but her steering wheel is stiff as a rock.

"OH MY GOD!"

Neve awakens to the sound of an early morning truck backing up. As the veil of her dream is slowly pulled from her heavy lids, she arches her back and stretches the fatigue from her veins.

It's been two days since Elliot's celebration of life. And since Neve had a meltdown in Dylan's arms.

She'd hoped her spontaneous visit would put it all on the table. That by standing her ground, she could finally get some real answers and be one step closer to closure.

Instead, she unravelled and wept in the arms of the very person who hurt her. She spilled her closely guarded secrets as the walls she spent years building crumbled around her.

And to this very moment, she doesn't know if her choice to leave was smart or stupid. Had she stayed, maybe they would've talked until all the kinks were ironed out. But would that have been the best time, given her state of mind?

She rolls to her side and stares out her window, wondering why Dylan hasn't reached out since. But then again, he *did* insist that she calls him after her session today with Alexander Galen. The emergency session he practically demanded of his own shrink, barely five seconds into receiving a call from him.

If that doesn't show just how much he cares about her, then what will?

She sits up and sinks into a wilting posture, trying to think of what to wear to her first therapy session in years.

If Galen is indeed the best psychiatrist in the city as Dylan put it, then who knows... A quick visit just might prove to be worthwhile.

σ

Three hours since she woke up from her highway dream, Neve sits by herself on a Victorian loveseat in Alexander Galen's office. She keeps tapping her foot as if it could shake off her anxiety.

What's taking him so long? Is this his lunch break?

She scans his spacious office, which quite frankly, looks more like the lobby of a luxury hotel. The large floor tiles are a soft cream color, and a thin strip of black stone is offset from the ivory walls. The entire space is of a neutral color scheme.

She wonders if it's intentional.

"Thank you for waiting," a sophisticated African-American gentleman enters.

Neve's eyes are immediately drawn to his graying curls and silver eyes. In his beige tweed vest, white shirt, and brown pants, he is reminiscent of a time long passed... when clothes were less about identity and more about character.

It's odd, meeting him. It is rousing a deep sense of nostalgia. But for what?

A generation she never belonged to?

"Hi," Neve rises to receive Galen's hand. "Thank you so much for seeing me on such short notice."

"It's my pleasure. Any friend of Dylan's is family," Galen smiles as he shakes Neve's hand. "Please," he indicates the loveseat, and then takes his own seat in an off-white tufted armchair across from her.

Neve retakes her seat and crosses her hands on her lap. There is just something about Galen that makes her compelled to impress him.

"I've looked over your file," Galen crosses his legs as he leans back in his chair. "It's been a while since you sought out therapy."

"Honestly, I sort of lost faith in the whole process after awhile," Neve admits. "No offense."

"It's not for everyone," he puts on his frameless glasses and jots something down on his notepad.

Neve cranes her neck up to sneak a glance at what he's scribbling. What could he have possibly deduced about her already?

"So what brings you in today?" he looks up.

"Right," Neve leans back, her posture stiff. "I know Dylan made it sound like an emergency, but it isn't." She drops her gaze and starts to scrape at her black nail polish. "The worst is already over."

"Which was... what?"

And it's like the words have wrapped around her tongue, holding on for dear life. "M—my best friend killed himself. A week ago."

"My condolences," he jots something else down.

Elliot's somber words flood Neve's mind, and the depth of his despair finally dawns on her.

Is this what you get when you finally summon the courage to seek out your last resort?

My condolences?

"Suicide is perhaps one of the most difficult issues to deal with," Galen says without taking his eyes off his notepad. "Even the thought of ending one's life is unfathomable for most people, which isn't surprising given that death is the most universal fear known to man."

"Right. Of course."

"What do *you* fear about it?" he stops writing and looks up at her. His gaze is so deep and inquisitive, it makes Neve feel like she's curled up at the base of a test tube.

"About death?" she asks.

"Is it the pain? The fear of the unknown? Leaving everything behind?"

Neve ponders it. "I guess for me it's about... time? Or lack thereof, I should say."

Galen's unblinking stare prompts her to go on.

"It scares me that one day I won't exist anymore," she says. "I keep imagining myself on my deathbed, all alone, with only a few seconds left. And it terrifies me that once I'm gone, I won't even be able to know that I *used* to exist."

"And how do you cope with these thoughts?"

"I don't, I guess. It doesn't matter how many times I think I've come to terms with it... after a while the thought creeps back and pounces on me like a cheap jump-scare."

He laughs. "An interesting way of putting it."

"Just to clarify, it isn't *my* mortality I'm concerned about. I just need to come to terms with my friend's suicide."

"Yes. Of course," he nods to himself. "Was there a note?" he glances at Neve over the rim of his glasses.

"No," she shakes her head, and watches him jot something else down. "Does that mean anything?"

Galen raises his head slightly, but his eyes remain glued to what he's writing. "There's no formula, I'm afraid. Everyone is different in how they perceive, perform, and react to suicide."

"But don't people usually leave a note?"

"If they have something to say, yes. But for most people, suicide is simply a way out—a means to end their suffering."

Suffering...

The back of Neve's eyes sting as she wells up. She swallows the painful pill in her throat, brows knitted to combat her vulnerability.

"Are you angry?" Galen asks.

"No," she says. "Not at him, anyway."

Galen's eyes narrow a bit, so Neve drops her gaze and starts to fiddle with her jacket's zipper.

This is it. If she's going to bring up her nightmare, now is the time.

"At yourself?" Galen asks with a voice completely devoid of empathy, and diverts his focus onto Neve's history forms.

"I know people tend to blame themselves in these situations, but in my case it's warranted."

"Warranted how?" he looks up. "Did you know he was suicidal?"

"Of course not," she blurts out as though she's just been condemned. "I mean—this wasn't his first bout of depression. He'd been battling it for years."

"Then why the 'warranted' self-blame?"

The image of her eighteen outgoing calls to Elliot flashes before her eyes.

"I don't know," Neve shakes her head. "I guess on some level, I feel like I could've stopped him."

"You just said you didn't know he was suicidal."

How on earth is Neve going to explain this to him? "It doesn't make sense, but I feel like my mind—my subconscious—somehow *knew* something awful was going to happen. I don't know how it's even possible, but I had a dream about his suicide the night before."

"It's not uncommon for deeply-brewing concerns to surface when you least expect them. In your case, manifesting in dreams."

"But my dream was too specific, almost identical to how things went down."

"And what was it about?"

Galen's words sound inviting, but his indifference makes Neve want to drop the whole thing.

She gets that he's probably dealt with hundreds of similar cases, but can't he at least pretend to care?

"I was standing high up on a diving board, holding an anchor. And I jumped. And the next morning the cops told me my friend tried to drown himself at the university's Aquatic Centre, chained to a fifty-pound weight."

Galen's stare deepens as his eyes dart back and forth between Neve's. "An anchor..?"

Neve nods once. "And I remember in the dream it all made perfect sense. I knew exactly what I was doing. It was like I'd already accepted my fate."

Galen removes his glasses, folds them gently, and slips them into his vest's pocket. He puts his pen and pad away and leans forward, his gray eyes filled with not just intrigue, but a deep concern. "Have you ever had similar dreams in the past?"

"Dreams about death?"

"Dreams that manifest into reality. Come true."

A wave of optimism washes over Neve. It's like Galen has harvested her very thoughts. "I have. But just a few," she understates.

"Can you give me an example?"

She's already here. Might as well take advantage of this opportunity. "I don't know if this is relevant, but when I was a kid, I had a dream about lying at the base of a pool."

Galen leans back and crosses his legs. "Go on."

"I couldn't tell if the pool was filled or not, but I couldn't move. It's like I was dead, but still aware of everything. And I remember this dark figure walking up to the edge, looking in."

Galen rests his elbow on the armrest and nestles his chin between his thumb and index finger. "Did this figure frighten you?"

"No," Neve admits right away. "I even remember wanting to let her know I'm fine, but I couldn't talk. I remember wondering if that's what death is like."

"For everyone to think you're gone, even though your awareness remains?"

"You could say that," she allows, her focus sinking through the air. "It was nice, somehow, to know that even though I'm dead, I can still see and hear. That I still have—" she searches for the right words.

"A vantage point?"

"Yeah," she looks up. "That I'm still *here*."

"How old were you when you had this dream?"

"I don't know exactly. Five or six, maybe?"

"And why were you so certain that the dark figure by the pool was a woman?"

"Oh—well, at the time I had no idea. It was just a dark figure. But *years* later, when I remembered the dream again, I was pretty much convinced."

"Why?" his gray eyes narrow, his question pulling Neve inside herself. And she starts to relive the night when it all came screaming back.

"A few years ago, I was at my best friend's party. A different best friend," Neve clarifies. "It was before she moved away to Paris. But anyway, her party had gotten way out of hand, so I snuck into the backyard to get away from it all."

The details of that night fill the corners of Neve's memory—the high-pitched chirping of crickets, and the biting freshness of the night air... It was way past midnight, and the full moon was brighter that she'd ever seen it.

"The water in the pool was black," she continues. "It was totally still. There wasn't a single ripple or leaf anywhere on the surface. And it was reflecting the moonlight like a mirror."

She remembers wandering over to the edge of the pool, struggling to see beyond the glossy threshold. And she remembers wanting to crouch down and dip her hand into the black water—to break through the reflective barrier and see into the depths.

But she didn't dare.

Because no matter how hard she tried to banish her doubts, she was convinced that something—that *someone*—was lying just beneath the surface.

The memory of that night haunts her to this day. Her breath is caught, her heart is pounding, and she is losing all sensation in her hands.

Because that was the night it all came full circle. The night Neve realized that the dark figure from her childhood dream was in fact her older self.

With a sudden SNAP, the side legs of the loveseat break under Neve's weight. She slides sideways and crashes to the floor, shattering the marble tile where her elbow lands.

"Are you alright?" Galen leaps out of his chair and makes his way around the coffee table.

Neve remains frozen, absolutely mortified. "I'm *so* sorry," she rises to her feet with Galen's assistance, but her gaze remains fixed to the splintered tile. "I'll pay for it. And the couch—"

"It's fine, just—are you okay?" he gently rests his hand on Neve's shoulder.

"Oh yes," she looks up and meets Galen's gaze, his bright eyes filled with concern.

"Are you sure?" his creased brows rise, deepening the lines in his forehead.

"Mmm hmm," Neve nods a bit too eagerly. "Really, it happens all the time. I'm so sorry."

Galen takes a small step back and stares at Neve with what she can only describe as... *heartbreak*? It makes her feel uneasy. It's the kind of look you give someone you love, not a complete stranger who just broke your furniture.

"I should go," Neve swoops down and yanks her purse from under the collapsed loveseat.

"My next patient won't be here for another—"

"Thank you so much for squeezing me in on such a short notice," she smiles and heads for the door.

"Wait—hold on," Galen strides over and rests the palm of his hand on the door. The silver pen wedged between his fingers clacks against the wood, making his interception feel all the more invasive.

Neve retracts her last step.

Registering her unease, Galen swallows and takes his intensity down a notch. "Miss Knightly, you have opened up to me about something very troubling. I can't in all good conscience let you leave without properly addressing it."

Neve lingers, struggling to think of a polite way to remove him from her path.

Galen takes advantage of the lull and reaches into his vest's pocket.

"Here—" he pulls out his business card, clicks his pen, and starts to scribble something down. "This is my home address. And this here... is my buzzer." He hands the card to Neve. "I'm afraid I'm booked solid for the next month or so, but you can come over to my home for a private session. It's on the house, of course. Say, tomorrow around noon?"

Sure! Do you want me to bring anything, or is your torture dungeon fully stacked? "That's… very kind of you, but—"

"Miss Knightly. Neve—" he levels with her, all his pretentions cast aside. "I know you think you have to live with this, but you don't."

Neve's focus sharpens as she tries to read him.

"What exactly do you mean by 'this'?"

"I'll explain everything," he smiles. "Tomorrow."

CHAPTER 11

RETROSPECT

Forty-odd blocks south of Galen's office, Neve ventures onto Mountain View Cemetery. She walks a faded stone walkway under a row of beautiful cherry blossoms, the shadows cast by their branches gliding over her like black lace.

With a gust of wind, tiny pink petals leap off the branches, chasing after the nonchalant breeze like a pack of love-struck teenagers.

It is such a spellbinding thing to behold, and yet Neve finds herself oddly disturbed by the pink hue of the blossoms. It is as though the roots of the trees have quenched their thirst with the blood of those lying six feet under.

How disrespectful for spring to invite itself to a cemetery—where only distant memories are capable of being revived. Memories of friends, foes, family, and strangers alike. Of people we may have loved or loathed, but irrevocably lost. People like Elli, whose grave beckons her from far in the distance, lonely and inglorious.

Neve drifts off the stony walkway and cuts across the open field littered with mismatched tombstones.

She weaves through them, skimming the names of people she will never know. It's heartbreaking how the weathered tombstones have taken moss as their companion, and how the newer ones shine bright, oblivious to how soon they too shall be forgotten.

And then there's Elli's grave: a rectangular mound of earth, still too soft to crown with a block of stone boasting an engraved cliché.

Though the cemetery is barren, it is anything but peaceful as Neve tries to shake the disturbing images in her head: of Elliot's cold body lying in a dark box. Of his pale, waxy face which will soon disintegrate beyond recognition.

She wants to scream. She wants to curse Elliot's mom for burying him in a pretentious suit he would have despised. For forcing Neve to stand idly by as they lowered Elliot's coffin into the ground against his dying wish. For having treated him as though his body is no longer his.

σ

~Three Months Ago~

At the front of the lecture hall stands Marcus Holt: one of the university's most revered professors, and the embodiment of Satan.

"Anyone?" Holt coaxes the crowd. "*Anyone* want to venture a guess?"

When no one takes the bait, Holt clasps his hands behind him and starts to pace the platform in his elitist attire.

Neve can't seem to stop staring at his hair: thick, slick, and side-swept. He looks like he's just crawled out of a men's magazine.

Douche.

"Op—he's doing his slo-mo runway walk again," Elliot whispers in her ear. "I bet you five bucks he'll trip on his scarf." He bites down on his grin and glances in Holt's direction.

"I'd gladly pay fifty to see that happen," she says.

"Show me the fifty."

"Show me five."

They both burst into an inaudible chuckle. Or so they think. Because when Neve looks up, she is met with Holt's unblinking glare.

Her smile vanishes from her lips.

"Miss Knightly?" Holt cocks his head, luring her in with his raised brows. But Neve lowers her head and feigns an apology with her silence.

Passive-aggressiveness may not be her style, but it's by far Holt's least favorite form of dissent.

"The principle of déjà vu—" Holt declares with a raised volume as he resumes his walk, "is actually rather simple. Any time you experience something, the information is first processed by the frontal lobe of your brain, and *then* stored as memory. But there are times when the fatigued brain fails to process this information in the correct order. As a result, you wind up remembering something *before* you register that you've already seen it. So you experience seeing something *twice*."

He stops center-stage and faces his audience, but no gasps of utter bewilderment or standing ovations ensue. Holt's disappointment is evident even at this distance. All this picture is missing is a tumbleweed rolling across the platform.

His chest deflates as he exhales. "The lesson here? Perception is circumstantial," he checks the time on his watch. "This weekend's assignment is out of body experiences—"

The entire class breaks into a frenzy.

"Five pages, double-spaced," Holt raises his voice over the commotion, "no Wikipedia, I'll know."

He then looks directly at Neve and holds her gaze for an uncomfortably long time, before proceeding to pack up his belongings.

"Wh—" Neve's jaw drops.

What the hell was that?

"Don't." Elliot rises from his seat.

"What?" she looks up at him, having no clue what he's talking about.

"Just let it go."

"Did you not see that?" she subtly points in Holt's direction.

"See what?"

"He's taunting me again."

"*He is not*," Elliot grimaces. "You're just looking for an excuse to start something with him."

"You *do* know he's a horrible teacher, right?" her glare follows Holt out of the lecture hall's exit. "The university just keeps him around because of all his research, or whatever."

"The man *is* brilliant," Elliot sighs longingly.

Neve looks up at him and scoffs. "I cannot believe you're taking his side."

"Yeah... nice try," Elliot throws his backpack over his shoulder.

"What?"

"You're not going to drag me into this."

"You're already in it," she says. "We *all* are."

"Let it go, Neve."

"He gave me a *D*, Elli."

"You passed."

She stares, baffled. "A 'D' is not even a valid grade in university. And he knows it! This is all just a sick game to him!"

"You *passed*. Seventy percent of the class didn't."

"Seventy-*three* percent. And you're only taking his side because he gave you a B+. You're such a whore."

"Okay, *one*: I don't think you actually understand how prostitution works. And *two*: you expect me to just waltz into his office and start bitching about the highest grade he's ever dished out?"

"Could ya?" Neve grins.

"*HELL* no."

"FINE!" she slides out of her seat and begins to cram her belongings into her bag. "I'm not afraid of him. And I don't need you to fight my battles."

"Hope you've updated your will."

σ

Neve's knock on Holt's office door was so meek, she might as well have caressed the damn thing.

"Yes?" Holt's cold and dispassionate voice oozes from the gaps in the doorway.

Neve takes a deep breath, forms a small 'o' with her mouth, and shakily exhales the tension. *He's just a teacher. He has office hours for a reason.*

She grabs the knob, steels herself, and enters.

Directly across from her, Holt is sitting behind a shamelessly large wooden desk, grading the paper at hand with palpable indifference.

Neve's grip of her graded assignment tightens as she approaches Holt with small steps. She waits at the head of his desk, waiting for him to acknowledge her. Instead, he remains preoccupied as though she's not even there.

He reaches for a red sharpie, uncaps it, and draws a thick 'C-' in the middle of the page.

As he casts the paper aside onto his amassing pile of disappointments, Neve wonders how he sleeps at night having spent the day stomping on his students' aspirations.

He snaps the cap back onto the sharpie and puts it down. He then intertwines his fingers, leans onto his elbows, and looks up at Neve for the first time.

"What can I do for you?"

Suddenly, she's aware of how dry her mouth is.

"Hi. Um—" she swallows, "I was hoping to discuss my grade on last week's assignment."

"Which was?"

The cup size I wish I had... "D."

Holt nods as though expecting her to continue. "I'm assuming you're not satisfied with that?"

It's not even a grade, you bitch. "Well, no," she says with a bit of hesitation. "It's a well-written paper."

Holt's gaze jumps to the corner of the room. "And, you're qualified to make that assessment?" He blinks a slow blink and drags his focus back onto her.

"Well—you asked us to think outside the box. To propose a new—"

"Ah ah—" Holt holds up the palm of his hand. "Let me stop you right there."

Neve cranes her neck back, utterly dumbfounded.

"Do you have any idea how many of these I mark every term?" he points at the pile of graded papers.

Neve squares her shoulders. "Hundreds?"

"*Thousands.*"

"It's your job," she says, and then watches as the last remnants of civility drain from Holt's face.

"Miss Knightly—" he leans back in his chair, "I've been doing this a long time. Long enough to be able to differentiate between a provocative assertion and asinine drivel. Often with just one glance. And since grading is subjective, I'd appreciate you letting *me* be the judge of the quality of your work."

"The quality of my work is impeccable."

"Impeccable!" he laughs. "Wow. Now that is a *big* word. Here—" he reaches out, "hand me your paper and I'll add a little 'plus' to your D."

Neve's blood is boiling. Even if her work *is* subpar in Holt's eyes, there is no need for him to humiliate her by calling it 'drivel'.

Whatever the hell *that* means.

"With all due respect, professor, you don't need to be so—" she hesitates, treading with more caution.

"Yes?"

Don't do it. DON'T DO IT. "Condescending." *Fuck.*

Holt's eyes narrow, a faint smile creeping onto his lips. "Are you sure you're in the right program? You might want to consider switching majors to Creative Writing. Or Poetry."

"I'm happy with the field I've chosen," Neve says, sounding far too rehearsed.

"Yes, well, Cognitive Neuroscience is exactly that: *science.* You're not here to romanticize a bunch of groundless assumptions, dress them up in ten-dollar words, and get an 'A' for effort."

"So you agree. It's not the *quality* of my work, it's the perspective that I've—"

"Perspective has no place in science."

"I humbly disagree."

"Miss Knightly, there's absolutely nothing humble about you. And in case I'm being too vague, that was not a compliment."

Don't let him see you sweat.

"Science is falsified all the time," she says. "There was a time when the brightest minds in the world believed—"

"Science—" Holt interjects, "is reality: quantified."

"Reality is relative."

"No. It isn't. And that's the whole point. There is only *one* reality and *infinite* possibilities. And science concerns itself with what *is*, not what *could be*."

"I'm just saying—"

"Your grade is final," he pulls another assignment off his stack. "You may close the door behind you."

σ

~Today~

At the opposite end of the cemetery, Romer sits by himself in front of a weathered tombstone. He reads *'Mason Bradley – Loving son and brother'*, and takes a painful gulp from the beer bottle he snuck onto the premises.

It's quiet today. Way too quiet. It almost feels like there is no 'rest of the world'. But then again, given where he is, that's probably appropriate.

"You know that line?" Romer finds himself saying, his deep voice straining through the tightness in his throat. "That fine line between, *it'll never happen to me* and, *I can never take it back*?" He reaches out and runs his fingertips over Mason's engraved name. "It's been strangling me like a wire," he wells up despite his best efforts, "and I just don't know what to do."

CHAPTER 12

GRAVE CIRCUMSTANCES

Neve can't seem to take her eyes off of Elliot's grave. All she can think of is how the mound will eventually weigh down on itself, becoming level with the field. Flat. Like the flat-line on a hospital monitor.

How did this happen..? He wasn't *that* depressed, was he? Why didn't he leave a note? *He* of all people would've had *something* to say.

Neve's bones feel too weak to support her weight, so she sinks onto her folded legs with her eyes glued to Elliot's final resting place.

It's not real yet. Despite the pain ripping her from within, none of it feels real yet.

Neve glances over her shoulder, half-expecting to catch Elliot sneaking up on her as if this has all been a stupid prank. And she can't help feeling cheated when the universe refuses to play along.

She looks back at Elli's grave and suddenly finds herself mid-conversation with him—as if he's sitting right there in front of her. "You just wouldn't shut up about your dad's receding hairline," she chuckles. "I kept telling you it skips a generation, but *nooo*, we just had to take pictures so that you could prove me wrong in ten years."

And now you can't.

Neve's sorrow wells up inside, filling every cavity with excruciating pain. So she presses the palms of her hands onto her lids before her disobedient tears can spill over.

It won't be easy. No one said it would be easy.

She reopens her eyes to a hazy world, and when she looks down, her focus closes in on a dandelion growing out of the mound.

Her brows furrow when she realizes the flower is sprouting from where Elliot's heart would be. And it wasn't there a second ago. It couldn't have been, or she would have seen it.

Neve scans the vicinity for other dandelions, but there isn't a single one. Except for long, untrimmed blades sprouting from the base of headstones, there is nothing but obsessively uniform grass.

When she returns her attention to the flower, her eyes widen in disbelief.

The marigold petals are now, mere seconds later, replaced with white, fluffy seed-heads. The kind you blow into the wind. The kind you make wishes upon.

It doesn't make any sense. As far as she knows, it takes weeks for a yellow dandelion to transform into a white globe.

Neve leans forward onto all fours and crawls up to the lonesome flower for a closer look. It's hard to put into words, but there is a quality to it that makes it seem... *unreal*? It almost looks like it's glowing, but maybe the sunlight is illuminating it from behind.

Like a naïve child who still believes in magic, she closes her eyes and bargains with the universe to wake her up from this nightmare. She then puckers her lips and blows softly against the delicate orb.

If only it were that easy.

She opens her eyes to watch the white umbrellas unfasten from the bulb. To watch the tiny specks fill the air like an explosion of daylight stars.

Instead, her gaze crawls up a pair of black, slim-fitting jeans and a gray sweater, and meets the wild eyes of a young man with dark, shoulder-length hair.

Neve stares, stunned by his sudden presence.

And she finds herself tilting her head back as the young man ascends.

What..? The numbing chill in her hands and knees is creeping up her thighs and forearms. And when she looks down, she realizes it is *she* who is sinking into the ground.

"Help!" she looks up just as the young stranger vanishes into thin air. And her deafening scream rips through the cemetery as her lungs squeeze out her fear. "No no, help—HELP!" she rakes the soil, but the earth is swallowing her up. She's sinking faster than a boulder swallowed by quicksand.

"HEEELP!"

And then her thoughts are even louder than her cries. *I'm not tall enough! I'm not tall enough!* She starts to tremble, realizing she won't be able to find footing on top of Elliot's coffin. If she keeps sinking like this, she will certainly suffocate to death.

'HELP ME!' she screams as her face becomes flush with the ground, but a strangled wheeze is all that squeezes past her throat. *This can't be it*, she weeps, bleeding hope and heat. *This can't be how I die.*

The soil at the rim of the cavity avalanches onto her face, taking all light with it. With her eyes firmly shut, she gasps for air as the burrow closes in on her. She reaches up to the sky like a dying tree desperate for rain, wondering if they'll ever find her body.

And suddenly, the grating against her skin ceases.

Is it over? Did animal terror numb her pain as she passed onto the next realm?

"NEVE!" a man's voice calls out to her from above, and she feels a tightness around her wrist.

A twinge of desperation burns through her chest.

She extends her neck as high as she can and flings her compromised vision onto the silhouette of her savior.

"ROMER!?"

"HANG ON!"

Romer tightens his grip and pulls with all he's got, but all he manages is to keep Neve from sinking any further. His knees have locked, his flexed arms are atremble, and his face is flushed beneath a sheen of sweat.

And she is not even budging.

Neve's heart is drumming in her ears. What if he can't pull her out? What if he isn't strong enough?

Her emotions flare once again, racking her body with sobs. "Pull me out, please," she begs, her flesh dense and prickling.

Romer strives for a better grip, but Neve's wrist slides out of his grasp. Screaming, she sinks into the mound another few inches, the soil's texture grating against her skin.

"NO!"

Romer grips Neve's wrist, her face now nearly a foot below grade. And this time when he pulls, an icy glow emits from his eyes.

The soil starts to grate downward on Neve's skin, the friction breathing warmth into her. And darkness wanes as she inches closer and closer to the surface.

As Neve's line of sight rises above the ground, she catches a glimpse of a tombstone further ahead.

There is a brownish stripe at the base of it that's becoming thicker and thicker. And Neve suddenly realizes what she's looking at is the buried section of the tombstone, rising above grade.

Every time Romer pulls, the stone block rises by a few inches, and once uprooted, it topples over with a quaking thump.

And it's not the only one.

Neve's terrified gaze leaps from one tombstone to another as one by one they collapse around her. It's like Romer's attempts at uprooting her have spread to his surroundings like cancer.

"I think you're stuck," he grunts.

She hears him, but she can't rip her gaze from the tombstones.

"Neve—" he strains, "listen to me—just relax!"

"I *can't*!"

"Yes, you can! If you just relax, I can pull you out. Just try it!" He steadies himself, his chest rising and falling, and then pulls with everything he's got.

But Neve's glimmer of hope is extinguished at the sight of the toppled tombstones slithering towards them. Every time Romer pulls, they creep closer and closer, converging like a pack of ravenous wolves.

"NEVE! FUCKING DO IT!"

And like a bolt of lightning ripping the sky in half, Romer's eruption slices through Neve's focus.

Before the paralyzing terror of her circumstances sinks back in, she finds the soil grating down on her once again.

He's doing it!

She unclenches at the thought, and with one final pull, Romer plucks her from certain death.

He grips the small of her back and secures her against his frame. And Neve wraps her arms around his waist, staring at countless tombstones bowing to them in concentric circles.

She's never seen anything so terrifying.

"Romer—" she tightens her grip as the drumming of Romer's powerful heart fills her ear.

When Romer doesn't acknowledge her, she looks up to find his focus outside of them. But it isn't on the fallen tombstones. His gaze is stern and distant, darting about the cemetery at large.

"Romer?"

"It's okay," he mutters absentmindedly and starts to rub her back. "You're okay."

Neve's brows knit. "What's wrong?"

He looks over his shoulder.

"We're being watched."

CHAPTER 13

PROPHECY

L ike streaks of charcoal dragged across a canvas, tattered clouds stripe the ashen sky. The soft breeze is spreading the gloom of the late afternoon, and urbanity is slowly dragging its feet home.

With Neve clasped onto his back, Romer pulls up to her building on his custom Harley.

Neve glances up at her apartment unit, dreading being by herself. Would it be wrong to ask Romer to come up? To keep her company until it doesn't feel like the world is going to crumble all around her?

Romer's metal insect growls, rattling under them.

"See? Told'ja," he grounds his feet. "You wouldn't be able to tip this thing over, even if you tried."

With her cheek resting on his upper back, "you don't know me," she says softly. "I break things."

Romer turns off his engine and leans his bike onto its kickstand. As it tilts over, Neve tightens her grip around his waist.

"Sss—" he winces. "I think you've crushed enough bones for today," he chuckles and then peeks at Neve over his shoulder.

Neve can tell he's trying to lighten the mood, but she just can't bring herself to join in.

"We'll figure it all out, okay?" Romer says through his jacket's collar and rests his hand onto Neve's.

His skin is soft, and surprisingly smooth. Not at all what Neve would expect from a carpenter.

"Want me to help you down?" he asks.

Neve exhales a somber sigh, and then unwillingly pries herself off of him.

Romer tightens his grip of her hand and steadies her as she steps off the bike. "Just swing your leg over and—there you go."

Even once grounded, Neve can't seem to gather herself. After the ordeal she's just endured, keeping her emotions at bay is just about all she has energy for. So she just stares through him, feeling broken.

"You okay?" he asks. "Need a front-hug?"

"I—" Neve gently lets go of his hand, desperately hoping what's brewing inside isn't registering on her face. But what started as a trickle of emotion is fast becoming a roaring flood. "I mean—you saved my life," she wells up in spite of her best efforts. "It kind of doesn't get any bigger than that."

With her remark, Romer begins to rub his wrists.

"Are you hurt?" she looks up just as his pupils constrict, his gaze fixed onto something behind her.

Neve turns around to find Dylan standing in the doorframe of her building's lobby, staring. And at the sight of him, she remembers her promise to call him after her therapy session with Galen.

How worried must he have been to come over to her place? How many missed calls—

The ferocious growl of Romer's bike startles her, and she leaps back as he rides off, the stench of his bike's exhaust lingering behind.

σ

Neve stares vacantly at the shower tiles. At the thin layer of condensation, and the veiny paths droplets of water carve on their way down.

She closes her eyes and leans forward.

Warm water seeps into her hair, combing the earth from her tangled tresses. She tilts her head back and welcomes the drumming of liquid bristles onto her face, desperate to erase the sense memory of being buried alive.

She steps back from the showerhead, wipes the heavy film of water from her face, and looks down.

The murkiness pooled around her feet is slowly vanishing into the drain. Out of sight, but not out of mind.

She sinks into deep thought.

It's always the same whenever it happens. Her body starts to feel tight and prickly, just like when her leg falls asleep. Any kind of movement becomes painful, and for as long as it lasts, she's incapable of forming a coherent thought.

It is always a limbo of intense, painful stimulation she can't seem to control. And now, coupled with her foreboding nightmares, she is beginning to wonder if something is terribly wrong with her.

σ

Neve leaves the bathroom in a cream, lacy tank-top and black pajama shorts.

Dylan looks her way, then puts Neve's sketchbook down and rises from the couch.

Looking at his soot-covered shirt, she remembers how he pulled her into a deep embrace when she told him about Elliot's grave. It was the longest he had ever held her, or so it seemed. It was as if the ground could swallow her up at any moment.

She hangs her towel on the door handle.

"What am I going to do?" she mumbles, then looks at Dylan. "How the hell am I supposed to explain all of this?"

Dylan puts his hands in his pockets, squaring his shoulders. "I honestly don't know."

Neve looks into her modest bathroom, at the pile of her soot-covered clothes on the floor, wondering if she'll ever be the same again—if she'll ever able to banish the image of those prowling headstones.

"Back at the cemetery—" Dylan draws her focus, "you said Romer thought you were being watched?"

Neve pulls her damp hair behind her ears. "Yeah. He was pretty convinced."

"Did he say what the guy looked like?"

"I don't think he actually saw anyone."

Dylan squints. "So it was... what? Just a feeling?"

"I don't know," Neve glides her fingertips under her eyes as though wiping away invisible tears, and nestles her rosy cheeks into the palms of her hands. She stares into space, thinking of the stranger who spawned and vanished right before her eyes.

"Talk to me," Dylan starts to approach.

"I think there's something really wrong with me," she mumbles, eyes unblinking.

"Look—what you're going through isn't easy."

"I don't expect you to believe me," Neve's hands slide down her face, arms dangling at her sides. She walks past Dylan and plops down onto her bed. "It's fine. I don't blame you."

Dylan remains silent for a moment.

"I don't know if there's anything I can say to make things better," he walks over and sits down next to her. "But for what it's worth... I do believe you."

With her gaze glued to the hardwood floor, Neve shakes her head at what she's about to say. "I sank into my best friend's grave, Dylan. I dreamed about his suicide."

Dylan opens his mouth to speak, but holds back.

Neve huffs. "I don't think I can ever sleep again. I mean—how can I?" she pulls her hair back. "Maybe I really do belong in a psych ward."

"Don't say that," he pleads softly.

"I'm not kidding, Dylan. I'm terrified of going to sleep. I mean—people are at their most vulnerable when they're sleeping. It's when they're supposed to feel their safest. Put the day's stresses—"

"There's something I need to tell you," Dylan cuts her off. "Something I've never—something less than a handful of people know about me." He licks his lips and looks down.

A swarm of possibilities inundates Neve's mind, each more disturbing than the last. *Is he sick? Is it cancer? Is that why he suddenly moved away? To get treatment?*

"Okay?" she pulls her legs onto the bed and wraps her arms around them. And she waits, shielded and prepared for the blow, but Dylan keeps staring at his wrist—at the veins bridging his palm and forearm.

What are you thinking? What are you going to say?

"Talk to me," Neve whispers.

Dylan opens his mouth, but doesn't look up. "Ever since I was just a kid, I've had these—" he swallows, "dreams... where it's impossible to tell the difference between what's real and what's not."

Dreams. Neve's eyes narrow. "How do you mean?"

Dylan exhales a shaky breath. "When I wake up, it's not like waking up at all. Everything I was feeling in the dream stays with me. And it feels... *real*."

"Dreams usually do."

"Yeah, while you're still dreaming," he looks up, "but what about when you wake up?"

"What about it?"

"When you open your eyes you're supposed to have this moment where you realize it was all just a dream. It's supposed to be a relief, knowing none of it was real."

"Right..." Neve says as a sense of unease washes over her.

"Well, what if that wasn't the case? What if your nightmare followed you back to reality?"

Neve stares, unable to breathe. The sharp stench of chlorine is suddenly flooding her senses. What on earth does Dylan mean by that?

Calm down. This has nothing to do with Elli.

"That's what it's like for me," he says. "What it's been like for as far back as I can remember."

"Hold on," Neve rests her hand on his lap, "what are you saying? That your dreams come true?"

Dylan nods, his lips pressed together. "Sometimes right away, and sometimes it can take months. Even years."

Neve's face darkens. "Like me," she says, her voice completely devoid of emotion.

Dylan drops his head, his face a portrait of guilt.

A murky feeling is pooling in the pit of Neve's stomach. If there's any truth to what Dylan is saying, then her premonition about Elliot's death was not a coincidence.

And if she'd known it to be possible, she would've never been so quick to dismiss her nightmare. She could've intervened. She could've topped Elliot from downing that bottle of pills. Everything, *everything* would be different!

"Why are you telling me this now? Why not when I told you about the red river dream? Or three years ago when we spent—oh I don't know—*every waking moment* together?"

"I didn't want you to know," he admits. "I didn't want to give you a reason to leave."

"So *you* left instead?" her voice breaks. "You did to me, what you were so afraid I would do to *you*?"

"That's not what happened," he shakes his head.

"Then what? What, Dylan? Do I actually *need* to beat it out of you!?"

"Look, it's—" He starts to rub his face. "You were better off without me, anyway."

Neve cranes her neck back. "What's that supposed to mean?"

"Doesn't matter. Forget it."

He grabs his jacket and rises from the bed.

"Dylan."

"Don't worry about it." He makes his way towards the front door.

"Dylan, what did you mean by that?"

"That I don't dream about rainbows and puppies, Neve!" he snaps in a way he's never done before.

And for a moment, Neve feels like she's looking at a total stranger. "Then what *do* you dream about?" she asks and watches Dylan's eyes fill with terror.

With chaos.

His lips are pressed together, damming the words he dares not utter. But then, like a crack in the dam's foundation, the truth spills from his lips. "Have you ever wondered what it's like to be choked to death? Doused in gasoline and set on fire? What it's like to try and breathe with blood jetting out from a slit in your throat—"

"Jesus, Dylan—"

"*I* don't have to," his index finger jackhammers his chest. "I know *exactly* what it's like."

"But—you said your dreams come true..."

Dylan's stiff posture slackens. "It's just a matter of time." He starts to put on his jacket.

Neve's heart sinks as she imagines herself across Dylan's tombstone, sobbing with no end in sight.

"Is that why you left? Were you in danger here?"

"I never meant to leave," he says dispassionately, like someone who's already given up on defending himself. "It's just how things played out."

He reaches for the knob and opens the door, but it slams shut under Neve's hand.

The world stops spinning with their eyes locked, Neve's heart pounding so hard it's making her entire body tremble.

And suddenly she is pinned back against the wall with her wrists at the mercy of Dylan's firm grasp.

Her lips clasp onto his like a magnet, and he leans in and kisses her so hungrily, she can't feel anything else but him.

His soft, hot lips devour hers, the sensation equal parts pain and pleasure.

She needs her hands free. She wants to touch him all over, but he pulls her arms up and crosses her wrists. He grips both of them with one hand as his other roams all over the contours of Neve's body.

The pleasure of his touch is over-whelming. She missed him so much. His voice. His smell.

She savors his taste, the pressure and traction of his lips, wishing moments like this could be kept.

That they weren't as fleeting as a thought.

Dylan slides his hand under her thigh and pulls her leg up against his hip. He releases her wrists, and with his other hand, lifts her up against the wall until they're both navel to navel.

Neve grips the back of his neck to steady herself, gasping a small moan when his hand slips up under her shirt. With her free hand, she starts to unbuckle his belt. And he gazes deep into her eyes, letting her know how long he's been waiting for this.

It's happening, Neve's heart flutters. *After all this time.* And suddenly there is blood gushing from a slit in Dylan's throat.

Neve screams and grips his neck, trying to contain the crimson spurt.

"Neve—" Dylan's strangled voice barely makes it out.

Neve looks up into his eyes to find confusion and not fear. And when she drops her terrified gaze back down to his neck, the blood that was spilling through her fingers—wet and slippery—is gone.

Gone... she stares with wide eyes.

Dylan rests his hand onto hers and taps lightly for her to let go, and in a state of shock and disbelief, she gently releases her grip to find his skin unscathed.

Nothing..? She pants, incapable of taking her eyes off Dylan's neck.

"I'm s-sorry," she stammers as he lowers her back down. And once she wills her gaze back up to meet his, all she sees is a pained frown weighing down on his brows.

"I don't know what came over me. The things you said probably put all these images in my head," she tries to make light of it, but Dylan just averts his eyes and starts to buckle his belt.

"It's not you," she approaches, but he shifts past her and grabs the doorknob.

"Don't go," she says, ego be damned. "Please."

"You should get some rest."

"Then stay," Neve's brows rise as she smiles. "Just come and lie down with me. We don't even have to talk. There's plenty of time for that."

Dylan gives her a look.

"Hey—*nothing* is going to happen to you, okay?"

Dylan nods, though his mind is clearly elsewhere. "There's something I need to do," he turns the knob and opens the door.

Neve's hand slides off his arm and she steps back, feeling smaller than she's ever felt before.

"Okay," she says softly, and he turns to face her in the door frame. "Do what you gotta do."

CHAPTER 14

REDEMPTION

The workshop's buzzer blends into the disc-sander's scratchy screech. Romer shuts off the machine, pulls his goggles up onto his hairline, and heads towards the entry. On his way, he takes a peek out the window and notices a seaweed-green vintage Porsche parked across the street.

At the sight of it, he stops dead in his tracks and bites down on the bitter smile creeping onto his lips.

He knew this day would come. He's been counting every waking moment. But now that it's here...

With a slight shake of his head, he makes his way back to his work station, pulls down his goggles, and turns the disc-sander back on.

He waits for the machine to gain momentum, but even once it has reached maximum speed, he finds himself just standing there, staring at it.

A few more agonizing moments of stagnation pass and he can no longer take it. He exhales a sharp huff and bangs his gloved fist against the power button.

He pulls his goggles off and casts them aside, then marches to the nearest window and sneaks a peek at the street.

The Porsche is still there.

He unlocks the window and pushes onto it, then sticks out his head to peek down at the entrance one floor below.

Where did he—

A loud creak startles him from the supply room.

He grabs a pipe wrench off the wall and marches towards the back of the shop, turning the corner just as Dylan jumps down from the clerestory window.

Romer drops the wrench and strides over.

Dylan rises to his feet, only for his jaw to be met with Romer's powerful fist. The punch propels him against the shelves, making them rattle.

"Ro—"

Romer grabs his collar and punches him again.

"Just let me explai—" Dylan chokes on the words as Romer knees him in the gut.

"YOU, SON OF A *BITCH*!" Romer grabs the back of Dylan's neck and shoves him down. "He then wraps his arm around Dylan's neck and pulls him back into a tight chokehold.

Dylan's hand creeps up to Romer's forearm, but his grip is weak and submissive. He isn't putting up a fight, which quite frankly enrages Romer even more.

"THINK I'M BLUFFING!?" Romer shouts into his ear. "HUH!? THINK I WON'T DO IT!?" Romer tightens his chokehold, but Dylan doesn't retaliate. His body is starting to weigh down on Romer's arm, his mind teetering on the verge of consciousness.

"You worthless piece of *SHIT*!" Romer releases his grip and shoves Dylan back down. "You think you can just worm your way back in?" he kicks a metal barrel over, the woodchips in it flying everywhere. "You think it's that FUCKING EASY!?" he shouts, body burning hot.

Dylan struggles onto all fours with his hand on his throat, coughing. The shelves are still quivering as if due to a small quake, but start to settle as Romer's rage wears him down.

He bends at the waist and rests his hands on his knees, burying the urge to weep—the urge to purge himself of the pain running through his veins.

He looks over at Dylan, and then makes his way back into the main space.

Over his shoulder, he watches as Dylan wipes the blood from the corner of his mouth and rises to his feet. But before their eyes meet, Romer looks away and leans forward onto the rim of his work table.

He drops his head and inhales a deep breath, but his shaking persists.

I've made my point, he thinks to himself. *It's done.*

"Is that it?" Dylan's coarse voice reaches him from behind. "Three years, and that's all you got for me?"

"Oh I'm going to kill you," Romer enunciates. "As soon as I'm done planning my escape to Mexico," he grabs a pencil and starts to whittle its blunt tip with a utility knife.

"You need to hear me out."

"No... I really don't," Romer leans over the table and starts to scribble meaningless notes on a scrap piece of paper. He waits for Dylan to start groveling, but no such satisfaction comes his way.

Rage is swelling back up inside him, burning like acid. Sour, and utterly intolerable.

He pushes off the table and straightens his back.

Every moment dragging by feels like the length of his sentence, stretching the space between them.

"Why," Romer asks. "Why didn't you help me?"

"I couldn't."

Dylan's response makes him sick to his stomach. "Let me guess," Romer turns to face him, "you were too busy throwing yourself a pity-party to give a shit about anyone else..? Well guess what asshole—*my hell* wasn't the kind you WAKE UP FROM!"

$$\sigma$$

~Three Years Ago~

Today was exceptionally chilly, especially for spring. Though the sun has already set, the blue sky is yet to yield to nightfall.

Twilight: Romer's favorite time of day. When the city comes alive with a vibrant palette of color and light. When early-birds and night-owls alike walk the streets.

Holding an alarmingly cheap bottle of champagne, he walks up to a stunning beachfront mansion. And although this visit could easily be his thousandth, the building's minimalist design takes his breath away, yet again.

He loves how the walls, columns, and ceilings are really nothing more than concrete rectangles cutting into each other. How the planes extend beyond one another, creating overhangs, depth, privacy.

Had he designed this house himself, it could not have been any more perfect than it already is.

If only Dylan's dad would be away more often.

With hopes of avoiding any unwanted encounters, he drifts towards the side of the mansion, hops over a small fence, and heads down the walkway towards the pool-house in the back.

He walks past rows and rows of bamboo planters and obsessively-trimmed bonsai trees, each step he takes revealing more and more of the infinity pool up ahead.

With the pool-house in his sights, he pulls out a folded envelope from his back pocket and grins at the 'UBC Faculty of Architecture' stamp on its upper left corner. And when he looks over the shoulder at Dylan's father's mansion, it finally dawns on him:

His dreams have materialized into reality.

Romer refolds the envelope and slides it back into his pocket. He can only begin to imagine the reaction on Dylan's face.

Today has been a lifetime in the making. Today just might be the best day of his life.

He fiddles with the bottle's cork, and unwittingly pops it a few feet shy of the pool-house's welcome mat. The swelling froth fountains all over his sleeve.

"*Goddamn*," he mutters and quickly unites his lips with the bottle's rim.

A few gulps into the endeavor, "*ugh*," he cringes. "Even *I* think this tastes like ass."

He checks the label, and then vows never to cheap out on celebratory alcohol again.

"KNOCK KNOCK, BITCH," he pushes the front door open and enters the pool-house.

There's no sign of Dylan.

"D!" Romer calls out. "I started without you," he puts the bottle down on the bar counter. "But don't worry—we're breaking into your dad's cellar later."

His glee is met with silence. Is Dylan in the main house, he wonders?

Nah… he thinks. Dylan hates it in there even more than he does. *He's probably just taking a nap.*

"D!" Romer shouts even louder as he swings open the nearest cabinet. He scans the dwindled selection of clean glasses and mugs, shrugs, and then pulls two bottom-heavy whiskey glasses off the shelf.

"Man—I'm buying you a new charger," he makes his way over to the guest bedroom. "I called like—"

143

He freezes at the threshold upon noticing a hand peeking from behind the bed.

Terror twists his core.

He drops everything and dives forward onto the floor to find Dylan with his eyes shut, sunken heavily onto himself.

"D—" Romer holds up Dylan's ghostly face and pulls up one of his eyelids.

His pupil is alarmingly dilated.

"What did you do..?" Romer barely gets out with what little air he had trapped in his lungs.

He frantically looks about the room and spots an empty bottle of prescription drugs on the nightstand.

What did you take?

He leaps to grab the bottle and discovers a folded piece of paper right underneath.

A letter he doesn't need to read.

σ

Behind the wheel of Dylan's vintage Porsche, Romer swerves out of the driveway and onto the main road.

"IF YOU DIE I'M GONNA KILL YOU!" Romer shouts as he cuts through the evening traffic.

"Hold on, hold on, HOLD ON!" he stomps down on the gas pedal, narrowly making it through a yellow light. But further down the road, a string of finicky traffic lights await the screeching of his tires.

"Oh, no no no, please—please turn green—TURN GREEN!" he screams, and inexplicably, the upcoming traffic lights start to flicker.

Regardless of whether they'd just turned yellow or red, they all revert to green like a chain reaction.

"Yes!" Romer jolts in place. "What the fuck—YES!"

He swerves left onto the leftmost lane and speeds up, not accounting for the aftermath.

WHIPLASH.

All color and light blend into horizontal strokes as his collision into an unsuspecting vehicle swerves him violently out of control. And as the Porsche spins sideways, all Romer can think of is how he needs to survive this so that he doesn't rob Dylan of the same opportunity.

They skid to a screeching halt with Romer's hand firmly pressed onto Dylan's chest.

Groaning, Romer rests his aching head back onto the headrest, unimaginably grateful to be alive.

The world is still spinning, and the pulsating pain in his skull is intensifying with every heartbeat.

He squeezes his eyes shut to ward off the pain, and opens them again to a blurry world.

He turns his stiff, aching neck and looks in the direction of the car he crashed into. And all he sees is the fuzzy outline of a dark blue vehicle with a huge dent in its passenger's seat.

The driver is clutching his head with both hands, screaming something, but Romer can't hear him over the ringing in his ears.

With his hand still on Dylan's breast-bone, all that Romer's aware of is the stretching silence between the beats of his dying heart.

He turns back around and looks at Dylan's sallow face. How he made it to the hospital, he can barely remember.

σ

"You know what they charged me with?" Romer asks, smoldering beneath his icy exterior.

Dylan just stares, his lips glued together.

"First Degree Man-slaughter," Romer says, feeling sick to his stomach. "They said if I hadn't driven back to the crash site on my own, they would've slapped me with a felony hit and run too."

Dylan lowers his head, a choked breath escaping through his strangled vocal cords.

"See, you may not have given a shit about *your* life, but I never—and I mean *never*—thought you'd throw *me* to the wolves."

"Is that what you think I did?" Dylan looks up.

"You ran away!"

"No, I didn't!"

"Oh so what—you just woke up one morning and just *happened* to be in New York!?"

"Yes! That's *exactly* what happened!"

Romer stares, at a complete loss for words. There seems to be just enough conviction in Dylan's eyes to make him second-guess himself.

"When I opened my eyes," Dylan continues, "I was hooked up to a bunch of machines in what I *thought* was a hospital in Vancouver. I didn't even know I was in New York till I overheard two of the nurses talking."

"You actually expect me to buy this bullshit?"

"I swear to God, Ro, I racked my brain for months, trying to remember how I got there, flight, packing, *anything*! But it was like all my memories had been erased since I—" he swallows, and then just stares at Romer with pleading eyes.

And all of a sudden it feels like life itself has been drained of Romer. "You had three years," he says in a firm, but broken voice. "Three whole years, and *this* is the best you came up with?"

Dylan stares at him, utterly baffled. "Do you think if I had three whole years to think of a bullshit story, this is the best I could come up with?" a faint frown darkens his expression. "Do you really think I came over today to make excuses?"

"It sure as fuck looks like it, given that's all you've done since you got here."

Dylan's shoulders slacken, his chest deflating. He looks like someone who's playing his final hand. "It was either military school, or a psych ward."

"Bullshit. *BULLSHIT*! Your dad has enough pull to do whatever the fuck he wants!"

"That's what I'm trying to tell you! Alex thought I needed round-the-clock care, but dad wouldn't have it. Come on *you know* what he's like!"

"And you just went along with all of it."

"I told you, I don't remember anything before I woke up in the infirmary. The drugs must've—"

"I DON'T CARE! YOU *LEFT*! And you didn't even bother to look back!"

"Christ—you make it sound like I was at a resort! Romer, when I woke up, my phone and wallet were gone. I had no way of reaching you. I had no way of reaching *anyone*! My hands were tied—"

"*Your* hands were tied," Romer starts laughing.

Dylan shuts his eyes and lowers his face into his hand. He presses down on his eyes with the length of his thumb and index finger. "The second I found out what happened to you—"

"What *happened* to me?" Romer interjects. "Don't you mean what I *did*?"

Dylan looks up, utterly gutted by what Romer just said. "Ro... it was an accident."

"Right. Well, that makes it okay then."

Silence.

Romer shakes his head. "You think *you* wanted to die?" he starts to well up. "You have *no* idea what it's like to live with this—with what I have to live with for the rest of my fucking life."

"I—"

"And do you know what the worst part of it was? Waiting for *you* to show. For you to tell me I'm not a monster for what I did. That I can survive this," he tilts his head back to keep his tears from falling.

Dylan holds his stare, not uttering a sound.

"And I *needed* that. I needed *something* to hang onto so I wouldn't drive myself insane." His breaths become rapid and shallow. "I counted *every* minute of *every* day, thinking any second they'll call out my name. That I was just a short walk in shackles away from hearing your voice through a fucking bullet-proof window."

"I called—" Dylan's voice breaks. "Romer, I called the prison a million times, but they wouldn't patch me through. So I flew back the first chance I got. I flew back four times, Ro, and *every time* they refused to let me see you. Telling me you're in solitary and don't get visitations. Or some other bullshit about you being dangerous... or unstable."

Romer's hardened shell cracks. He *was* in and out of the SHU over the years. But what are the odds of every one of those instances coinciding with Dylan's visits?

"Dad swore to me he'd get you the best lawyer money can buy. They tried every avenue they could think of. But in the end, the best they could do was getting your sentence reduced."

"I was there," Romer says, remembering the cold, condemning stares of the jury piercing through him. Judging every inch of him as if he's a worthless piece of trash. A rabid dog that ought to be put down.

Twelve years.

Twelve years is what would have been the length of his sentence without Dylan's dad's help.

Would that have been fair? A year of confinement for each year Mason Bradley spent on this earth?

No.

Fair would have been getting locked up for all the years that kid had coming to him. Fair would've been the length of the future that was robbed of him.

"Ro, I'm sorry if my efforts didn't reach you, but I swear to God, I really did try."

Romer says nothing. There's nothing left to say.

"I don't expect you to forgive me. I don't. But you need to know that even if *I've* changed in your eyes, you haven't changed in mine."

Hard truth.

"Because of you," Romer swallows the painful pill in his throat, "I've changed in *everyone's* eyes."

"Ro—"

"Get the hell out of my shop."

Chapter 15

PRELUDE

Neve stands before an enormous map of an ancient city. Black and white, beautifully meticulous, and rendered by the skilled hands of someone long gone.

It's like looking at history itself.

Although she doesn't recognize the city the map belongs to, there is something strikingly familiar about it. The oddly-angled streets and pathways, the wide, snaky river...

It feels like she's been there before.

Beneath the map, the amber light of an antique banker's lamp has set the surface of a *large desk ablaze. And basking in its warmth is a leather-bound book.*

Neve approaches the desk, cutting through the thick smell of opium. She reaches into the sweltering light, her hand casting a shadow over the book. She gently strokes the velvety texture where the title would be, and then succumbs to her curiosity and opens the book to a random page.

At the bottom of the left page, the number '6' is stamped, which Neve finds odd given how far into the book she is.

She skims over the content, but can't seem to understand any of it. Though the letters are familiar, it's almost like she's trying to make sense of a dead language, like Latin.

She leans in to inspect the text more closely.

The ink bleeding around some of the more complex letters makes her realize the book was typed using a classic type-writer.

She flips to much further in the book and is surprised yet again to find the page number boasting a single digit '6'.

But this *page is filled with elegant sketches vaguely resembling dry branches. And framing the page are dozens of formulas and cursive annotations which Neve once again can't seem to decipher.*

The book suddenly begins to flip without being prompted, landing abruptly on the very last page.

At the sight of the third '6', a dark shadow crawls onto the desk. Neve's eyes seek the body it belongs to, and—

Neve jolts awake with a gaping mouth, her wide gaze flung onto her white ceiling.

Him again, her heart pounds. *Not him again.*

Stiff as petrified wood, she scans her apartment, terrified that she may in fact not be alone. Neither sitting, nor reclined, she waits for her mind to adjust to reality. For her nerves to calm. But the longer she waits, the more anxious she feels.

This is now the third time she has dreamt about him. Their fourth overall encounter in under a week, all of which trailed after Elliot's suicide.

Neve grabs her covers and yanks them away. She inhales a deep breath, and then sits up and pulls her pillow against the headrest. And then she just stares into space, wondering who this mysterious stranger is, and why he has begun to plague her dreams.

Has the trauma of Elliot's suicide made her mind conjure some Grim Reaper as a coping mechanism?

No, that's ridiculous. She would have to be insane to do something so extreme. She might be confused, lost, and undeniably scared... but she is *not* insane.

She grabs her sketchbook off the nightstand, pulls her pencil from the coil binding, flips to the next blank page, and starts to draw him.

His features are so deeply engraved in her mind that it's almost like tracing an invisible portrait. She cascades her pencil downwards, capturing the waves draping onto his broad shoulders. She shades in his blade-like brows resting low above his wild eyes. And with diagonal strokes, she adds depth to the curves and contours of his chiseled face.

Even in Neve's artistic rendition, his essence feels venomous.

Neve holds up her rough sketch and stares at it, then shuts her sketchbook and drops it by the foot of her bed. She pulls up her knees and wraps her arms around her legs, feeling like her depiction of him has somehow validated his existence. Made him real.

Her recurrent nightmares, the incident at Galen's office, Elliot's death...

Something is going on, Neve thinks to herself, her eyes staring blankly ahead. The dots are in place. She just needs to connect them.

Even if it involves taking Galen up on his offer.

σ

Galen's home is something else. From the moment he welcomed Neve in, she has been utterly captivated by every inch of it. By the exposed brick walls, aged to perfection. By the eighteen-foot windows flooding the living space with diffuse light. By the softly-aged leather furniture, and by virtually every color and texture her senses come to encounter.

His loft is lavish. But unlike his pretentious office, everything in his home is imbued with authenticity.

She'd stay here forever if she could. She'd happily sleep right here, on his incredibly comfortable couch if he'd let her. It would be like sleeping on a giant marshmallow.

Directly across, there's a colossal library mounted to the wall. Thousands of weathered books shy away from her, exposing their spines. And directly behind her, narrow bookshelves span from floor to ceiling, wedged between the slender windows, silhouetted. The entire wall looks like black and white stripes. A contrast of light and enlightenment.

Rich, and resonant.

A high-pitched hiss draws her focus towards the kitchen in the back, blending with the clattering of spoons. The rich aroma of espresso is filling the loft, making Neve feel right at home.

"And how do you like your coffee, my dear?" his voice travels from the depths of the kitchen.

Heavy cream, two tablespoons of honey, and zero calories. "Black is fine, thank you!"

Smiling in his direction, Neve notices an exquisite spiral staircase leading up to the mezzanine. To what she assumes to be his bedroom.

What a lovely view it must have from up there.

She's glad she came. It would've been a shame to miss this opportunity. To miss becoming acquainted with Galen's far more appealing private persona. The side of him Neve doubts he shares with just anyone.

"Here we are," Galen emerges with a wooden tray topped with a pair of semi-circle mugs, a cute little creamer, and a small sugar bowl, all porcelain white. There's also a matching vase hosting a single pastel-pink peony.

The man knows how to impress.

"Smells wonderful," Neve says.

"So—" Galen bends slightly at the waist to extend the tray. "How have you been doing?"

Neve takes the mug closer to her.

"It's been a hectic couple of days," she admits, and then sinks into deep thought. How is she going to bring up the cemetery? Or her recurring nightmares?

"You might want to give it a minute," Galen nods at Neve's mug. "It's probably scalding hot."

"Right. Thanks," Neve smiles and lowers her mug as Galen rests the tray down on the coffee table and takes a seat across from her.

The chair he sinks into is almost identical to the one from his office, except for being maroon, leather, and easily over fifty years old. The wooden armrests have lost their varnish along the edges, and the well-worn hide has minor rips near the stitching.

It must be his favorite chair.

Neve watches as he carefully empties the creamer into his coffee, making the lightening blend rise by about an inch. He then proceeds to put spoonfuls of brown sugar into the brew. Six and a half teaspoons, to be exact.

It's so endearing, Neve can't suppress her smirk. It's like watching a child playing a grownup.

"If I were to be quite honest, my intent for having you over today was rather, self-serving," Galen takes a sip from his drink and sinks back into his chair.

Neve finds his frankness surprising. Was meeting him at his home the dumbest thing she's ever done?

"How so?" she asks as casually as she can manage, desperately hoping Galen isn't about to allude to any 'favors'.

"I'm not sure if Dylan has already briefed you on my background?"

Background? "That you're his godfather?"

Galen smiles. "That too, but I was referring more to my academic background."

"Well, he *did* mention your interest in philosophy. He said it's what gives you an unconventional edge."

Galen nods appreciably and places his mug on the side-table.

"Philosophy is indeed my one true passion. I used to absolutely love teaching it, even if it was only one class per week."

"You don't teach anymore?"

"It's been years, I'm afraid. It's nearly impossible to make a living out of questioning the validity of... well, everything!" he laughs.

"Yes," Neve smiles. "I can imagine."

"And how about yourself? What are you currently pursuing?"

A dark cloud casts its shadow over her. "Cognitive Neuroscience," she admits with zero enthusiasm.

"A rather ambitious subject," Galen says, suddenly seeming far less relaxed. "Are you enjoying it?"

Oh great. Let's talk more about it.

"Honestly, it wasn't what I expected," she says.

"How so?"

"Don't get me wrong, I think it's fascinating. But it all just became so dry. And quantitative. It just didn't feel like I was learning about a person anymore."

He nods.

"I don't know," Neve shrugs it off. "I guess it just didn't resonate with me."

Galen stares. "Why did you use that word?"

"Um—" Neve retraces her steps, "*resonate?*"

"That's right."

An awkward smile creeps onto her lips. "I don't really know. It just came to me, I guess?"

All of a sudden it feels like she needs to pore over every single word before it comes out of her mouth.

Guess this is a therapy session, after all.

"What attracted you to Cognitive Neuroscience in the first place?"

"Well, I've always been curious about the human mind. I figured it made more sense than Chemistry if my ultimate goal was medical school."

"And what intrigues you the most when it comes to the workings of the mind?"

"I'm sorry—" Neve interjects before they stray too far off topic. "I really don't mean to be rude, but I was under the impression that we were going to continue yesterday's session."

Galen smiles courteously, but it's obvious he isn't too pleased. "Your dreams," he acknowledges.

"Yes."

"Very well, then. Let's dive right back in."

She should not have interrupted him. If she'd just let things take their course, maybe his 'self-serving' intentions would've naturally been brought to light.

But now that she has changed the topic, she might as well stay the course.

"I need to understand how it can be possible to dream about something before it happens," she cuts right to the chase. "Is there any scientific explanation that can account for something like that?"

"My approach to deciphering life's mysteries has always been from a philosophical perspective. And philosophy—as I'm sure you can imagine—is highly contested."

"I would love to hear your take," she says.

Galen sinks into thought, but not quite in the way someone would if they were pondering a question. He seems torn. Like someone who's faced with a big dilemma.

He clears his throat and leans forward in his seat, locking eyes with her.

His gaze is soul-deep.

His focus is unwavering.

It makes Neve wonderfully nervous, the way she would feel if she was about to open a treasure chest.

"What was it like when you broke the couch in my office?" Galen asks.

Well that wasn't random.

"I'm sorry?"

"I'd like you to explain as precisely as possible the thoughts, sensations, and emotions you experienced right before it broke under you."

"What does that have to do with my dreams?"

"It may not," Galen allows. "But I'd appreciate you explaining it to me anyway."

"I... honestly don't even know where to begin."

"Whatever comes to mind is often the best place to start," he smiles.

What it was like... Neve clings onto the first thing that pops into her head. "I start to feel numb, like when my leg falls asleep."

"I remember you saying it happens all the time?"

"Not *all* the time. Not when things are good. But if I'm under a lot of stress, or scared, or nervous... It usually happens when I'm having a panic attack."

"And what about on a cognitive level?" he asks.

And Neve realizes she's never bothered to assess her mental state during one of her episodes. She was always preoccupied with steadying her breathing, or holding back from breaking down in public.

"At first," she starts, "the thoughts in my head are jumbled."

"Jumbled how?"

"I get flooded with all these random thoughts that make absolutely no sense. It's hard to explain, but it's almost like there are ten of me in my head, and each of them is saying something without letting the others finish. And it's not a coherent conversation either. They all talk over one another about totally unrelated topics."

Galen's fascination dims into something darker.

"But they're *thoughts*, not voices," Neve clarifies.

"That must be maddening."

"It is. In the beginning. But then eventually all the scrambled thoughts... *blend*. They combine into one, unified thought," Neve exhales the tension in her gut. "And then I can breathe again."

Without breaking eye-contact, Galen leans back in his chair. He rests his elbow on the armrest and rubs his lower lip with the knuckle of his index finger.

His stare is intense. He looks like someone who is gauging the risk of an impossible leap.

Has she done it?

Has she passed his test?

Will he now give her the answers she seeks?

"What I'm about to tell you," he intertwines his fingers, "is difficult to understand, and even harder to accept. It is a ground-breaking revelation akin to discovering that the world isn't flat."

His intensity is subtle, but quite powerful. And his analogy is far too bold to take lightly.

"Can I trust that you will keep this information to yourself?" he raises his brows.

She's already come so far. How can she turn back now? "Yes. Yes, of course," she reassures him with an eager nod. If what Galen has to say can shed even the faintest light onto what's ailing her, then this will all have been worth it.

"Are you familiar with 'Modal Realism'?"

CHAPTER 16

THE FRAY THEORY

"Modal Realism..." Neve samples each word like a fine wine, trying to trace back to its origin, but instead she finds herself standing amidst a barren vineyard. The words sound so ambiguous and bland, she can't even venture a guess.

"I'm afraid I've never heard of the concept."

"Modal Realism is a theory proposed by American philosopher, David Kellogg Lewis. It claims that *all possible worlds exist*, and are *just as real as the actual world*."

"What do you mean by 'possible worlds'?"

"Exactly that: if something is possible, it exists."

"Like in a parallel universe?"

"Yes, but not quite. A parallel dimension would mean that there is only one alternative to our reality. But Lewis was convinced that there are *infinite* other dimensions out there. He believed that a possibility in our dimension is the reality of another dimension. And vice versa."

Staring, Neve licks her lips. What does any of this have to do with her dreams?

"That's a very interesting proposition," she says.

"Indeed," Galen nods. "But here's the catch: Lewis thought these alternate worlds are isolated from one another. That each dimension is self-contained and cannot influence the others."

"And I'm guessing... that's not the case?"

Galen's smirk broadens into a full-fledged smile. "Can you imagine?" he nearly whispers. "Can you just *imagine* the possibilities if Lewis was wrong? If there actually *was* a way to access alternate dimensions?"

"But how would that even be possible?"

"Through us, or course," Galen fans out his hands. "Through our minds."

Neve drops her gaze to keep herself from staring. What Galen is claiming sounds far more like fiction than science. Or even philosophy for that matter.

And considering just how many possibilities there are in the world—how many combinations of people, things, and events—'infinite' is just way too big for her to even conceive of. And to claim that *all* of these possibilities actually exist?

"Have you ever wondered why you often dream in third-person?" Galen asks. "And why you always look slightly different in your dreams than you do in real life?"

A tight sensation grips her core.

She *has*. Countless times. But she always assumed that's how dreams work. That dreaming is just a way for the brain to take a break from reality, and play.

Was she wrong? Is there more to it?

Neve's gaze crawls back up and meets Galen's.

"We look different in dreams, because dreams are windows to our alternate realities. When you dream in third person, you are observing another 'you', who *does in fact exist*."

Neve's throat is closing up. The air in her lungs is trapped. Her stomach feels heavy. Why is her body so quick to react to such an absurd claim?

"A dream, Miss Knightly, is simply a glimpse into the life of your Proxy."

Neve rummages through her mind, remembering some of her most vivid dreams. She recalls one of her alternate selves who was running for her life, but was caught, nonetheless. And another 'Proxy' who somehow understood Japanese. She even remembers a dream where she had a younger brother she raised by herself after her parents—*their* parents—died in a plane crash...

Those other Neves were all so different, but while dreaming, their lives and their realities made perfect sense. So much sense, in fact, that Neve never found herself questioning anything in her dreams.

They felt... *real*.

Suddenly the idea doesn't feel as absurd anymore.

Neve had no reason to be dreaming those dreams. And it was always a mystery why her mind would fabricate scenarios that have nothing to do with her reality.

She looks up at Galen who happens to be smiling, patiently waiting as Neve wraps her mind around his bold claims.

Every possibility in our dimension, is reality in an alternate dimension...

Come to think of it, given how many possibilities there are in the world, it is a bit odd that only one of them becomes reality, and all the others are wasted.

It's a shame to think that so many beautiful things that *could* happen never do. But if Galen is right, that means *no* possibility is ever wasted.

It means that the universe is far richer than Neve could've ever imagined.

"Is that why a dream doesn't have a beginning or an end?" she asks.

The crow's feet around Galen's gray eyes crinkle as he smiles. He nods with a slow blink.

"Dreams appear fragmented because they're not *entirely* the constructs of our minds. They're a blend of our alternate realities and our subconscious. And this phenomenon—establishing a connection to your Proxy—is called Resonance."

Resonance...

Is that why Galen seemed intrigued when she said neuroscience didn't 'resonate' with her?

The outline of Galen's face is starting to blur, and Neve simply can't understand why she's having such a visceral reaction to Galen's claims.

Philosophy isn't science, it's speculation, she tries to rationalize, but it isn't suppressing her panic.

"So... what you're basically saying is that dreams feel real, because they *are* real?"

"This isn't an easy pill to swallow. Surprise and doubt are both perfectly warranted reactions."

"What happens when you die in a dream?" Neve asks and watches Galen's expression harden.

Was that a dumb question? Or is Galen reluctant to discuss the subject because of Dylan?

"If what you're saying is true," she says, "then if I dream about dying—"

"You are in fact witnessing the death of another you," he completes her sentence, and looks away.

Does Dylan know all this? He must. The theories must have come up at some point. Even if not in a conversation between a doctor and his patient, then surely in one between a godfather and his godson.

Is that why Dylan believes he's doomed? Does he think the death of his Proxies is somehow related to his own?

Neve immediately banishes the thought. Because accepting Galen's claims would in a way be the same as acknowledging Dylan's nightmares as a kind of reality—as brutal tragedies that actually *happened* to him. And that is not something Neve is willing to accept. Not without putting up a fight.

"Is there any proof to back these theories?"

"The proof is all around you," Galen indicates his surroundings. "Whenever you experience something out of the ordinary, you are Resonating with one or more of your Proxies."

"What exactly would be 'out of the ordinary'?"

"The near-magical nuances of life which lie just outside the realm of science: premonitions, déjà vu, dreams. Pretty much any topic which falls under the category of 'peculiar' or 'paranormal'."

"Paranormal? As in ghosts?" Neve squints.

"Yes. Even apparitions are accounted for."

"How?" she slides to the edge of her seat.

"Would you like to venture a guess? Keeping the existence of multiple dimensions in mind?"

She mulls it over for a moment. "Well, if there are *infinite* alternate worlds out there, then there must be infinite alternate versions of the same person."

"Proxies," Galen allows. "And you are absolutely right. Some of these Proxies are highly similar to one another, and others are vastly different."

"So how do ghosts play into this?"

"Take yourself for example: at this very moment, you have countless Proxies who are sitting exactly where you are right now," Galen points to her seat, "but each is contained within her own dimension."

"But, how is that even possible?"

"This is where Lewis fell short. He believed Proxy dimensions are contained in isolated bubbles, when in fact, they are spatially overlapped. They all coexist in the exact same space."

"So, right now there is another *me* sitting here?" Neve asks, half-expecting to be able to feel her.

"Correct. And it's quite possible that she is yet to have this exact conversation with *my* Proxy. And as a result, she has absolutely no idea that *you* exist. She is unaware of you, just as you were unaware of *her* a few moments ago."

Neve sinks into thought.

If she has a Proxy that's sitting exactly where she is, then she must also have a Proxy who decided to skip today's session. And another who never even met Galen in the first place. And so on and so forth, until every single possibility is played out.

And suddenly all she can think of is the dandelion stemming from Elliot's grave.

The one she blew into the wind.

She envisions the white umbrella seeds, luminous in the sunlight, floating backwards through the air and reuniting with the bulbous stem. She imagines the white globe folding in onto itself, converging and un-growing in time, until the flower has reverted to its marigold self.

Young, and full of promise.

And then she finds herself back up on that diving board in the Aquatic Center, tightly clutching a metal anchor. And she realizes how having done just *one thing* differently, she would now be living a whole other reality—one that one of her Proxies is living because *she* did things differently.

Because every single decision, regardless of how seemingly insignificant, has the power to derail.

Because it's in the nature of paths to diverge.

Neve's heart breaks, realizing that she has in fact lost Elliot more than once. *Far* more than once.

But if so, wouldn't the reverse also be true?

"When someone dies, there are still infinite living versions of them in Proxy dimensions, aren't there?"

Galen nods. "And Resonance allows you to catch a glimpse of them through your Proxy's eyes."

A ghost is just a Proxy in an alternate dimension? Is that why there are people who swear they've seen ghosts move objects? *Oh Jesus Christ.*

Despite her efforts to contain her emotions, she is welling up. "Is that why when someone we love dies, we can still feel them? Like they're still with us?"

Galen confirms with a single nod.

Neve still can't bring herself to believe him, but a part of her desperately wants to. Because then, if she ever was to see Elliot again, it wouldn't be as a faded memory, or a daydream of what could've been.

She'd be seeing him as he *is*.

"What else?" Neve asks softly.

Galen leans over and grabs his mug.

"There are multiple ways in which someone can Resonate. And far more often than you'd think. For the majority of the population, it happens almost daily," he takes a sip from his drink.

"Daily!?" Neve's brows shoot up.

Galen chuckles with his lips tightly-pursed, then swallows the gulp of coffee in his mouth. He leans to his side and puts the mug back down on his table.

"Daily," he nods. "And not just through dreaming. Any time you think an unprovoked thought, or are suddenly overcome by a groundless emotion, struck by an epiphany, or conceive of a unique idea, you are in Sync with one or more of your Proxies."

Neve's mind wanders to the first time she caught a glimpse of Dylan's blood-red hair. Her gut tightens as she recalls the explosion of nervous pleasure in her chest the first time their eyes met.

"Love at first sight?" she asks, hoping Galen won't find it a juvenile question.

"It is the experience of meeting someone you have loved intimately in a Proxy dimension. And that is precisely why your first-ever meeting feels more like a reconciliation of two split halves."

This is big, Neve thinks. *This is way bigger than discovering that the world is round.*

"But if what you're saying is true, then that means each of us—through our Proxies—gets to see and do *everything* there is..."

"You are absolutely correct," he smiles. "It is what I like to call cross-dimensional self-actualization: no place left unvisited. No action untaken. Absolutely nothing of what life has to offer missed out on."

Neve can't help but smile at the thought.

"The instant you and your Proxies are born, your paths begin to diverge outwards like a fraying rope. Each Proxy's path in life is like an individual strand. And step by step, from moment to moment, you are creating a unique life for yourself. A life very similar to some of your Proxies, and highly different from others."

"And whenever you establish a connection to one of your Proxies..?"

"Resonance," Galen concludes.

"That's... incredible."

"It is. And in keeping with the analogy of a fraying rope, we've dubbed this premise: the Fray Theory."

"How exactly do premonitions tie into all of this?"

"A premonition occurs when you—through your Proxy—experience something in an almost identical dimension; something which winds up happening in your own realm soon thereafter. Give or take a few negligible differences."

"And what if it doesn't?"

"Then you're unlikely to even notice anything out of the ordinary," he says. "Déjà vu operates in much the same way, but with shorter lags in time."

"I thought déjà vu was a mistake in information processing; just a physiological error of the fatigued brain," Neve recalls Holt's lecture.

Galen laughs, almost as if at an inside joke.

"The Fray Theory is not the sole authority on the subject matter, I'm afraid. Though I honestly believe it should be."

"So *any time* there is a glitch in reality, it's due to Resonance?"

"Is that so hard to believe? The mind is the most fascinating, and by far the least understood enigma there is. It can move back in time simply by recalling a memory. And by imagining, it can bring things into being, even if only as a thought. And I believe in due time, those of us who indulge our minds will be able to transcend our physical limits."

"Transcend, how?"

"I believe that with introspection, discipline, and training, one day we'll evolve to be capable of much more than just 'experiencing' Resonance in a passive way. We'll be able to actively initiate it."

Neve marvels at the idea, completely spellbound by Galen's genius.

Speculation or science, it's so refreshing to watch him dismiss the most universally-accepted principle: the singularity of the universe itself!

"Transcending our physical limits..." she repeats, "but wouldn't that basically mean breaking the laws of physics?"

Galen's smile lights up his face.

"There will come a day, Miss Knightly, when we no longer need to reach for objects. We can summon them with our minds."

Neve's gaze darts to Galen's porcelain mug.

White. Just like the tombstones at the cemetery.

Is that what Romer was doing? Telekinesis!?

Neve goes to speak, but Galen is pulling his phone from his vest's pocket. So she bites down on her lip as he puts on his glasses.

Upon reading what appears to be a text message, Galen's brows furrow. "I'm sorry my dear. I'm afraid we're going to have to cut this short."

CHAPTER 17

THE REQUEST

G alen takes off his glasses as he rises from his chair. Though he's standing perfectly still, the concern in his eyes makes it clear his mind is racing a mile a minute. He glances towards the front door, and then begins to slowly fold his glasses and tuck them back into his vest's pocket.

Whatever the interruption, it seems important. So without asking questions, Neve rises from the couch and pulls her purse over her shoulder.

Galen looks at her, his eyes wider than an owl's.

"Hang on a moment—" he indicates for her to stay put, and scurries down the hallway next to the loft's front entry.

Feeling awkward just standing there, Neve slowly makes her way towards the front door.

Moments later, Galen reemerges from the room at the far end of the hallway, tightly gripping a leather-bound book.

"Take this," he pulls on the mouth of Neve's purse and slides the book inside.

His invasiveness alarms her.

"Read it," he says, "thoroughly, and as many times as it takes for things to sink in."

"What is it?" Neve looks down at the book.

"It's my life's work."

"Wh—" she looks up. "Professor, why would you trust me with something so valuable?"

"I can't explain," Galen shakes his head. "Not right now. Please, just go home and start reading. I'll call you later," he opens the front door, making it even harder for Neve to argue.

She's beginning to feel scared. It's like he's asking her to do something illegal.

"I appreciate the gesture, professor," Neve starts to pull the book back out of her purse. "I just don't think I'd have the time to—"

"Please," Galen pushes down on her hand, his eyes glossed over with paranoia. "You *need* to trust me."

Leave. Leave now.

"Yes. Okay," she nods and lets Galen lead her out into the main hallway.

She reaches out to press the elevator button, but Galen's hand flies up and blocks it.

"No—" he looks up at the floor the elevator is stalled at. "You should take the stairs."

She'd say goodbye, but he seems too preoccupied to even notice. So she pulls her purse up to her chest and backs out into the stairwell.

Her paranoia grows with every step she takes, and then she is just shuffling down as fast as she can, having no idea what it is she's running from.

Five floors down, she bursts out of the building's side-exit into a dim and narrow alley.

The stress of her obscure circumstances is fueling her anxiety. So she leans onto the cold brick wall and tries to steady her breathing.

For some reason, her mind wanders back to when Galen's interest in her was first sparked.

It wasn't when she mentioned her dreams. It was when the loveseat in his office collapsed under her. And again today, his revelations about the theories followed revisiting the same incident.

She pulls her purse up against her chest and rests her chin onto it.

Why would Galen entrust her with his life's work? What on earth did he mean when he said inviting her over was 'self-serving'?

Has he been stalled in his research? Does he think of Neve as a potential case-study to help him with a breakthrough?

That sure would account for his personal touch of inviting her over for coffee and conversation. But it doesn't explain him parting with his work so hastily.

What was so damn important that he had to get her out of there like that?

A flash of darkness in the corner of Neve's vision startles her.

She pushes off the wall and looks down the length of the alley. Whatever she saw came and went too quickly, but from where? The door she just emerged from is the only side door to the building.

The thought of someone hiding behind the hedges propels her onto the main street; where there's light, noise, and people.

With warm light draping over her skin and fresh air filing her lungs, she doesn't feel quite as scared anymore. But at this point she just wants to go home.

Today is fast shaping up to be as distressing as yesterday. There's only so much she should have to put up with.

With a cleansing breath, she sets out towards her apartment. But a few steps in, she notices someone staring at her from down the block.

He's dressed in all black, and appears to be in his late thirties.

Is *he* the flash of black she saw a few seconds ago?

Probably not. He is way too far down the street.

And yet, there is something about the way he is eyeing Neve that makes her skin crawl.

She finds herself taking smaller and smaller steps with her attention firmly on him. But the moment his gaze drops down to her purse, Neve stops dead in her tracks and tightens her grip around it.

Without a second thought, she turns and starts in the opposite direction towards Dylan's apartment.

This makes way more sense, anyway. His place is only a few blocks up the street. She can kill some time there until her irrational sense of doom passes.

Maybe they can even discuss the theories. Might be fun to swap notes about each other's dreams and experiences. Galen might have sworn her to secrecy, but surely his own godson is exempt from the rule.

She puts a bit more distance between herself and the man in black, and then looks over her shoulder in his direction.

And he is nowhere to be seen. He must've turned the corner and gone about his business.

A wave of relief washes over Neve. But with her focus misplaced, she ends up bumping into someone.

"Oh—pardon me," she backs up.

At the sight of her obstruction, she immediately feels sick to her stomach.

"Miss Knightly."

"Professor Holt," Neve acknowledges on impulse.

She can't believe it. As if it weren't bad enough to have run into the prick off university grounds, she has now made actual physical contact with him.

Guess I'll be scrubbing myself with bleach all night.

Holt flaunts what he surely thinks is a charming smile. "Fancy running into you here," he slides his gloved hands into the pockets of his wool overcoat.

"Yes, small city," she flashes a shamelessly phony smile. "Very, *very* small."

"What brings *you* to this lovely neighborhood?" he asks, judging Neve's attire with no attempt at hiding his disconent.

"Well actually, my boyfriend and I own a condo a couple of blocks over."

Wow, Neve. That wasn't even remotely true. Why not just go ahead and throw in a Lamborghini while you're at it?

"Is that right?" Holt nods impressively. "Well good for you. I myself have invested in a few properties around the block."

I hate you. We're not friends. Die.

"Right, well—it was really great running into you, professor."

Seeming a bit disappointed, "right," he extends his hand for a shake. "Likewise."

His gesture confuses her. Is this an honest peace-offering, or another one of his traps?

With the fate of her final exam still hanging in the balance, Neve errs on the side of caution and shakes his hand.

His nod signals the end of their unholy encounter, so Neve retrieves her hand and resumes her walk towards Dylan's place.

And for a moment, she ponders the likelihood of one of her Proxies actually getting along with Holt. If every possibility is reality *some* dimension, then there must be another version of her who—

She shudders at the sheer thought and sneaks a glance in his direction. But instead of Holt, she spots the same stranger she saw earlier down the block.

He is now roughly the same distance from her as when she first spotted him. Which means—

RUN.

She crosses to the middle of the street and snags an approaching taxi in the nick of time.

CHAPTER 18

RESONANCE

Neve keeps glancing behind her through the taxi's rear window as she directs the driver one block at a time. By the off-chance that her stalker is following her, the odds of Neve losing the tail is much higher if she throws a few twists and turns into the mix.

After ten or so minutes of aimless driving through downtown's veins, Neve directs the driver to Dylan's place. She overpays cash to save time, bolts out of the taxi, and darts across the street to Dylan's.

She keeps pressing his buzzer, but to no avail. Her impulse would normally be to assume he isn't home, but he hasn't returned any of the texts she sent him during her drive, either.

Is he upset with her over what happened at her apartment? He did say there's something he needs to do, but that was yesterday.

Panic-striken, she scans the vicinity.

In spite of her aimless drive, she saw the man in black only a few blocks away. What if he's still in the area? What if all of this was for nothing?

The main door to the building squeaks behind her and one of Dylan's neighbors steps out.

Neve flashes him an innocent smile and then slips into the lobby behind him. She pulls the door shut to make sure no one else can sneak in like she just did, does another quick scan of the street, and when she doesn't see any signs of her stalker, decides to skip the lift and takes the stairs all the way up to the top floor.

But what if Dylan's not home?

What is she going to do then?

She *could* call the police. Even if her fears aren't warranted, and even if they laugh at, or scorn her for wasting their time, it's still within her rights.

Panting, Neve emerges from the stairwell into the hallway of the sixth floor. But before her fist can land onto Dylan's front door, it swings open to reveal him with damp hair.

His skin is a bit flushed and glistening, and he is wearing nothing but a white towel around his waist.

"Hey—" he frowns off Neve's expression. "What's wrong?"

"I buzzed—" she says while staring at his insanely ripped body.

"Yeah, I was in the shower. Is everything okay?"

"Yeah. I think? This creepy guy was stalking me a few blocks down, so—"

"What guy?" Dylan's tone drops, deep and urgent. "What did he look like?"

"Can I come in?"

"Oh—yeah, of course," he paves the way for her, and then scans the hallway before closing the door.

Lingering in the foyer, Neve watches as he applies the heavy-duty bolt-locks to the front door. And with her fresh experience of being followed, the locks no longer seem like a frivolous precaution taken by a wealthy father. They seem... *necessary.*

But Yaletown is a posh neighborhood. One of the safest in the city. Are those locks meant to keep out someone in particular?

Could it be the same man Neve is trying to evade?

"Just give me a sec to throw something on," Dylan makes his way towards his bedroom.

"Oh—sure. Take your time." Neve watches him go, astounded by just how much his body has changed over the years. From the back he looks like a whole new person, even in spite of his signature red hair.

With relief settling back in, Neve makes her way into the living space and sits down on the couch.

From Dylan's bedroom, the sliding and banging of drawers are followed by hasty swooshes of fabric. A 'click', a sharp 'hssss', and the wobbling of a metallic bottle follow, and Neve can't help but crack a smile.

He still uses mousse in his hair.

Slowly, the events of the day creep back into her mind. She pulls Galen's book out of her purse just as Dylan walks back out into the living space.

He's wearing a pair of dark jeans and a navy-blue T-shirt that's way too small for him. The collar is so stretched, Neve couldn't tell it was a v-neck at first.

"Sorry about that," Dylan pulls the rim of his shirt down, covering the exposed sliver of his milky skin.

"Wait, is that—" Neve's eyes narrow as she points to Dylan's shirt.

"Yeah—" he smiles and looks down, then starts to smooth out the shirt's fold-lines near his abdomen. "You helped me pick it out on Boxing Day."

Three and a half years ago, Neve reminisces. She can practically see the clouds they breathed into the chilly air, and feel the smolder of her raspberry tea seeping into her hand.

"What's that?" Dylan walks over and takes a seat next to her.

She looks down at the book. "Galen lent it to me."

"Nice," Dylan's brows rise, his smile waning a bit. "What's it about?"

And just then, Neve realizes the book has no title. "Um—I haven't had the chance to check it out yet."

Gliding her hand over the soft leather cover, she's overcome by a peculiar feeling. By comfort shrouded in mystery.

And all of a sudden it feels like there's something she was supposed to remember.

Something important.

She slides her nail along the side of the book and opens it to a random page.

It's type-written, Neve marvels. Just like the book from her nightmare last night.

That one didn't have a title either.

"You okay?" Dylan rests his hand on her back.

Neve looks up at him. "Has Galen ever mentioned the Fray Theory to you?"

Dylan shakes his head with a small, unknowing pout. "Can't say that he has, no."

Neve's brows knit.

"That's really weird," she starts to skim the text in the book. "So, he *never* brought it up when you guys talked about your nightmares?"

"Honestly, I think he secretly hated talking about my dreams. He'd keep trying to change the subject."

Neve can definitely identify with that. Galen was dismissive with her too when they first met.

"Why do you think he would do that?" she asks.

"I have no idea. Maybe he thought I was trying to get attention," he shrugs it off. "So after a while I just stopped bringing them up altogether."

"I doubt that's what he thought. You're not exactly an attention-whore," she laughs to lighten the mood, but Dylan just looks at her with a ghost of a smile.

"But I get it," she looks down.

"Get what?"

"Why you stopped bringing it up. How exhausting it can be to keep screaming into the void."

Neve tries to shake it off, but the straws are fast piling up: her childhood therapy, Elli's death, Galen's highly questionable behavior...

"What's going on, Neve?" Dylan glides the back of his fingers along her draping hair, and pulls the onyx veil behind Neve's ear.

"I don't know why he hasn't—I mean—maybe it'll make things worse for you," she says, remembering her promise to Galen. A promise she would break in a heartbeat if Dylan's happiness was at stake.

And she wholeheartedly believes that it is.

"Our session yesterday was cut short, and he was booked solid for the next little while, so he invited me over to his place so we can—"

"His place?" Dylan smiles with genuine surprise.

"Yeah," she says awkwardly, letting him know she too was taken aback by Galen's offer.

Silence stretches out between them.

"Cool," Dylan starts to pick at the fraying threads along the rips in his jeans. "Are you going to take him up on it?"

"I... sort of just came back from there," she holds up the book.

σ

Neve follows along as Dylan reads the introductory chapter of *The Fray Theory*.

"It's more or less what he and I talked about," she says once Dylan's reached the end. "So, what do you think?"

"I don't know…" Dylan mumbles and relaxes back on the couch. "I mean, it's fascinating."

"Just don't know if you believe any of it?"

"Well, that's the thing. It's not something you can falsify either."

"I wonder how he came up with it."

"He's spent pretty much his whole life pondering the meaning of it all," he says with a hint of sarcasm.

"If only they were true," Neve says longingly.

"You *want* them to be true?"

"I don't know. I guess it's nice to imagine another Elli out there who didn't go through with it."

With the mere mention of his name, she wells up. "Ugh, sorry," she quickly collects her tears with her cardigan's sleeve.

"Babe," he swings his arm around and pulls Neve in, planting a firm, loving kiss on her temple. "I'm so sorry you lost him," he whispers.

"We would've been friends," she says. "He would have warmed up to you in no time."

Her gaze falls back down onto the book and she notices the page number, bottom center.

Five… she frowns, then reaches out and flips to a page lined with a faint pencil grid. On top of the grid, there are twelve square diagrams in black ink.

Dylan turns his attention to the diagrams as well.

The first diagram is a black square with a squiggly line cutting diagonally across it.

At the bottom-left corner, where the line begins, there's a black ink dot labeled 'birth'. And at the top-right corner, where the line ends, there's another dot labeled 'death'.

"I think this is a two-dimensional representation of a person's life," she mutters under her breath, and looks to the other diagrams.

At first glance, they all seem identical to the first one. But there is a major difference between them: although each line starts at 'birth' in the bottom-left corner, it ends at a slightly different 'death' node.

"Same birth, different deaths," Dylan mumbles.

Neve looks at the final diagram which appears to be a composite of the previous: all eleven lines are layered onto one another, starting at 'birth', and then diverging outwards.

It vaguely reminds her of the 'fraying rope' Galen mentioned during their session.

"The Fray Theory is about multiple dimensions," she starts to think out loud. "This last diagram must be a representation of someone's *possible* lives."

"What are these intersections?" Dylan points out a few instances where the lines cross one another.

Neve lifts the book up for a closer look.

Next to each intersection, there's a small marking: the letter 'R'.

Resonance?

She lowers the book back down onto her lap and looks about the page for a reference to the 'R'. She soon discovers a formula near the top-right corner of the page.

Nothing complicated. Just a symbol that looks like a sideways six, an equal sign, and a zero.

$\sigma = 0$?

"What's this?" she points it out to Dylan.

"That's Sigma," Dylan indicates the sideways six, "the eighteenth letter of the Greek alphabet. Haven't you studied this?"

"Yeah, I think so," Neve recalls frantically copying one of her colleague's math homework right before class. "It's been awhile."

"It's also a mathematical symbol that represents Standard Deviation," Dylan says.

"It measures how far you deviate from average?" she squints, it all slowly coming back to her. "Okay, but what does it have to do with multiple realities?"

Dylan taps his finger on the formula. "Maybe it's referring to how far you deviate from each one of your Proxies? The bigger the number, the larger the difference between the two of you?"

"So if Sigma equals zero, that means you and your Proxy are almost identical?"

"If you have infinite Proxies, you're bound to have billions and *billions* of them that are almost identical to you. I think this formula means something else." He looks up and into space, his thoughts unfolding.

Neve watches him, feeling overcome by nostalgia. Being here feels just like one of their old study dates.

A curious smile overcomes Dylan, and he shifts on the couch to face Neve better.

"Alright," he raises his hands like someone who's about to pitch a brilliant new idea. "Imagine you're done with med school, that you're a world-renowned cardiologist like your mom."

"Ugh."

Dylan chuckles. "Now imagine one of your Proxies dropped out of school and wound up becoming this super famous artist. She lives in LA, owns her own art studio, and charges a ton of money for each of her pieces."

Intrigued, Neve pulls her legs up on the couch and faces him with a tight smirk.

"Now... imagine there is this big, glamorous event that only the world's elite are invited to."

"In which dimension?"

"*Both*," his brows rise.

A faint smile colors Neve's expression. "This event is the common denominator," she nods, "where both of my realities overlap."

"It's when your deviation from your Proxy is zero: you are both in the same place, at the same time."

"We're in Sync," Neve says, her mind wandering back to how Galen put it: that you 'feel connected' to something much bigger than yourself whenever you Resonate with your Proxy.

She looks down at the formula, nearly certain that 'R' stands for Resonance. But when she looks up to meet Dylan's gaze, her smile melts right off her lips.

"What's wrong?"

"Hmm?" Dylan snaps to attention. "Oh—nothing."

And Neve notices him pull his index finger off one of the 'death' nodes on the final diagram.

Her fears come full circle, reminding her of what their conclusions *really* mean.

"Can I just—" Dylan pulls the book onto his own lap and flips back to the table of contents. His finger traces down the list until it arrives at 'Dreams'.

"Dylan," Neve watches him flip to the designated chapter and start to read.

And the fold between his brows becomes deeper and deeper as his green eyes glide from left to right.

He flips to the following page, but a few words in, slams the book shut.

"It's okay," Neve starts to rub his back.

His breathing is rapid and shallow, and his body quivers every time he exhales.

"You're fine. Just keep taking deep breaths," she says, knowing exactly what he's going through. She reaches up and runs her hand through Dylan's hair, just like how she used to whenever they cuddled up on the couch.

"I'm okay," he tries to brush it off, but it's clear he is nowhere near over the hump.

"Let me get you some water," Neve rises from the couch, but pauses. She bends down and takes Dylan's face into her hands, and plants a gentle kiss between his brows.

His eyes fall shut, and for the first time, Neve feels what *he* felt every time he kissed her worries away: the joy of his frown unfurling beneath her lips.

Parting with Dylan's smooth skin, Neve heads for the kitchen.

"I'm fine, Neve," he calls after her as she opens the fridge. "It's nothing new."

Neve turns to face him with a pitcher of water in her hand.

Nothing new? Since when has he—

An aggressive knock on the front door makes her jump out of her skin.

"Jesus—" she puts the pitcher down on the black stone countertop. "I'll get it."

"Just leave it," Dylan's hushed voice reaches Neve from behind as she walks over to the door. She peers through the peephole, and suddenly jolts back with a horrified gasp.

"What's wrong!?" Dylan springs to his feet.

'Oh my *GOD*!' Neve mouths as she rushes back to him. "It's that guy," she whispers, "it's the creep that was following me!"

CHAPTER 19

QUANDARY

Despite gripping Dylan's switchblade in her hand, Neve can't rid herself of the fear wringing her insides. Hiding in his bedroom, she watches Dylan through a hairline gap between the door and its frame. Bursts of aggressive knocking continue to shake up the air, and Neve can't imagine what will happen once Dylan swings the apartment door open.

How did her stalker find her? And how did he get into the building? Did a neighbor let him in? If so, how did he know which floor Neve ran up to? It's not like the lift would have given her away, she took the stairs.

Unless… The stalker isn't after *her*. He's after—"

Neve flings her focus back onto Dylan as he looks through the peephole. His intensity diminishes a bit, making Neve wonder if it's because he knows the man behind the door.

Is this whole thing just a huge misunderstanding?

Another burst of aggressive knocking.

"What do you want!?" Dylan shouts.

"RCMP! Open up!"

The police? Neve's glare tightens as Dylan glances in her direction, looking completely puzzled.

Is her stalker just an undercover cop? But even if so, why is he after *her*?

Her heart drops.

Is this about the cemetery? Romer was convinced that they were being watched. Oh, she's in so much trouble. And she can't even explain what happened!

The sound of Dylan unclasping the locks beckons her attention.

No, don't! Tell them I'm not here!

The instant Dylan opens the door, a group of men in black uniforms flood the foyer. Two of them grab Dylan by his shoulders and arms, and bend him over the kitchen counter.

A choked grunt escapes Dylan as his face collides with the stone surface, and Neve jolts back, covering her mouth at the sight of her stalker walking into the apartment following the initial flurry.

His hollow gaze scours his surroundings until it fixates onto something further ahead of him. He then heads towards the living area, out of Neve's narrow range of vision.

"What's going on?" Dylan demands.

"You're under arrest," says the thick-necked alpha applying his handcuffs.

"For *what*!?"

Moments later, the stalker reappears in the foyer, slipping Galen's book into a protective plastic case.

What..? Neve gawks at him. The book was in her purse. How did he know she even had it!?

Something's wrong. Something's seriously wrong. And not the kind Neve can fix by bursting out of the bedroom and claiming the blame.

These men seem dangerous.

All this over a book?

Neve's stalker scans his vicinity, gives the alpha in charge a terse nod, and then disappears into the hallway with the book in his possession.

"What the hell is going on!?" Dylan demands.

The man who cuffed him grips the back of his neck and pulls him off the counter without uttering a word. He then—with the aid of two others—escorts Dylan out of the apartment.

Those who remain behind start to toss the place.

But they got the book, Neve thinks. *What else are they looking for?*

She can't think. Everything is happening too fast. She needs to buy herself some time till she can figure something out. But with the men guarding the front door, running is out of the question.

She needs a better place to hide. But where? The closet? Under the bed? They'd find her in *seconds*.

The moment the men are out of her direct line of sight, she slides out of the bedroom and scampers all the way down the adjacent hallway, opens the very last door, and sneaks into the laundry room.

She gently shuts the door behind her, but realizes it doesn't lock from the inside.

Shit!

As she turns around in a state of panic, her eyes are stung by the glare of a big, bright square in the ceiling.

Her pupils constrict, but once her eyes adjust, she realizes what she's looking at is not a light fixture, but a rooftop-access hatch!

It's almost unbelievable.

She bolts to the back of the room and climbs the narrow metal ladder two rungs at a time. She fiddles with the snap-closure of the hatch, and then pushes up against it.

The hinge squeaks, pinning her in place like a thumbtack on a map. She can't seem to open it any further without it making more noise, so she rests the weight of the door onto her back and struggles through the narrow gap.

Once her feet have cleared, the door falls shut with a loud and echoing bang.

RUN.

She breaks into a sprint towards the rooftop exit, ready to explode through it. But at the touch of the door handle, she suddenly hesitates.

What would a cop do in a situation like this?

Cover all exits.

Her realization punctures her like a bullet wound, her hope spilling out.

She turns around, expecting to be met with one of the men in her pursuit. Instead, she witnesses a row of rooftop hatches trailing behind the one she just emerged from.

Her eyes widen. The very last hatch is open, its door resting onto its retaining arm.

A sound comes from inside Dylan's unit.

They're coming.

Neve pushes on the stairwell exit and swings it open so hard that it slams against the inner wall.

She then sprints past Dylan's hatch towards the opposite end of the roof, and climbs down through the neighbor's open hatch into their laundry room.

She bangs her fist against the retaining arm and catches the hatch door as it falls down on her.

A moment later, she hears the same squeak that gave her away, and watches the back of a man's head emerge from Dylan's hatch—just in time for him to witness the rooftop exit door swinging shut.

With a burst of static, he relays this information over radio, and Neve knows her diversion was at least somewhat successful.

She lowers the hatch door into its frame, locks it, and exhales the breath she's been holding onto.

She crawls down the ladder and curls up in the corner of the room, but it's no good. She's still in full view of anyone who might walk by on the roof.

A coarse and assertive voice draws her attention from inside the apartment unit. She is almost certain it belongs to one of the cops who partook in Dylan's arrest.

Between him and the cop manning the roof, her only viable escape routes have been compromised.

She squeezes her eyes shut, trying to think a way out of this mess. She's already managed to outsmart them once, so it's not impossible.

Think! What else would a cop do?

What *wouldn't* he do?

Her eyes fly open.

She checks that the coast is clear up on the roof, and then bolts towards the dryer and looks inside.

It's a long shot, but it's her only shot.

She pulls the hamper towards her and rakes out the dry clothes, sizes up the inside of the machine, and with substantial effort, crawls into it.

Tight, bumpy, and painful.

But she fits!

She reaches out, grabs a handful of clothes from the hamper, and starts to restock the confinement. It doesn't take much to conceal her, but she pulls it all back in. She just can't risk tipping off the owner. The hatch being locked from the inside is already a huge discrepancy.

She grabs the dryer door and shuts it as gently as she can. With it, what little light was seeping through the folds in the clothes is snuffed out.

And now it's a waiting game.

There's barely enough air in here to sustain her for a few minutes, and she's already starting to feel dizzy from the thick scent of fabric-softener.

Her heart is drumming against her ribcage, and her folded legs pressing onto her chest won't let her take a deep breath. But if there's the slightest chance that she can evade those men—those aggressive and frightening men—

Dylan.

With the thought of him, a pang of anxiety stabs the inside of her chest.

If Galen's book was what those men were after, then this entire thing is undeniably her fault.

What is she going to do?

What are *they* going to do?

Her thoughts and breathing cease immediately as the door to the laundry room is swung open.

"Here we are," a woman's voice announces. "What exactly has she done, again?"

She? So it *was* her they were after.

Another burst of static is followed by a muffled mumble. Either they've caught onto her little stunt and she's about to be yanked out of the dryer, or—

"Thanks for your time," says the coarse voice, and then the laundry door moans shut with a small click.

Neve breaks into a silent sob.

Her purse, along with her keys and wallet are still back at Dylan's.

If they didn't already know who she is, they sure as hell do now. And even if by some miracle Neve manages to snag her keys back, going home would most likely mean walking straight into their trap.

What has she gotten herself into?

What was Galen so afraid of?

What if the book isn't even *his*? Did he use Neve to smuggle out someone else's property!?

With every labored breath, the consequences of knowing about Galen's theories become even more terrifying.

Knowledge is power. And people kill for power.

What is she going to do?

CHAPTER 20

HOLLOW

Romer sits by himself on a small stretch of beach, gazing at the blue harbor beyond. Light and warmth come and go as mild gusts of wind drape off the sun, making the atmosphere waver back and forth between blue and gray. And today, instead of squawking seagulls or giant cruiseship horns, it's Neve's shrill cries that echo in his mind.

He remembers the way she looked up at him, her big, brown eyes amber in the sunlight. How her tears had cut trails through the dirt on her cheeks, and how her heart was drumming against his lower chest like a little hummingbird.

But what he remembers most vividly is how just moments before, her grip was hard enough to crush the bones in his wrist. Hard enough for Isaac's blade to break upon contact with her flesh.

He squints as his mind draws parallels between the two incidents.

At the prison yard, *his* life was on the line. At the graveyard: Neve's.

Survival mode. Life or death.

Is that what it takes.? Is that why whenever his emotions are heightened, inexplicable things start to happen all around him?

He rises to his feet, pats the sand off the back of his jeans, and starts towards his workshop.

Up ahead, a row of industrial buildings run along the train tracks like a brick fortress, separating the harbor from Gastown. But unbeknownst to even the locals, Romer knows a way through which cuts his trip in half.

He dips under a broken chain-link fence, then cuts across the tracks towards a narrow gap separating two abandoned factories.

He turns to his side and slips into the divide—an efficient shortcut, but not a comfortable one.

Halfway through the passage, his phone vibrates.

He retrieves it from his back pocket, careful not to scrape his leather jacket against the walls.

Neve... A faint smile sweetens his lips.

Think I'm ready for my cape.

He clears his throat and receives the call. "Hello?"

"Romer—thank God!" Neve breathes heavily into her phone. "I'm so sorry. I'm just—I didn't know who else to call."

Her urgency alarms him. "What's wrong?"

"The cops are after me," Neve whispers. Her voice is somehow loud *and* muffled.

Romer frowns. "Why?"

"I don't know for sure. They came over to Dylan's looking for *me* I think, but arrested him instead."

"Well that makes perfect sense."

"I don't know what to do."

"Where are you? Why are you whispering?"

"I'm in Dylan's neighbor's dryer."

Silence.

"Is that slang for something?"

"What? No, no I'm hiding. I'd leave, but there's no way to know if they're still searching the area."

Is this a prank, Romer wonders?

He tilts his head back and shuts his eyes. "Neve—I got a lot of work to do."

"I swear, I'm not messing with you. This guy was following me on the street, and less than an hour later, he shows up at Dylan's with a bunch of cops."

"How do you even know they were after *you*?"

"I overheard one of them."

"What did you do?"

"I hid in Dylan's room, then I—"

"*No*, forty-watt. What did you do that made the cops come after you in the first place?"

"Well, that's just it. I'm not even sure they *were* the cops. They said they were RCMP, but something was really off about them."

"Like what? Their belts didn't match their shoes?"

"They didn't ask for Dylan's ID. Just barged in and arrested him. They didn't even read him his rights."

Romer suddenly feels a tight, painful heaviness in his gut. "What?"

"The Miranda rights? You have the right to remain silent," Neve starts to recite from memory, "anything you say—"

'*May be used against you in a court of law—*'

Romer's mind wanders back to the worst day of his life.

Suddenly he is standing in the middle of a police barricade, staring at the bloody body of a child being strapped to a stretcher.

All he sees are flashing sirens.

All he hears is the wailing of a broken father.

And all he feels are the steely handcuffs biting his trembling wrists.

"Romer?" Neve's voice frees him from his waking nightmare, but the wretched self-hatred continues to wreak havoc inside him.

He leans forward and rests his forehead onto the cold brick. He feels faint. There isn't enough air. It feels like the walls are closing in.

"Romer, say something."

"I'm fine," he clears his throat. "I'm listening."

"Look—I know we barely know each other, but I really need your help. I have no idea what to do."

Pull yourself together, he squeezes his eyes shut, banishing his crippling weakness.

"How long have you been hiding?" he asks.

"I don't know... maybe ten minutes?"

"Hang up right now and turn off your phone," his sharp whisper fogs up his screen. "They're probably going to search the whole building."

"They've already searched this unit."

Romer puffs his cheeks and exhales. "Well, in that case, your safest bet is to just stay put."

"Need I remind you I'm in a dryer?"

He chuckles. "You must look like a pretzel."

"I feel like one, too."

"At least you're in a cage of your own choosing," he says, and immediately regrets it. Did he just give away his dirty little secret?

It's fine. She doesn't know anything.

"Do you think Dylan's okay?"

Is Dylan okay? Romer hadn't considered it since before the legitimacy of the cops was brought into question.

"I'm sure he's fine." Romer picks up his pace, eyes glued to the bright slit at the end of the passage. He doesn't know what he can possibly do to help, but if Dylan actually *is* in some sort of danger...

Just as he is about to step out into the open, an uneasy feeling pins him at the brink. He remains put, concealed by deep shadows, fearful of what could be brought to light should he step out.

He inches to the very edge of the wall and sneaks a glance towards his workshop.

Down by the entry, several black SUVs are idling. Their windows are tinted, so Romer looks up to the second floor where he detects dark figures lurking about—strangers who must have broken his padlock in order to enter his shop.

He glances at either ends of the street. Amongst the casual crowd, there are several well-built men in dark clothes trying to appear inconspicuous. One of them is dawdling on the sidewalk, pretending to be on his phone. Another is sitting on a bench, reading the paper. And the third is snapping photos of the area with a long lens camera.

To someone not looking for it, it would be so easy to miss the dead giveaways: like how the men make intermittent eye-contact with one another, but don't openly acknowledge each other. Or how each one is engaged in an activity he can quickly abandon.

But who are they? The cops? *No.* The cops would need a warrant to break into his place.

Unless they've already got one. But for what? He hasn't done anything.

The cemetery...

Someone must have reported him to the cops. No doubt whoever was watching them at the cemetery.

And Neve was with him. It all makes sense now.

He slides back into the depths of the passage. He can't go back to prison. He won't.

Three years was already a lifetime.

Retracing his steps back towards the train tracks, he remembers still being on the phone with Neve.

"Hey—you still there?" he asks.

"Yeah," she says after a brief pause, her voice soft and broken.

Romer sighs. "Don't worry. He's gonna be fine."

"Okay," she says with an even meeker tone. "What do I do, Romer?"

"Just stay put, for now. Wait for the dust to settle. And lose your phone. I will too."

"If they were tracing our call, I think I'd be in cuffs right now," she says.

"You really want to risk it?"

"But how do we stay in touch?"

Romer ponders it, and then checks the time on his phone. "Okay, here's the plan: stay put for as long as you can, unless there's a fire, or whatever, and once you know *for sure* the coast is clear, sneak out and meet me at—" he hesitates, deciding to take a more cryptic route. "Meet me at that place where I *'fell'* for you. Wink wink."

After another stretch of silence, "when?" she asks.

Romer breathes a sigh of relief.

"Midnight."

CHAPTER 21

ASUNDER

D ylan opens his eyes to pitch black. His head is throbbing, his mind feels foggy, and his entire body is atremble. Despite his best efforts, he can't seem to retrace his steps to the juncture that has led him here.

Wherever *here* is.

He goes to swallow, but something rubbery seems to be lodged in his mouth. He reaches up to remove it and finds his left hand following along.

A weak frown registers on his face as he realizes his wrists and legs are tightly bound.

He inhales a deep breath through his nose, taking in warm, stale air. He screams at the top of his lungs, but his gag soaks up his voice like a sponge.

Things are seeming worse by the second.

The wild growl of a v8 engine fills his ears, and he instantly places himself inside the trunk of a car. And with a sudden jolt, he skids to his side and strikes the back of the tight confinement.

The car must've been idling at a traffic light when he came to. That would explain the trembling, but as for why he is tied up and being transported in a dark trunk, he can't even venture a guess.

With his energy slowly returning to him, he starts to feel around for the trunk's release latch. And in no time, he realizes the pull-grip has been cut off.

Shit.

With a bit of struggle, he repositions himself and starts to claw at the inner lining. If he can just break through to the brake lights, he will be able to shove them out of their sockets. If he's lucky, he just might be able to alert someone on the outside.

Come on! *COME ON!*

His raking becomes more and more savage. His nails are breaking, bleeding, but he ignores the sting. His warm, slippery blood is running down his fingers and pooling in-between, but he keeps at it.

Claustrophobia is a state of mind. All suffering is a state of mind, he reminds himself over and over until the words unhinge from their meaning.

His harrowing circumstances are fast becoming a haunting reminder of a deeply-buried memory.

It seems history is adamant to repeat itself.

σ

~Three Years Ago~

Silver light pours over the windowsill. It's almost too bright to look directly at.

It must be a full moon tonight, Dylan thinks, and then looks at the clock on his beaten night-stand.

It is 3:12 a.m., and the barracks are as still as a frozen lake.

Lips pursed and jaw clenched, he exhales through his nose. It's been about twenty minutes since a bed-frame has creaked, or since one of his roommates has muttered something unintelligible in his sleep.

And in the blink of an eye, it's already 3:15 a.m., leaving him with exactly fifteen minutes and not a moment to spare.

He rolls to his side and slides off his bed onto his knees. From underneath the bed, he pulls out a small backpack, jacket, and boots.

With his eyes darting from one cadet to another, he sneaks out the room and carefully shuts the door behind him.

One down, he breathes a silent sigh of relief. His least consequential obstacle is now behind him.

He looks down the hallway in both directions. The coast is clear as far as he can tell, but directly across, the door to cadet Colton's room is ajar.

Every muscle in his body tenses.

Has he been caught? Is it over, already?

And in that moment, Dylan realizes he hasn't even thought of a plausible explanation for being out and about so late.

He looks down the hallway towards the latrines, and quickly decides not to stick around for an actual problem to present itself. He takes the stairs all the way down to the main level, and then starts to put on his boots and jacket.

He throws on his backpack, and lurks over to the exit, peering at the grounds through the small glass window.

Once again, the coast is clear.

As he exits the building, his face is stung by the crisp night air. He inhales a deep, oxygenated breath, and sets out towards the plush forest framing the academy.

Though the odds of running into a security guard are slim at this hour, he doesn't risk cutting across the open field. It's far too big a risk to shave only a few minutes off his excursion. So he keeps within the dark shadows of the night with his sights set on the trees in the distance.

Soon enough, he reaches the brim of the forest and crosses the threshold into the heart of nature.

The darkness is sweeping, the moonlight barely managing to penetrate the thick foliage. And Dylan is still far too close to the premises to even entertain using his flashlight.

So he hurries through the winding trail, assessing each step based on the outlines of trees and bushes.

The rustling of dried leaves beneath his boots is roaring in the dead of night, sending his heartbeat to a gallop. He needs to be especially careful not to drift off onto one of the embedded training grounds, or stumble into a man-made ravine.

Or worst of all: trip an alarm.

His eyes eventually adjust to the darkness, able to better detect the ditches compromising his gait. But even once he has picked up the pace, the end of the trail seems nowhere in sight.

Is he lost? Or is it just harder to tell the progress he's made because of the lack of light?

He reaches for his map, confident that by now he is far enough from campus. But just as he grabs his flashlight, the crunching of brittle twigs startles him.

Dylan swings his head towards the source of the noise and sees a pair of hands spring up into the air.

A gesture of peace?

"Identify yourself," Dylan demands with a rather assertive tone. If it's one of the junior cadets, he just might be able to feign authority and send the kid on his way.

"I don't want no trouble, man," a surprisingly lax voice reassures. "Just doin' a late-night delivery."

Dylan switches his flashlight on and holds it up. "Step into the light," he orders, and watches a lanky twenty-something year-old step forward.

It must be him. "Are you Bryce?"

"The one and only," Bryce cracks a smile.

Dylan unclenches a bit. "Are we set?"

"Ssss, yeah… there was this little hitch."

"What?" Dylan's tone drops.

"Well, most of what they had were either panty-droppers or guzzlers, so I grabbed you a hatchback. It's a total mom-car, but easy on gas if you—"

"What about the passport?"

As though he just remembered there was more to their deal, Bryce pulls out a navy passport from the inside of his jacket pocket.

"Got it right here," he taps it onto his open palm, boasting a playful smirk.

Dylan flicks his flashlight at it. "Hold it up."

"It's legit man. I'm a pro," Bryce flips to the page containing Dylan's photo, and then holds it up to the light.

Dylan steps forward with his stern gaze fixed to his commissioned ID. He then looks up at Bryce and takes a second to read him.

Frail build, unkempt hair, and dilated pupils. But he doesn't strike Dylan as the type that screws over his customers.

Dylan puts his flashlight away, and then pulls out twelve hundred-dollar bills from his back pocket.

He completes the exchange and begins to inspect his ID more closely.

It's good, he nods to himself. He would never be able to tell it apart from his real one. "You weren't kidding about being a pro," he half-chuckles.

"A happy customer—" Bryce counts the cash, "is a returning customer," and tucks it away in his fanny-pack, having no idea that once Dylan gets to Seattle, he plans on leaving the car at the rental branch and taking a bus across the border into Canada.

He slips his passport into his pocket. "You rented the car under an alias, right?"

"Yeah, we cool," Bryce bobs his head.

"So, where is it?"

"That way—" Bryce nods towards the end of the trail. "It's a dark gray hatchback in the third stall of the cemetery parking lot." Off Dylan's look, "I know, it's eerie as fuck," he chuckles, "but at least I don't gotta worry about running into no one at this hour. Unless it's Halloween," he scoffs, "learned *that* the hard way." He reaches back into his fanny-pack and pulls out the car keys.

Dylan reaches out to grab them, but nearly jumps out of his skin when he hears a piercing scream. The morbid sound floods the forest like light engulfing a silhouette.

"Shit—" Bryce panics like a spooked gazelle and bolts down the trail, vanishing almost instantly.

Another scream trails the echoes of the previous, luring Dylan's attention. And he can't tell whether it belongs to a girl, or a young boy.

He looks in the direction of Bryce's flight; towards his one and only shot at getting to Romer before his trial. But the tortured voice of a complete stranger has pinned him in place.

"Fuck," he curses and segues off the trail towards the screams. With each and every step, the victim's voice becomes magnified, until Dylan emerges at the brink of an enormous cemetery.

Must be the one Bryce mentioned.

He remains hidden behind a large tree, gawking at the astonishing sight before him.

Roughly fifty feet ahead, three cadets are standing ten-hut with their backs to him, decked-out in their combat uniforms. The fourth is circling six younger cadets on their knees who are assembled in a perfect line. They've all been stripped down to their boxers and numbered on their torsos with what appears to be mud.

And not until one of them bends over does Dylan realize their wrists are tied behind their backs.

With his forehead on the ground, the bent-over cadet slavers from his gaping mouth. His sobbing has become so intensified that no actual sound is leaving his throat.

Meanwhile, the circling cadet is going on and on about what it takes to become a *real* soldier. How graduating from this academy is the kind of honor you earn. And most importantly, how facing your fears before you're dispatched onto the battlefield is detrimental to your survival.

Don't you mean 'instrumental' you overgrown tool?

Dylan scowls at the loathsome roid-monkey and the self-proclaimed alpha of the academy, Tobias Colton. The prick is quite possibly the only person in the world Dylan would shoot right in the face, and feel nothing.

Colton concludes his monologue and comes to a stop by the weeping cadet. He stares down at him for a few moments, and then suddenly swoops down.

"GET THE FUCK UP!" he barks into the cadet's ear, jolting the kid back up onto his folded legs. "And you call yourself a GODDAMN SOLDIER!?"

"I'm claustrophphph—" the cadet stammers, "ph-phobic," his posture wilting under the weight of his fear. "I sss-swear."

Claustrophobic?

Dylan follows Colton's line of sight to what seems to be a rough and poorly assembled rectangular box.

A coffin.

And directly next to it, there's a dark, rectangular patch. And it's not a shadow.

It's a freshly-dug grave.

Dylan's wide eyes dart back to Colton as he tosses something the size of a sugar cube into the air.

"Luck of the draw, solider," Colton flashes a smug grin. "Unless, of course, one of your comrades wants to volunteer?" He looks to the other candidates, but they all avert their eyes.

"*NO*," the young cadet begs as Colton's crew grab and drag him over to the coffin.

"Quit being a little bitch!" Colton barks as the kid is stuffed into the box. He then slams the lid down, snuffing his victim's pleas for mercy.

"And you might want to stop panting so much," he bends down and shouts at the box. "That air's gotta last you the next four hours."

Boasting a wide grin, Colton crosses his arms and backs up, spectating as his crew pummel nails into the coffin's lid. And Dylan finds himself in full stride towards Colton like a grenade of rage.

He comes up to Colton from behind and kicks him in the hamstring.

Colton heaves a grunt and falls to his knees, at the sight of which the others cease their hammering.

Dylan takes advantage of the lull and marches up to the coffin, shoves the nearest cadet out of his way, and starts to pull the nails with the hammer's claw.

"Well, look who it is!" Colton rises back to his feet. "Ain't this past your bedtime? Shouldn't you be all tucked in right about now, crying to mommy in your sleep?"

Ignore him. It's what he does.

"What the hell are you even *doing* here?" Colton walks over. "Have you been following us?" he teases with a playful voice, and then rests his hands on his hips. "Feelin' a little left out, are we?"

Dylan pays him no heed. All he wants is to get the kid out and be on his way.

"Transfer students usually do," Colton goes on as Dylan yanks the final nail out and opens the coffin to reveal the sodden face of a child. "But hey—there are always ways to fix *that*."

Fingers dig into Dylan's shoulders and yank him back, and the ground soars up and collides with the base of his head.

The impact sends a stab of pain down his spine, and for a few moments, he can't see.

He reaches up to his pulsating head, but his arm springs back down to his side as a savage kick lands onto his ribs.

Dylan recoils as more join in, targeting his torso.

Colton pulls the young cadet from the coffin and throws him down on the grass. He then marches up to Dylan, shoves his crew out of the way, and kicks Dylan in the stomach so hard that it knocks him onto his back. He then steps onto Dylan's ribcage, leaning his weight onto him.

Gasping for air, Dylan grips Colton's calf, forms a fist with his other hand, and strikes Colton's ankle.

The goon grunts and staggers back, and then with a vicious growl, bears back down and starts to kick Dylan in the gut with everything he's got.

With every inch of him tense and writhing with pain, Dylan feels the fourth kick crack, and the fifth break his ribs. And then, whatever Colton is barking at him he can no longer hear over the sound of his own screaming.

The ground is suddenly pulled from under him.

The sky is moving.

Please, his heart sinks. *Please don't.*

And a wet grunt escapes him as the cadets drop him into the coffin, knocking every wisp of air from his lungs. Upon impact, one of Dylan's cracked ribs dislodges, scraping at his insides. And his howls of agony become deafening as the cadets slam the lid shut, eradicating all light.

Dylan's strangled voice, his labored breaths, and even the drumming of his heart bounce off the walls, their echo saturating the tight space.

He prays for an end to his misery—for his body to go into shock, for him to pass out—but his stubborn mind hangs onto consciousness as he splinters from within. And despite his best efforts, he breaks down and starts to sob as they lower him into the ground.

The darkness becomes even darker. The stuffy air becomes thicker, and the inevitability of his doom, bitterly real. Tonight has deteriorated into a waking nightmare, and he doesn't know what terrifies him more—dying from the pain, or surviving to feel it.

σ

~Today~

Claustrophobia is a state of mind, Dylan repeats to himself within the confines of the trunk. *All suffering is a state of mind.*

He has survived worse than this. *Much* worse.

Upon hearing what sounded like a gunshot, he is thrust towards the deep end of the trunk. The squeal of skidding tires fill his ears, his balance shifting as the car swerves from side to side.

Dylan recoils as more gunshots follow, convinced with each blast that the next bullet will be the one that gets him.

But instead, he once again collides with the deep end of the trunk as the car crashes into something.

The whiplash vibrates through his skull, fogging up his mind. But having survived thus far, already feels like a miracle.

His vision is flooded with light as the hood of the trunk is flung open.

A man wearing a black ski-mask reaches in, grabs Dylan by the collar, and drags him closer. He then pulls out a small syringe containing a blue serum, and plunges it into Dylan's neck.

The prick stings sourly, but the liquid flowing into his veins is sweet and calming. And within seconds, the hauntingly familiar eyes of his captor begin to shift out of focus.

All boundaries blur into abstract patches of color.

All sound is fading away.

Dylan's muscles relax, and with a heavy body, he sinks into a peaceful abyss.

CHAPTER 22

LEEWAY

The dark seems endless like a starless sky. But Neve can barely move an inch in the confines of the dryer. With each breath, her limited supply of oxygen depletes even further, and she's too afraid to crack the door open. Good luck can only stretch so far, and a part of her is just waiting for an onslaught of bad luck to restore the balance.

She wonders what her mug-shot would look like. What it would be like to have her fingerprints taken. But that's all assuming the men in her pursuit really *were* the cops.

There was just *something* about them. Something about the way they carried themselves. About their demanding attitudes and entitled behavior. They just seemed *dirty*. The dangerous kind of dirty. The kind that has law-enforcement in its pockets.

But regardless of their true identities, what were they planning on arresting her for? Theft?

The man who took *The Fray Theory* was treating it like a precious artifact. But the book is far from a priceless antique that needs to be handled with care. It's practically still a manuscript—with sketches and formulas sprinkled throughout.

So its value can only lie in its content.

Since Neve keeps arriving at dead-ends, she puts her reservations on hold—just for a moment—and decides to look at this whole thing from an entirely new perspective: for argument's sake, she assumes the theories are not philosophical conjecture. That they're not science fiction teetering on the verge of being science fact. She assumes that they are, beyond a shadow of a doubt, one-hundred percent true.

And with the shift in her perspective, her mind is inundated with countless peculiar instances that she could never before explain. Things she brushed off, or told herself she was imagining. Subtle things. So subtle and seemingly insignificant that their mention to others sparked little to no interest.

Things like having the feeling that you're going to run into someone today, and then do. An unfounded rush of stress, which days later you realize coincided with a tragic car accident in a different city. Dreams, déjà vu, and other bizarre experiences alike.

And it suddenly dawns on Neve that she isn't just privy to the theories, she embodies them. She, Dylan *and* Romer are living proof that not only do Proxy dimensions exist, but that they're also accessible.

But even if Neve's brazen new assumptions have merit, then how come she has never met anyone else with similar abilities? The three of them can't be the only people in the world who can gain access to their Proxies.

If cross-dimensional Syncing is the next stage in human evolution, why haven't there been reports of other people with paranormal abilities?

Are they all locked up in madhouses? Paid off? *Killed* off? That sure would explain why the incident at the cemetery never made the news. It should have at least stirred up some concern amongst the locals.

And *nothing.*

She was smart to fear those men in black. If they are powerful enough to influence law-enforcement *and* the media, they're the last people on earth she'd want to mess with.

She can't stay here. She needs to get as far away from Dylan's as she can. Regardless of what Romer said, there is no reason to assume those men won't return to search the premises a second time.

She gradually increases the pressure on the dryer door, and with a soft click, it swings open, wrinkled clothes spilling out. She shoves the rest of them out and inhales as big a breath as she can manage in her uncomfortable position.

With aching limbs and stiff joints, she cautiously struggles out of the dryer onto all fours.

So far, so good.

With nothing in particular alerting her to trouble, she begins to erase all evidence of her intrusion. She shoves the wrinkled clothes back into the dryer and repositions the hamper back to where she found it.

She listens once more for approaching footsteps, and then walks to the back of the room with her eyes on the rooftop hatch.

From down here, there's no way to know whether the coast is clear up on the roof. So with a giant leap of faith, she climbs the metal ladder, and carefully unlocks the hatch.

She pushes up against the glass door and ascends very slowly, peeking over the rim in all directions.

They're gone.

She emerges onto the rooftop and rests the hatch door onto its retaining arm, just in case.

The late afternoon sky is a soft shade of blue, but every breeze that swooshes past lifts her body heat.

Neve keeps low on her way over to the rooftop ledge. Hiding behind it, she scans the balconies and roofs of adjacent buildings, half-expecting a sniper to have her in his crosshairs. But beside a few balcony-dwellers, little else commands her attention.

She diverts her gaze down onto the street below.

The traffic isn't unusual for this time of day, and the people strike her as the typical Yaletown crowd.

Good, she nods to herself. With so many potential eye-witnesses around, she can cause a big scene if it ever comes to it.

Now or never.

She dashes to the rooftop exit and bursts through the door, ready to fly down the stairwell. But before taking the first step, a man's hand clasps onto her mouth and pulls her back behind the door.

Darkness swallows the space as the door swings shut. Pinned to her captor, Neve kicks and screams into his hand, trying to rip his grip from her waist.

But it's no use. He's too strong.

She goes to grab Dylan's blade from her pocket, but the numbness overtaking her is making it nearly impossible to move. Numbness that's paving the way for the peppery sensation of pins and needles.

It's happening again—an encore of the cemetery.

Her captor seems to be saying something, but she can't hear him over her chaotic thoughts—over the dissonant voices of her Proxies.

It's like listening to white noise.

To nothing.

And then, she hears her name as though from the bottom of the ocean.

A man's voice. A familiar voice.

The excruciating prickliness is slowly waning, the thoughts in her head are fading, and the voice of the man speaking in her ear is becoming clearer.

Closer.

Neve's eyes flicker open, and from the corner of her vision, she catches a glimpse of a swatch of gold.

The grip on her mouth softens, and as she turns her head, a lock of silky blonde hair brushes against her cheek.

Romer.

CHAPTER 23

FULL CIRCLE

On her way down the stairwell, all Neve can think of is Dylan, and whether or not he's okay. Because if anything were to happen to him, she'd *never* be able to live with herself.

With Romer a couple of steps ahead, they reach the bottom of the stairwell.

Romer walks up to the door and pushes onto it, scanning the surroundings through the narrow gap.

"Are you sure you weren't tailed?" Neve whispers, then follows him out into the building's side alley.

"They were too busy tossing my shop," he looks over his shoulder down the alley, and then turns to Neve. "You've got a *lot* of explaining to do."

"I will," she nods. "Once we're safe."

Romer exhales a frustrated sigh through his nose.

"Fine. Come on," he turns and starts towards the laneway lining the back of the building.

Neve follows suit with a surprising degree of faith in his judgement. If he was able to sneak in and out of Dylan's building without being noticed, then it's probably safe to assume he knows what he's doing.

Nearing the end, Romer slows down and inches towards the edge of the wall.

"So, what's the plan?" she asks as Romer sneaks a peek down both sides of the laneway.

"First, we need to find somewhere to hide."

Great. As long as it's not inside a home appliance. "What are our options?" she asks.

Romer licks his lower lip, deep in thought. "We really should call his dad."

He's right, Neve thinks. It's naïve of her to have assumed that because Dylan was 'arrested', he would be entitled to a phone call.

"Okay," she nods as Romer pops the battery back into his phone. "But make it quick."

"Yep," Romer turns his phone back on, but instead of pulling up his contacts, he opens his browser.

"What are you doing?" Neve asks.

"I don't have his dad's number," he says as though stating the obvious.

Right. Why would he?

Neve glances behind her towards the main street, wondering if it would be safer for them to be out in the open.

She turns to run the idea by Romer, and catches a glimpse of his screen as he inputs <marcus holt ubc> in the search bar.

"Um—why are you typing that?"

"Typing what?"

"Marcus Holt."

"Because that's—his *name*?" he looks up at Neve, a confused frown twisting his brows.

Copper beard. Pale skin. GQ style.

Neve banishes the thought. Especially since—

"No. No, Dylan's last name is *Sterling*," she objects.

Romer rolls his eyes.

"Sterling is his mother's last name," he says, and then drops his gaze back onto his phone, mouthing 'typical Dylan'.

Tongue-tied. Dumb-struck. Nauseous.

"Why?" she asks. "Why would he do that?"

"*I don't know.* Calm your tits."

She stares at Romer, at a complete loss for words. The thought of Dylan and Holt sharing blood—

"Look—don't take it personal," Romer says.

"Personal?" she asks, still reeling from the shock.

"It's just his way of honoring his mom's memory."

Neve says nothing.

"She died giving birth to him—"

"Yeah—I know," she interrupts, shaking her head out of frustration.

"The hell is wrong with you?" Romer frowns.

"Nothing—" she says a bit too hastily. "Nothing. I just didn't know. About his dad, I mean. Dylan never introduced us."

"Then he really *does* love you, 'cause his dad is a *raging* asshole."

Neve sinks into thought.

Holt *is* a raging asshole, no doubt about it. But she always felt like he has some sort of vendetta against her—as though his distaste for her was personal.

Is it because of Dylan? But that would mean Holt has known about her *long* before she became one of his students. As far back as three years ago, when she and Dylan were in the thick of it.

Oh God...

Neve closes her eyes, but the humiliating reality of her situation is practically burnt in her mind: Holt must've been laughing up a storm in his head when she lied about living with her boyfriend in the condo they own.

The condo Holt owns.

"LOAD, BITCH!" Romer barks at his phone.

Neve jolts at his eruption, and then the futility of what they're trying to do starts to sink in.

"Turn it off," she says. "It's been too long."

"Let me try one more time."

"Forget about Holt. It's Galen we need."

σ

Neve follows Romer through a network of laneways and alleys—through the tight capillaries of the city's circulation. And in no time, she is back in the same walkway she emerged into from Galen's building.

"Now what?" Romer asks as they reach the same door Neve burst through mere hours ago.

"Guess we're going to have to wait for someone to leave."

"*That's* your plan?"

"What? You said it's risky to be out in the open. If we're not going to press his buzzer, and we can't call him, this is pretty much our only option."

"Or is it..?" Romer turns his head with a broad and boyish grin, then reaches into the inner pocket of his jacket and pulls out a Swiss Army Knife."

"Um, what are you doing?" Neve asks as he kneels down in front of the exit.

"I'm going to carve 'Neve & Dylan 4 ever' on the door," he fans out the knife and starts to size up his options. "Inside of a heart."

"Romer, if we're caught breaking in—"

"Relax..." he slips a wavy metal extension into the keyhole. "I got this."

"I think I still have Galen's number stored on my phone."

"No—" Romer dismisses with a small shake of his head. "All things electronic tend to leave a trace. Last thing we want is to drag more people into this."

He peeks into the keyhole, twists his wrist up and a bit to the side, and then Neve hears a soft click.

"Boom."

σ

Neve and Romer run up the stairwell to Galen's floor, but upon entering the hallway, Romer's hand springs up against Neve's belly, holding her back.

The front door to Galen's unit is ajar, but there is no indication of people coming or going.

Romer draws out his knife's top blade. It's short and fat, but seems to be sharp enough to inflict some serious damage.

He sets out towards Galen's unit with his weapon gripped firmly in his fist. And although Neve knows he'd disapprove, she follows him nonetheless.

He peeks into the loft, and then his hand flies up again, holding Neve back at arm's length.

"What is it?" she whispers.

"Head back into the stairwell," he whispers back. "Wait for me there."

"What are you going to do?"

"Can you *please* just do as I say?" he turns to Neve with an agitated glare.

Though Neve can't see into Galen's unit, the alarm registered on Romer's face ignites her anxiety.

She shifts her weight back onto the balls of her feet, but can't bring herself to walk away from him.

"I'll wait for you here," she says.

Romer parts his lips to say something—to object, most likely—but instead, he just stares at Neve, his wide gaze darting between her eyes.

Before Neve can break the silence, Romer huffs an agitated sigh and sneaks another glance into Galen's loft. "You still got D's switchblade?"

"Yeah," she nods, her frown deepening. "Why?"

CHAPTER 24

ENTROPY

Leaving Neve behind in the hallway, Romer cautiously enters Galen's loft. The place is completely ransacked. All the furniture has been gutted, the stuffing spewing out like entrails of road-kill. Tables have been flipped over, drawers, boxes, and containers have been purged of their contents, and broken pieces of antique artifacts are scattered all over the floor.

This was not a burglary.

The culprits must've been looking for something specific. Could it have been the book Neve said the cops took from Dylan's?

But this doesn't look like a police raid either. If it was, the place would've been sealed off.

Neither a burglary, nor a raid. And yet, it is both.

Stepping over and around the ravaged remains, Romer crosses the living area and enters the kitchen in the back.

It's more or less in the same shape as the rest of the loft. And there's still no sign of Galen.

Was he even here when all of this happened?

Romer retracts his steps to be on his way, but a small noise draws his attention towards the far end of the kitchen.

Is it Galen? Is he in hiding?

Romer cautiously approaches what he assumes to be the pantry, tiptoeing around the broken shards of glass and porcelain. He tightens his grip on his knife, just in case his hunch proves to be horribly wrong.

Keeping his distance, he steels himself and pushes on the door.

It swings open to reveal an enormous beehive: a double-height cylindrical cellar, home to some of the world's finest vintage wines.

The way all the bottles point to the center of the room reminds Romer of miniature war cannons. And on the ground and along the wall, giant wine barrels lay on their bellies in the shape of a crescent.

At the far end of the room, Romer notices a small puddle of wine. But it isn't pooled anywhere near a spout, which makes him wonder if the spill *is* in fact, wine.

σ

Neve lingers in the door frame of Galen's entrance, one foot inside the unit, the other out in the hallway.

The state of the loft is absolutely tragic. Nothing shy of a massacre.

These horribly mutilated objects were relics with mystery. History. And now they are sprawled across the floor in pieces, robbed of their integrity.

Cops wouldn't stoop this low—ravaging priceless artifacts like savages.

This mess is too hideous *not* to be personal.

Neve wonders if the culprits responsible for this mess would have unleashed the same hell at Dylan's, had they failed to recover Galen's book.

And she wonders about the text Galen received, right before he abruptly terminated their session.

What could it have possibly said that frightened him as much as it did?

Was it a warning? From whom?

The ding of the elevator nearly makes her heart stop. But its doors remain shut.

Different floor.

Neve exhales a huge sigh of relief, and then steps into the loft and shuts the door behind her.

The last thing she needs right now is for one of Galen's neighbors to walk by and start bombarding her with questions she won't be able to answer.

It's too weird being back here already. Especially given the huge discrepancy in the loft's condition.

Neve was standing right here when Galen rushed back with *The Fray Theory* from down the hallway to her left. And she remembers the door at the far end swinging shut behind him.

She knows she should stay put, but her curiosity is proving to be much more compelling than her fear of consequence.

She looks in the direction of the kitchen.

Detecting no signs of Romer, she throws caution to the wind and ventures into the hallway towards what she assumes to be Galen's office.

She knocks out of courtesy, and hearing no sound, opens the door to reveal what used to be a quaint and charming study.

The state of this room is more or less on par with the rest of the loft. But there is something unnerving about it that Neve can't seem to quite figure out.

Her heartbeat is rising up to twice what it should be. Her insides are twisting tight enough to bend her at the waist. But what could her insincts know that her brain has yet to discover?

Remembering her promise to Romer, she begins to back out of the room. But all of a sudden, she finds herself pinned in place.

Neve's eyes fill with awe and wonder. She realizes what she'd initially registered as wallpaper, is in fact a *gigantic* map—a meticulous, hand-drawn map of an ancient city with a winding river snaking through the heart of it.

And it dawns on her that she's dreamt of not only this map, but this *entire room* last night, *before* she visited Galen's home for the very first time.

She also remembers how in her dream, regardless of what page she flipped to, 'six' was the number of the page she landed on.

Come to think of it, the number six also appeared in her dream of merging into a sea of identical cars.

Neve's vision starts to blur as she thinks of the beautiful stranger who's been plaguing her dreams as of late.

The mysterious apparition who incited something ferocious in her at the cemetery, nearly costing Neve her life.

And last night, when she dreamt of this room, it was the very sight of him that made her scream her way into consciousness.

He was standing right in front of her—right there by that console with the vintage typewriter on it.

Just then, Neve notices a small, white envelope in the typewriter's paper rest, and walks over to take a closer look.

It's odd, how the entire room is in shambles, and yet this envelope is resting delicately onto the paper rest, completely undisturbed.

Was it put here *after* the break-in?

Neve picks it up and reads the hand-written 'N. K.' designation at the bottom right corner. And although the initials could belong to nearly anyone, she feels convinced this letter was meant for *her* to find. And even if not, aren't the initials a good enough excuse for her to give into her curiosity?

She flips the envelope over.

The wax used to seal it is a deep, lapis blue. And the elegant impression that is stamped onto the wax simply reads: 'Q'.

Neve breaks through the seal and retrieves what appears to be a personal letter.

The penmanship is beyond exquisite. Aristocratic even. And it vaguely reminds Neve of the scribbled annotations she discovered in Galen's book.

> *My dear,*
>
> *This letter is not a revelation, but a simple reminder of what your soul already knows to be true.*
>
> *Dreams are devoid of logic. They neither begin, nor end. In dreams, we do not question reality. We bend the laws of physics, and defy gravity. And I know it's hard to believe, but you are not dreaming.*
>
> *I have waited long for this day. For the day your self-awareness transcends your physical limits. But awareness is worthless without action. Talent, wasted without creation. Life, unlived without purpose.*
>
> *You have a choice. You can either welcome your calling, or settle for mediocrity. Settle for dreams that are only dreamt, destined never to come true.*
>
> *And your dreams are of the kind, which must.*
>
> *~Q*

The inky letters on the page blur into squiggles.

Welling up, Neve lowers the letter with quivering hands, feeling as though she's just recalled a deeply buried memory.

She can't imagine what's causing her to have such an emotional reaction... to such a vague letter from a complete stranger.

And truth be told, she doesn't want to know.

Where the hell is Romer?

CHAPTER 25

CAPRICE

Galen is nowhere in sight. And with each passing second, Romer's becoming more and more convinced that the puddle he's staring at in the back of the room, isn't wine. He should grab Neve and get out of here. *Now.* But like a wiper-blade, a flash of black swoops down across his vision and tightens around his neck.

Panicked, Romer drops his Swiss Army Knife and reaches up to his throat, but a swift blow to the back of his knees knocks him onto his shins.

Ridges of a man's boot are pushing down on his spine, but the thick cord around his neck is pulling him back.

Romer pats the ground frantically, but his knife is nowhere to be found. He reaches up to reduce the tension around his neck, but he can't seem to dig his fingers under the cord.

The throbbing in his temples intensifies each time his heart pumps blood into his head. It feels like someone is drilling a hole into his skull. The tension above his Adams apple is making him gag, and his lungs are on the verge of collapsing.

He is frozen in a lethal limbo and fast running out of hope. This is Isaac all over again.

As his blurry vision paves the way for a black-out, something akin to an idea emerges in his mind.

His focus sharpens. His senses heighten. He leans forward into the cutting sting of the cord, lowering himself as close to the ground as he can tolerate.

And he feels the surge of a faint vibration outside of himself. He's felt it before, like a foreshock before a seismic earthquake.

Romer concentrates his will on what he needs to do. He lets the vibrations seep into him, and then—with the mere thought of it—the wine bottles and the barrels lining the perimeter EXPLODE.

With that, the crushing pressure on Romer's spine is lifted, and the tension around his throat, released.

Romer slips away and backs off from his attacker.

And as tides of wine flood the cellar, he watches a man in black—ravaged by the shards of glass lodged in his skin—collapse into the shallow sea of aromatic garnet, floating face-down.

Heaving wet coughs, Romer struggles to his feet with his eyes glued to his assailant. He watches him sway from side to side as the dissipating waves of wine splash against his lifeless body.

And all Romer can think of is how he'd rather die than go back to prison.

σ

Neve starts to back out of Galen's study. It was a bad idea to come here—to have involved Romer.

They should just—

Someone's arm wraps around her neck, and Neve instantly knows it isn't Romer's.

The chokehold is extremely firm. Firm enough to snap her neck. And an explosion of terror rattles her as she realizes snapping her neck might be *exactly* what her aggressor is trying to do.

With that thought, her body starts to fall asleep.

Shit—no, no, no!

She is running out of time. Once the prickliness starts to take over, it will be beyond excruciating to lift a finger.

With the nagging numbness in her flesh already compromising her, Neve pulls Dylan's blade from her back pocket.

A small jolt sends a rush of prickliness through her arm, and she suspects having unwittingly sprung the blade out.

She rotates the blade in her hand, grips it firmly, and stabs her attacker in the leg.

His scream is terrifying. But it's almost as much a relief as the breath Neve manages to take before he cuts off her air supply again.

Only this time, his grip feels weaker.

Much weaker.

The peppery prickliness overcoming Neve's flesh is excruciating. Her nerves are firing so violently that even the smallest movements feel impossible.

But this is life or death.

She goes to pull the blade out, but it seems to be lodged in her attacker's bone.

So she twists it instead.

His second howl is deafening. Murderous, even.

He grabs the back of Neve's neck and SLAMS her forehead into the wall.

A strangled grunt leaps out the back of her throat.

He then clutches her jaw, and BASHES the back of her head against the opposite wall.

At the verge of collapsing, Neve's knees give out from under her. But her aggressor tightens his grip of her jaw, and pins her to the wall.

The darkness surrounding Neve's vision closes in, seeping into the black mask of the man holding her life in his hands.

Neve searches his eyes for a hint of compassion, for mercy, but what she finds instead is certainty:

He is going to kill her.

Help—Neve grabs his wrist with both hands, but they unclasp a moment later when he punches her in the gut.

He punches her again and again, until a string of blood spurts from her mouth and vanishes onto his black clothes.

Where are you? Neve thinks of Romer as another punch lands on her frail frame.

He wouldn't leave me... He'd be here.

Unless he couldn't.

With the thought of Romer in peril, Neve's heart quickens, pumping an overabundance of adrenaline through her veins. The rush of prickliness paves the way for calm and clarity, and then Neve is standing strong, her body tougher than wrought iron.

As the man in black reaches for his weapon, Neve hears the hardwood floor creak, louder and louder, until it suddenly collapses under her weight.

Neve's hair floats up as gravity pulls her through the floor. With her voice trapped in her throat, she crashes into one floor after another, paving a vertical path all the way down through the building.

Her plunge ends abruptly when she crashes onto a hard surface, the earth-shattering impact shaking up the space like a mild earthquake.

Neve lies amidst the wreckage of her fall as debris pours from the oculus above.

As her density gradually returns to normal, Neve starts to feel the bulging corners of the bed of rubble underneath. With a weak grunt, she props herself up into a slouch, and looks about what appears to be an underground parking lot. And behind her, within the pile of rubble, she finds the man who attacked her lying on his back.

Without taking her eyes off him, Neve shifts her weight onto all fours and backs away from him. But he doesn't even flinch.

Is he passed out? Faking it?

Keeping her distance, Neve rises to her feet and walks around him for a better look.

There is a film of dust over his unblinking eyes. And blood, pooling at the base of his skull.

Neve chokes on her gasp and backs away.

She can call it self-defense. She can call it a freak accident. She can rationalize it any way she likes, but when it comes down to it, she's just killed someone.

Heavy stomping reaches her ears from a nearby stairwell. She snaps out of remorse and dives down, rummaging through the rubble for Dylan's blade.

She salvages it from beneath a broken plank, and in the process, also discovers her assailant's weapon; the gun he tried to pull on her, right before the floor collapsed under them both.

She grabs it and dashes towards the parking lot exit, bursting through it.

σ

At the sound of progressive crashes, Romer bursts out of the cellar, his drenched clothes clinging to his body.

"Neve!?" he shouts as he makes his way through the kitchen. "NEVE!?"

He reenters the living space just as a pair of men in black step into the loft from the hallway.

Romer staggers to a stop, bracketed by floor to ceiling libraries on either side of him. His eyes dart about the space for something to use as a weapon, but there is nothing within reach except fragments of things once whole.

Concealed in masks, the strangers in black start to take aim.

At the sight of this, Romer senses a faint vibration outside of himself, and time slows down to a crawl.

He watches a pair of red laser dots glide over the pillaged furniture towards him, and next thing he knows, he is raising his hands to eclipse the red glare threatening to blind him.

With this gesture of his hands, hundreds of books fly off their shelves and start to assemble midair like tiles. They snap together like a puzzle of mismatched rectangles, and within seconds, Romer finds himself shielded behind a floating barrier of books.

A barrage patters on the other side of the barrier.

Romer dives down and lands at the foot of a spiral staircase.

Looking up, he remembers that Galen's loft is on the topmost floor of this building.

Like Dylan's.

With hope radiating from his eyes, he springs to his feet and bolts up the stairs.

He emerges into Galen's bedroom with his eyes to the ceiling. But unlike Dylan's apartment, there's no rooftop hatch to aid him in his escape.

It isn't until he turns and looks over the railing of the mezzanine that he realizes the book barrier has already crumbled into a massive pile.

Where are they?

Stomping draws his focus to the staircase, and he once again finds himself in crosshairs.

Suddenly, the objects in the room start to glitch. Some vanish and reappear in the exact same spot, while others reappear slightly displaced.

It's like flipping through a flip-book—except the pictures are in a random order. The kind of chaos Romer had always sensed, but never *seen*.

Within this state of flux, he senses the shooter's grip tightening around the trigger. And then—with a silver glow radiating from his eyes—Romer's mind throws his enemy back against the wall.

The invisible force is so powerful, however, that it pushes back onto Romer, thrusting him backwards.

The window his back collides with shatters upon impact. And the air is suddenly fresh and cold.

Romer gawks at the building's exterior.

In trying to save his own life, he's just expelled himself from a six-storey building!

His heart drops even faster than he is, knowing in mere moments, all will fade to black.

Do something! DO SOMETHING!

Further up the street, he spots a black SUV. And it's high enough to absorb most of his momentum.

Beckoned by his mind, the car rips from its spot and charges down the street, leaving behind trails of burnt plastic as it skids to catch Romer's fall.

σ

Neve bursts out of Galen's parking lot and onto the main street, her mind and heart racing one another.

What should she do!? Run? Hide?

But Romer—

The sound of glass shattering draws her attention upwards, and she looks up to find Romer airborne, enveloped by a cloud of glistening shards.

Merge.

Her flesh starts to fall asleep, prickly and painful. One by one, her Proxies snap onto her like magnets, increasing her body's density in a chain reaction.

She becomes denser and heavier one infinitesimal jolt at a time, the pain more and more bearable with each fusion.

And then, she is no longer her-*self*.

She is her-*selves*—an indestructible anchor who is connected to all shared dimensions.

She hears a soft groan, and then DROPS by half a foot as the ground beneath her collapses into a wide and shallow crater. But not once does she take her eyes off the silhouette falling from the sky.

As though her will is tangible, it pushes back up against Romer, decelerating his plunge. And then he is suspended midair, close enough to reach out and touch her hand.

The screech of skidding tires fills Neve's ears, and she looks down to find a black SUV charging at her in a solo stampede.

No.

Neve turns on the balls of her feet and sinks into a defiant stance, her ruby eyes glued to her impending doom.

"NEVE!" Romer's scream cuts through her.

CRASH.

The car's front caves in upon impact, rippling like a collapsing accordion. The powerful collision wipes Neve clean from under Romer, the backs of her feet scraping the asphalt as she resists the momentum.

A fatal crash. A violent clash of metal and flesh, and yet, it is the hammer that breaks, not the nail.

And within seconds, the dense fusion loses steam, lurching to a rocky stop.

Neve staggers back and looks at the dent her body inflicted on the SUV. It's almost like the front of the car is wrapped around an invisible column.

Dazed, and struggling with her balance, she peers through the windshield at the trail of destruction she carved into the road.

And like light at the end of a tunnel, she discovers Romer lying on his side in the middle of a shallow crater—where *she* had stood mere moments ago.

He's moving. He's alive.

With a throbbing head, burning skin, and a body much too heavy to support, her knees buckle and the ground soars up to catch her fall.

CHAPTER 26

AFTERMATH

R omer rolls onto his back in the middle of the crater. His left side is writhing with bone-splitting pain. He was so adamant not to land on his head that his shoulder wound up burdening the worst of the brunt.

But he's alive.

Thank you, he squeezes his eyes shut, *thank you*, *thank you*, *thank you*, reliving the horrible sensation of freefall. For the life of him, he can't believe they're not scraping him off the ground.

As his lungs settle into a normal rhythm, he rolls back onto his side and struggles onto all fours.

Like he feared, his left shoulder is in pretty awful shape. He can barely put any weight on his left arm.

With a gust of wind from further up the road, he catches a whiff of burnt plastic. People rush past him in a flurry of noise and color, far more fascinated by the crash to concern themselves with his wellbeing.

Probably a blessing in disguise.

His eyes follow the ravaged road to the wrecked SUV, and he catches a glimpse of Neve's body before the aggregating crowd blocks her off.

She's fine, Romer exhales a big sigh of relief right before confusion consumes him.

How could she have possibly survived a crash like this? Anyone else would have been killed on impact. And she completely decimated the car *and* the road!

The cemetery…

He remembers how incredibly dense Neve's flesh felt in his grasp, and how impossible it seemed for him to pull her out of that grave.

But how did she suspend him in the air?

Romer glances up at Galen's building and locates the broken window he emerged from. Seems like the men who shot at him are steering clear of it.

Probably on their way down.

As he struggles to his feet, he catches a glimpse of Dylan's bloodied switchblade by his foot. And right next to it, there's a slick and unusual gun not unlike the weapons the men upstairs were aiming at him.

He quickly snatches both weapons before anyone notices, and makes his way into the alley across from Galen's.

The shock of his impact with the ground is slowly wearing off. He's starting to feel the bone-splitting pain pulsating through his flesh and bones.

And then he can't stand it anymore, and stumbles back against the alley wall, struggling to breathe.

His mind keeps reliving what it felt like for the ground to race up to him—the rush of his plunge like the sudden dip of a rollercoaster.

But gravity abandoned its resolve. The turbulent wind in Romer's ears allayed to a soft whisper. And when he looked down, he saw Neve's glossy hair rise up like black ink in clear water, her eyes aglow with the most ravishing shade of red he's even seen.

Until what he had intended as his own salvation swiped her from beneath. Until the air became thin again, and the ground, hard.

He winces as a sharp stab of pain shoots through his left shoulder. And it's familiar. He knows exactly what he needs to do. So he slides all the way down against the wall, sitting on the cold ground.

"C'mon," he mutters under his breath as he grabs his left wrist. "C'mon," he repeats over and over, but the courage he seeks keeps evading him.

Do it fast.

Do it hard.

He swallows the tension in his throat and YANKS his arm as hard as he dares, popping his shoulder back into its socket.

He inhales his scream, body trembling from the painful jolt. "F—*fuck*—" he shudders, the scars Isaac adorned his body with pulsating like fresh wounds.

Today is just not his day.

He takes a few deep breathes, and then sneaks a glance at Galen's building entrance.

No signs of the men in black. *Yet.*

From the inside of his jacket, he takes out the gun he found in the crater, and pulls out the magazine to check the ammo.

The hell?

He cranes his neck down for a closer look. Instead of bullets, the magazine is stacked with glass darts containing a faint blue serum. Are these what they were shooting at him upstairs?

He jerks his head towards Galen's building just as two men in black emerge from the lobby.

Romer slides the magazine back into its chamber and hides the weapon behind him. He then slumps forward and pretends to be passed out.

He can only hope they'll spot him before they spot Neve, or there's no telling what will happen to her.

Come on... Over here, Romer peers through the veil of his draping hair. And the instant he is discovered, he shuts his eyes, relying on his ears to keep track of the men's whereabouts.

His heart's pounding against his chin. And despite trying to keep calm, he can feel himself trembling.

With the crash drawing everyone's attention, they can kill him on the spot and get away with it.

He hears a click from a few feet away as one of the men cocks his gun. And then another.

This is it, Romer thinks. *I'm done.*

He feels a kick against the side of his foot, but he's so paralyzed with fear, his body doesn't react.

A firmer kick lands higher up on his calf.

"He's out," says one of them.

"The ambulance is en route," says the other. "Do we want it here, or—"

"We shouldn't be transfering them together," says the first. "Not after what happened. It's too risky."

"What about the girl?"

"They'll take care of her. Let's clear this one out."

Romer feels their hands on him. And that means even if they plan on killing him, they don't intend on doing it here.

And if their hands are full with carrying him—

Romer grabs the gun he's been hiding and puts a dart in each of their necks.

Completely stunned, the men stumble back. They reach for their guns, but are already starting to fade.

Before either can pull the trigger, their weapons slip from their grasps and fall to the ground.

And moments later, they both crumble in place.

Still in awe of his luck, Romer struggles to his feet and stares down at their listless bodies.

What now? Should he snag their weapons? Check their IDs in case he'd ever need to report them?

He immediately decides against both. There's no way for him to know when and how poking the bear might wind up biting him in the ass. He's already in enough trouble as is.

He looks down at the weapon in his hand, and with his wine-dampened shirt, starts to wipe off all fingerprints. His *and* Neve's. He drops it down by the unconscious men's feet, and then inches towards the main street.

From around the corner, he sneaks a peek in the direction of the crash.

Two police vehicles are already on scene.

That was fast.

Romer canvases the area: three officers seem to have their hands full with keeping the crowd at bay, and the fourth is questioning potential witnesses.

With a giant leap of faith, Romer throws on his hood and ventures back onto the street.

He weaves into the boisterous crowd, looking as inconspicuous as he can manage. Every step brings him closer to Neve, and yet it feels like she's miles and miles away.

And as though the cops, the crowd, and his aching body weren't challenging enough already, the sirens of an approaching ambulance start to drown out the city's cacophony.

You've got to be kidding me, Romer frowns, then glances at the cops managing the horde of onlookers. They don't strike him as particularly dangerous. But the ambulance—which is now turning the corner—is a whole other story.

The crash *just* happened.

The only way for the ambulance to have made it here so quickly, is if someone called for it prior to the accident.

Smart, Romer thinks to himself as the ambulance infiltrates the scene. There is probably no better way to transport someone you plan on killing without anybody questioning it. This must've been their plan even before things got out of hand at Galen's.

And it suddenly dawns on Romer why it was so easy for he and Neve to escape Dylan's building and break into Galen's: they were walking into a trap.

With the numerous obstructions blocking Neve from his vision, Romer can't tell whether or not she's conscious. And if she's not, that leaves him with next to no options. He can't exactly wrestle her away from the paramedics, especially now that he knows they can't be trusted.

And he doesn't trust the cops either.

So what does that leave him with? Should he get a head-start towards the hospital and try to intercept them there? But what if the ambulance isn't even headed to the hospital?

He's starting to panic. Everything's happening too fast. They're already bringing out the stretcher.

But on the bright side, it looks like Neve is awake and talking to the paramedic.

If Romer can only get close enough, he just might be able to warn her about them.

He glances back at Galen's, and then towards the alley. When he doesn't detect any signs of immediate threat, he starts towards the back of the ambulance, where it's significantly less crowded.

But a few steps into the endeavor, he notices one of the cops approaching in full stride. And judging by his unblinking stare, he is singling Romer out.

Are the cops in on it? Should he run?

He can't anyways. Not in his condition.

In the precious few moments he has left, Romer sizes up the ensuing threat, desperately hoping his luck hasn't already run out.

Tucking his blonde locks behind his ears, Romer winces as a sharp stab of pain shoots through his left shoulder. And with his chin lowered, he takes a whiff of his damp, wine-soaked shirt.

Even if the cop isn't with the men who attacked him, reeking of alcohol is still not something Romer would want to have to explain.

"Don't I know you..?" the officer bridges the gap and stands fortified between the young man and his objective.

"You're asking me if *you* know *me*?" Romer quips with his mind on Neve.

They're sliding the stretcher into the ambulance.

And without warning, the cop's inquisitive squint broadens, brightening his expression.

"You're that kid," he says with a self-satisfied grin, "Romer Anthony. I was the one who processed you a few years back, remember?"

What—you wanna chat? Romer sneaks a glance in Neve's direction.

The ambulance is taking off.

"Is there something I can help you with? Or are you just brushing up on your solo good cop/bad cop routine?"

With that remark, the cop's face darkens slightly, but he masks it as though it's second nature. "Fancy running into you here," he grins from ear to ear, his tone loaded with subtext. "You wouldn't happen to know anything about this, would'ja?"

"Nope," Romer crosses his arms. "Just a regular, impartial bystander."

"That right?" the officer takes a half-step forward, standing far too close for comfort. Close enough to smell the wine vaporizing off Romer's clothes. "Then why the hell are you so nervous?"

With a burst of static from his radio, the officer lowers his chin to his collar. He listens as someone relays information about a pair of unconscious men in the alley up the street.

His gaze darts back up and meets Romer's. "Roger that," he says into his mic, and then slowly raises his head without breaking eye-contact.

Romer fights the impulse to swallow, determined to keep his cool. But if someone has ratted him out about what he did in that alley, it's already over.

The cop takes a deep breath through his nose and shakes his head disapprovingly as he exhales.

"You need to get your shit together, kid," he eyes Romer's clothes, and then bumps shoulders with him on his way to the alley.

OW.

σ

The howls of the ambulance are becoming more and more distant.

In spite of the pain, Romer runs as fast as he can towards St. Paul's Hospital, having no idea what to do once he gets there.

Should he try to sneak in through one of the back entries? *No.* There will be cameras for sure. But it's not like he can just waltz into the emergency ward and demand to see Neve, either.

He'd have to say he's a relative. But considering he and Neve look as much alike as wheat and coal, it will likely be a pretty unconvincing argument.

Unless he tells them that they're married?

But then again, what if they're not even taking her to the hospital?

From further up the street, he hears the sudden squeal of skidding tires, followed by a THUMP, and then a blaring screech akin to nails on a chalkboard.

And then he's running even faster.

It's got to be her.

σ

Roughly ten blocks up from where Romer was first alerted to the turbulence, he's faced with yet another crowd of onlookers.

This time, he weaves through them with far more vigor, ignoring people's protests.

And then he finds himself gawking at a sunken ambulance blocking traffic across multiple lanes.

Its axels are badly deformed. One of its tires has rolled to further up the street, and the other three are nowhere to be seen. And from where he stands, there is a long trail of scratches dug deep into the asphalt.

Romer closes in on the vehicle and starts to circle it for a better vantage point.

The rear doors are wide open. Two of the three paramedics are sitting on the edge of the landing, hunched over. And the third is flying off the handle about what incompetent morons they are.

Romer can't help but snicker. It sounds like Neve gave them quite a scare.

Relieved, he quietly slips away, distancing himself from the scene.

He finds a quiet corner and pulls out his phone with hopes of getting back in touch with Neve. And just then, he realizes he forgot to take out his battery after popping it in to call Dylan's dad.

Is that how those men tracked he and Neve over to Galen's? Is this entire thing his fault?

He shakes off the guilt and mulls over his options.

Neve might have turned her phone back on, but in light of his epiphany, Romer can't bring himself to risk calling her.

He pulls out his phone's battery and tries to think of how else to reach her.

What would *she* do next? With her phone off, she won't be able to reach out to anyone. And she isn't too likely to go home either, knowing about the men who broke into his workshop.

So what other options are there?

Come on, think! She's a smart girl. Smart enough to hide in a dryer...

And with that, Romer remembers the rendezvous plans he and Neve made when she called him earlier today, desperate for help.

He may very well have foiled those plans when he decided to step up and go to *her*. But in light of their new circumstances, what if Neve *does* follow through and go to the gallery with hopes of reuniting with him? What if instead of waiting for midnight, she's already made her way over?

CHAPTER 27

ENIGMA

Dylan opens his eyes, or so he thinks. It's much too dark for him to be able to tell. The air around him is cool, but stale. The ground he's lying on feels chilled against his bare skin. His mind is foggy, and there is a heavy murkiness to his blood.

This whole thing feels like an encore of his brief captivity in that damned trunk. But unless his senses are betraying him, he's in a much larger box.

His gag is gone. And it seems like his wrists and ankles are no longer bound.

That man...

Dylan recalls the masked man who stuck a needle in his neck. The stranger with eyes Dylan was certain he recognized.

But who was he?

Tears break in his eyes as his fear rips him from within. Because if his hunch is right—if the man who claimed him from that trunk is the same murderous monster who's been plaguing his dreams—then this right here, is where Dylan will die.

This dark and lonely abyss is the last place he will ever be. And he will most likely leave it in pieces.

Unless he can escape before it's too late. And that means he can't wait to regain his full strength.

He rises to his feet, but still reeling from the drug in his system, staggers to his side and hits the wall.

There is a soft rustling sound.

He glides his arm along the wall, listening to the swish and crackle of the papers pasted onto it.

And his wrist bumps against a small, bulky object, which a quick feel reveals to be a battery-powered light-switch. Its cord seems to be stapled to the wall, running up towards the ceiling.

It's looking like his cage is much more civilized that he'd initially thought.

He tightens his grip around the switch and stares into the void, imagining all the horrors that could be awaiting him. Horrors the likes of which he has not only seen, but endured time and time again through his Proxies. Except, in *this* realm—*his* realm—there's no waking up from death.

He swallows the painful pill in his throat, raises his chin, and flicks the switch on.

A blinding rectangle of light frames the ceiling.

Dylan squints, his eyes stung by the bleach-white glare of LED lights. And his very first instinct is that he's inside an industrial storage unit.

At the far end of the rectangular space, black sand bags are stacked up against the wall. But aside from those—and give or take a few crates scattered along the periphery—the room is more or less empty.

But in contrast to the room itself, the walls are as burdened as can be. The rustling sheets of paper that Dylan felt earlier belong to an enormous panorama: a rich collage consisting of maps, charts, newspaper clippings, photographs, color-coded notes, and much more.

The volume of information is staggering. But even more astonishing is how with just one glance, Dylan can tell just how intricately-connected everything is.

On the wall to his right, a large map of Vancouver beckons his focus, and he turns to face it.

But it isn't the map itself that he finds fascinating.

Splayed over it, there are three colorful networks of thread—red, black, and blue—vaguely resembling spider webs.

The red network—the largest, and by far the most elaborate of all three—is speaking to him in a way he can't quite articulate.

So much red. Pins and thread. A beautiful web of connections so labyrinthine that it takes a moment for Dylan to realize what it actually represents:

Him.

The network is a visual representation of not only anchors like his apartment and Galen's office, but of countless other random locations that he has visited over the years.

Someone has been watching him for a *very* long time. Not just *watching*, but tracking his every move!

His thoughts come to a screeching halt, and then all Dylan can think of are the mysterious shoeprints he discovered in his apartment.

The urge to simultaneously laugh and cry is rising up in him. He knew it. He just *knew* it wasn't all in his head! Alex was convinced it was just paranoia—that Dylan's crippling fear of his nightmares was slowly driving him mad. But after years of trying to explain to Alex the nature of his nightmares and the severity of his pain, Dylan finally stands witness to proof.

And it doesn't even matter if anyone believes him. Because now he knows the torment he has suffered his whole life was not a sickness in him.

It was real.

He flings his focus onto the other two networks. The smallest, and by far the least sparse network, is the one in blue thread.

It takes Dylan little time—taking note of Romer's workshop and the British Columbia Penitentiary—to realize who it belongs to.

Dylan cranes his neck back. He has barely been in touch with Romer since he returned from New York. So why on earth would the Reaper care to keep tabs on *Romer*'s whereabouts?

At a total loss, Dylan diverts his attention to the black network, and his gaze is immediately drawn to the pin from which nearly all the threads stem:

Neve's apartment...

Dylan backs away from the wall and looks at all three networks in unison. Neve's and Romer's barely overlap. There *is* a spot in Gastown close to Romer's workshop, but that's it.

And that makes Dylan's red network the common denominator amongst all three.

Dylan starts to feel sick to his stomach, his short-lived bout of vindication, eradicated.

He stares at the way the red network bleeds into the black and the blue. And he can't shed the feeling that he is the one responsible for putting Neve and Romer in the Reaper's crosshairs.

He starts to pace the perimeter, scanning the wall for more clues. It's beginning to seem that practically everything knowable about them is *somewhere* on these walls—info as broad as school transcripts, and as invasive as genetic profiling.

But why such an astounding investment?

He comes to a section on the wall that's riddled with data, charts, research summaries, and complex mathematical formulas.

He scans the sea of letters, numbers, and symbols, failing to understand any of it. And then, from within one of the summary paragraphs, the world 'suicide' leaps out at him.

His heart skips a beat, and then he's just reading, his eyes darting from left to right, all the way down the paragraph at hand.

The rage swelling up inside is making him shake.

His focus wanes, and then he is staring at nothing, wondering how Alex could betray him like this.

Because how else could—whoever the *FUCK* has put this room together—know about all the things Dylan told Alex when he confided in him in therapy? How could *anyone* know about the degrading details of Dylan's disturbing nightmares unless Alex hadn't divulged them!? Or know about Dylan's guilt over his mother's death, the shame of feeling like a burden on *everyone* around him, and even about the numerous times he begged Alex to put him out of his misery..?

Alex *betrayed* him. Day after day, as Dylan poured out his heart and soul, Alex kept on insisting that his nightmares are just fabrications of his own troubled mind. That his premonitions are nothing more than coincidences.

And not *once* did he mention the Fray Theory.

Why would he do this? Why would he spend years soaking up Dylan's words like a sponge, but offer no insight in return? Why withhold the theories from his own godson, but readily hand them over in a neat little package to a girl he's *just* met!?

His face goes slack, realizing he has no idea what happened to Neve after his arrest. For all he knows, they could've taken her as well.

With a pang of anxiety wringing his core, he looks to the network in black.

He skims over Neve's anchors, most of which are within walking distance of her studio apartment. But further south—next to Mountain View Cemetery, a hand-written note is pinned onto the map.

Dylan leans in and reads:

> *The Anvil's frightened reaction to sinking into the mound shows a lack of understanding of her condition.*
>
> *Her Merging appears to be triggered and propagated by extreme duress, which as of yet she is incapable of consciously controlling.*
>
> *The Kinetic's poorly-executed influence on the tombstones is indicative of the same. If not for his determination, he would've likely failed at uprooting the Anvil.*

Anvil. Kinetic.

Good, Dylan nods to himself. *We're finally getting somewhere.*

His gaze lands on the report pinned directly next to the note he just read.

He flips up the pages one by one, skimming over the unimaginably complex mathematical calculations he'd never be able to understand in a million years.

Over formulas not only packed with highly advanced symbols, but some that are over a page long!

Formulas which seem to account for—

Teleportation!?

And just like that, the broken links between his fragmented thoughts are mended, and for what feels like the first time in his life, he can see clearly.

It's all beginning to make sense: Dylan's relentless feeling of being shadowed. The mysterious prints he found in his apartment. Even the means by which he was brought here—to a room with every inch of its walls covered.

A room with no apparent doors or windows.

But it can't be possible, can it? Teleportation is far too big a leap for mankind to even come close to, no matter how elaborate these formulas may seem. But at the same time, dismissing what's right before him would mean denying what he's felt deep in his bones practically his entire life.

He reads on:

> *Teleportation (also known as Glitching), is conceptually simple. Instead of walking from A to B, a Glitch takes a shortcut.*
>
> *He Syncs with a Proxy in another dimension who's already at point B.*
>
> *This temporary fusion makes him vanish, but once the bond is broken, he reappears in*

his own dimension at point B, thus completing the jump.

Jesus... Dylan skims over the remainder of the text until he arrives at a section titled: ANVIL.

Material Syncing (also known as Merging), is the rarest form of Syncing known to man.

It is a temporary fusion with one's Proxies, resulting in an immediate increase in body density.

But this overlap can only occur with Proxies who are at the exact same spatial coordinates as the Primary who initiated the connection.

Since Merging occurs at a molecular level, it initially confuses the electrical flow of the nervous system, causing numbness. As things progress, the buildup of electricity leads to rapid firing of nerve endings, causing the same prickly sensation as a limb falling asleep.

Once the Merge is complete, the rapid firing ceases, and the temporary morph (a.k.a. Anvil) is linked—physically and psychologically—to all dimensions in question.

Dylan exhales a trembling breath and looks to the hand-written note about Neve and Romer.

The cemetery. The mound would've been freshly-poured and soft. If Neve is an Anvil, and if she was in

Sync with enough of her Proxies, she would've been dense enough—*heavy* enough—*Jesus Christ.*

He backs away from the wall, fingers raking into his thick hair. Through cross-dimensional Syncing, the laws of physics can be bent.

Even broken.

Bewildered, he makes his way around the room. And he sees and reads and marvels at what feels like decades' worth of research on the science of Syncing. Science that is further reinforced with Neve, Romer, and himself acting as prime examples.

But why them? Why *only* them? They can't be the only people in the world who are capable of Syncing.

What's more, if Neve's ability is the rarest of them all, then how come most of the research in this room is concerned with *him*? And if they've all been under surveillance for this long, how come they are being apprehended *now*?

Dylan huffs a sharp, exasperated sigh. And then another, releasing the tension he's been bottling up.

It's too much. All of this is too much.

How is he supposed to deal with facts that have completely massacred his understanding of reality? With answers that have raised even more questions?

And how does Alex play into all of this?

Dylan takes another scan of the space, but not at the collage of intel.

He's looking for an escape.

Because even if he *was* brought here by a Glitch who has little use for a door, that doesn't mean this place doesn't have one.

He starts to feel around for indents or protrusions in the walls, working his way around the room. Upon arriving at the fourth wall, he leans forward onto the sand bags to check behind them.

Except, they aren't sand bags.

At the touch of rigor-mortised flesh, Dylan cringes and rips himself away, his mind racing back to the gunshots he heard when he was trapped inside that dark trunk.

Do these bodies belong to the cops who arrested him? Is this the work of the masked man who stuck him with a needle?

If so, then he couldn't possibly be the Reaper from his nightmares, can he?

Backing away from the bodies, Dylan brushes his hands over the rough texture of his jeans, desperate to wipe away the sense-memory of cold, dead flesh.

He looks around again, this time taking notice of the small crates scattered about.

He walks over and starts to dig into them, hoping to find something that can aid in his escape—keys, a weapon, a miracle?

Instead, he discovers a rather thin pillow, a worn blanket, a lamp, and several other personal items—basically little else besides the bare necessities one would require to sustain himself for a few days.

And then, beneath a collection of files and folders, Dylan catches a glimpse of something familiar.

His heart sinks.

No. He reaches in and pulls out Neve's sketchbook from under everything else, his pale face a portrait of terror.

This isn't an old keepsake. It's Neve's most recent sketchbook. He was flipping through it while she was in the shower just... *yesterday..?*

Feels like ages ago.

But how the hell did it wind up here? And why?

He flips through it at the speed of shuffling cards, the black and white sketches blurring into abstract shades of gray. And right before the blank pages take over, a familiar face jumps out at Dylan and he slams the sketchbook shut.

It was an illusion, he tells himself. Just an illusion, no doubt caused by the drug that's still lingering in his system. That must have been it. *An illusion*, he keeps on insisting until his mind starts to believe it.

But his trembling hands speak another truth.

He swallows and starts to flip backwards from the end cover, one page at a time, until he is faced with a frightfully realistic rendition of his worst nightmare.

He stares at the Reaper's feral eyes. At his sharp, sunken brows. At his squared hairline, and his dark hair flowing down past his shoulders.

He stares at the face of the man who has haunted him, hunted him, and hurt him for as long as he can remember. The man Dylan always *knew* exists, while desperately hoping that he doesn't.

A killer whose existence has now been validated by someone other than Dylan. And regardless of how Neve came to know the Reaper's face, and regardless of why she chose to draw him, Dylan is now certain of one thing:

He is going to die.

CHAPTER 28

RENDEZVOUS

Midnight was the plan. The *old* plan. In truth, Neve was not expecting Romer to actually show up. She had prepared herself for a long and lonesome wait, followed by inevitable disappointment.

Instead, barely an hour since she and Romer were split up at Galen's, his arrival at the gallery put all of Neve's doubts to rest.

Too bad their rendezvous was as brief as a blink.

Fully conscious of her surroundings, and skeptical of practically everyone, Neve follows Romer with a twenty-foot gap.

'*Keep your distance, but make sure we're always on the same block,*' was the last thing he instructed; far enough to avoid falling into the same trap, but close enough to run to each other's aid should something arise. So with half her focus on Romer, Neve zigzags through the congestion.

With twilight on the horizon, Gastown is as lively as ever. And Neve finds it ironic how the very thing she has always cherished about this neighborhood is precisely what's grating on her every nerve. The only thing keeping her from snapping at all the dawdlers blocking her way is not wanting to draw attention to herself.

Romer is now idling at the intersection up ahead, waiting for the pedestrian light. So Neve lingers by a small gift-shop, occupying herself with the colorful postcards on the rotating racks.

Every single one of her actions feels artificial. Can people tell? It doesn't matter. It's not the crowd she's putting on an act for, anyway.

She looks up just in time to meet Romer's gaze.

What is it? Danger? What are you trying to say?

Her flustered thoughts are immediately silenced when Romer winks at her over his shoulder, then resumes his walk across the street. And it isn't until the pedestrian light's countdown begins that Neve realizes she's falling behind.

σ

Neve follows Romer into the underground parking of the Vancouver Convention Center.

"Are you sure about this?" she whispers, trying to keep up with him. "I think we're still way too close to your workshop."

"Mmm hmm," Romer responds absentmindedly as they come to a stop next to a side-exit.

The door itself has no handle, but there is a digital lock on the wall right next to it.

Romer pulls a keycard from his wallet and holds it above the lock. He closes his eyes as though saying a prayer, then slides his card down through the slit.

The little beady light on the system goes from red to green, at the sight of which Romer's fists spring up in the air triumphantly.

With a satisfied grin, he swings the door open and holds it. "After you."

"Should I even ask?" Neve flashes him a skeptical smile and enters a sterile, white stairwell.

Snickering, "I *can't* believe it worked," he walks in after Neve and leads the way up the stairs.

"I'm guessing you used to work here?"

"Part-time security. Good money."

"When was this?" she asks.

"A *while* ago."

"They didn't ask for it back after you quit?" Neve indicates the keycard as Romer tucks it back into his wallet.

"I—" he clears his throat, "I didn't exactly quit."

Fired, Neve wonders? That sure would explain the shame registered on his face.

Romer starts to double his steps.

Did she press a button?

"Does it work on all the doors in this place?" Neve quickly asks with hopes of slowing him down.

"Only the building's circulation."

"Well then—where exactly are we going to hide?"

"The roof," Romer says rather proudly.

"Uh... Shouldn't we be looking for a dark hole to crawl into?"

"Oh, trust me, this is *perfect*," Romer stalls at the next landing and faces her. "We're literally *right* next to the seaplane terminal."

Neve stops halfway up the flight. *Why would that matter?*

"Vancouver Island is probably our best bet. We'd be separated by a big body of water," he resumes his climb up the next flight, "but we would still be close enough that—"

"What about Dylan?"

Romer's head peeks from behind the wall. "What about him?"

Neve's expression darkens. "You're joking, right?"

Squinting, Romer steps back down on the landing. "What did you *think* we were going to do?" he says as he leans against the wall and crosses his arms. "We have *no* idea where he is."

"Well—what happened to calling his dad?"

"We can call him from Vancouver Island."

With that remark, she finds herself at a complete loss for words. So she just stares, waiting for Romer to come to his senses. Or to burst into laughter over his tasteless joke.

Arms still crossed, Romer squares his shoulders.

"They were trying to *kill* us, Romer."

"I know. I was there."

Without uttering a sound, Neve starts to make her way back down the stairs.

"Where are you going!?" Romer squeaks, but Neve doesn't even acknowledge his question.

I can't believe him... I can NOT believe him!

And the pounding of Romer's footsteps becomes louder and louder, until—

"Hey, hang on!" he grabs Neve's arm and pins her in place. "I asked you where you're going."

"Let go," she says.

"Not until you tell me where you—"

"I don't *know*," she huffs, losing her patience.

"Exactly, which is why we need to—"

"They're going to *kill him*, Romer!"

"They're going to kill *you*!"

"Let me go, let—AH!" she screams as Romer pulls her over his shoulder and lifts her up.

"OW! *Jesus*," he winces and tightens his shoulders.

"Put me down, Romer," Neve demands as he turns and resumes his climb up the stairs. "ROMER!"

"By all means, throw a tantrum in the mix."

Draped over his shoulder, she starts to pound on his lower back. "Romer... RO—I *swear* to God!"

"There's more cushion south of the equator."

"ARGHHHH!" she tries to rise, but he clamps her back down.

"Could you grab the door, please?" he asks with a cheery voice, and then pushes through the exit with the bottom of Neve's shoes. "Thank you!"

"ROMER, I—" Neve's voice locks in her throat as they emerge onto the Convention Center's rooftop— onto a secluded green summit with the blue harbor draping beyond.

Neve's bewildered eyes glide over the lush carpet of grass, and she marvels at the thousands of daisies sprinkled onto it like powdered sugar.

She *knows* this place... The memory of her horrid nightmare is draping onto it like a sheer veil.

Romer lowers her down onto the slanted roof, but she can't rip her gaze from her surroundings.

Yet another one of her dreams has materialized.

What will happen next?

"You okay?" Romer's voice beckons her focus, but she just stares beyond him at the watermelon sky.

"Neve?"

"Do pink clouds rain blood?" Neve finds herself asking. As though the answer could undo the horror of being drenched in blood pouring from the sky. As if it could make her forget the steely voice of the man she's now come to fear with every fiber of her being.

"Okay, *what* are you talking about?" Romer asks.

Neve doesn't utter a word. *Why* is she here? How many stars would've had to align in order to bring her to this very spot? And at this exact moment?

"Hey," Romer reaches out, but she recoils at his touch. "Okay, now you're scaring me."

"I—"

Where does she even begin?

Concern taints Romer's expression. He sighs, and then sneaks a glance towards the seaplane terminal.

"We can't go," Neve says decidedly. "We can't just take off and leave him here."

"Neve—we do *not* have a choice. If we stay here they're going to find us, and then we won't be of any help to anyone."

"I just can't leave him," she shakes her head. "He got caught up in all of this because of me. If I wasn't dumb enough to take Galen's book—"

"Oh don't do that," Romer frowns.

"If you want to go, just go."

"And just leave you here?"

"Why not? You don't seem to have a problem with leaving *him* behind."

"They *have* him!" Romer cranes his neck forward. "What—you're just gonna walk into the lion's den?"

"I'll figure something out," she heads for the door, but Romer grabs her by the arms.

"Look—" he takes his intensity down a notch. "I get it, okay? I know you think you're doing the brave thing. The *right* thing. And I know you love him—"

"Don't talk down to me," Neve pushes off of him. "I'm not a child you need to handle."

He tightens his lips and exhales through his nose.

"And you don't know a thing about me."

"What I know—is that we're in the middle of a shit-storm. *Not* a fairytale. And you thinking this is one of those love conquers all situations—"

"Stop telling me how I feel, Romer!"

"I wouldn't have to if you had your goddamn head screwed on straight!"

"*ME*!? You're the one blowing hot and cold every five seconds, still hung up on some *bullshit* feud!"

A small twitch tugs at the corner of his mouth. He scoffs and looks away with a nonchalant smile, but the fury brewing inside him melts it right off.

"What's wrong?" Neve coaxes. "Don't like it when people tell you how it is?"

"You have *no* idea how it is," he glares.

"I may not know exactly what's going on, but it's obvious you've been just *waiting* for the day you'd get to stick it to him! You're so goddamn petty that you can't—"

"I lost EVERYTHING because of him!" an icy glow emanates from his eyes. "*EVERYTHING*! MY HOME! MY REPUTATION! MY *FUTURE*!"

Neve backs off against the heat of his rage, feeling like a hare at the mercy of a ravenous wolf.

She was not expecting such an explosive eruption.

"I'm sorry," she says.

"No you're not," his eyes narrow as he shakes his head. "You don't even know what sorry *is*."

"What the *hell* is it with you and apologies!?"

"Here's an idea: why don't you get your goddamn facts straight *before* you run your mouth off? Hmm?

Maybe that way, you wouldn't be apologizing every five seconds."

Neve clenches her jaw, her heart pounding.

"What?" Romer throws his chin up.

She'd say something. Fire back. But she can't even formulate a coherent thought.

"That's what I thought," he walks right past her.

Neve remains still, feeling utterly paralyzed.

This can't be it. Running can't be the only option.

But what else can they do? Just stay here and wait for a miracle while her nightmare keeps replaying in her mind?

She turns and looks at Romer down the slant. He's sitting at the southern brim of the rooftop, rubbing his shoulder.

And Neve realizes that the only thing keeping her back is her ego, so she swallows her pride and makes her way down towards him.

Romer turns his head slightly, letting Neve know he's aware of her approach. But even once she's sat down next to him, he doesn't acknowledge her.

So she just looks at him. *All of him.*

His leather jacket is badly scraped, his white shirt has a pink tint to it, and the loose strands of his hair are swaying in the wind like golden willow branches.

He looks completely haggard.

Neve looks back out into distance.

She follows the slender strings of headlights and brake lights flowing through the city's veins, seeking Dylan from amidst all possibility.

The first time she lost Dylan, it was like dropping a priceless jewel into the ocean. And no matter how hard she tried to swim into the depths, she couldn't reach him. She couldn't find him. So she just kept on treading water, waiting for north to find *her*.

"I really am sorry," she says softly. "I know it's not an excuse, but it's been a rough couple of weeks—"

"If you want me to feel sorry for you, you've got the wrong guy."

"I don't," she faces him. "I'm just so sick of feeling like a victim, you know? Of being the consequence of the things that *happen* to me."

"Yeah, well," Romer leans forward and rips off a long blade of grass, "sometimes you're dealt a hand you can't win."

Silence.

"What happened between you two?" Neve asks.

Romer looks up as if he's bursting at the seams. But instead of spilling what's eating away at him, he just stares at Neve like she's a complete stranger.

"Look," she starts, "I know you think it's none of my business. And maybe it isn't. But I feel like I'm walking on eggshells around you. *Both* of you. And given everything that's happened, I just don't think keeping each other in the dark is the best idea."

"It's not my secret to tell."

Neve's fingertips fly up to her pulsating temples. "I just don't get you," she shakes her head. "You're willing to hop on a plane and leave him behind, but God forbid you rat him out?"

Romer looks away, exhaling an exasperated sigh.

Neve stares for a moment, then rises to her feet and heads up the slope towards the rooftop exit.

"Neve—" he calls after her. "I'm not Dylan! I'm not going to chase after you!" A few more seconds pass. "NEVE! GET BACK HERE!"

And as though caught by an invisible lasso, Neve is suddenly yanked backwards by a powerful force.

Screaming, she crashes into Romer, and they both slide to the very edge of the roof.

"*OW*!" Romer groans and clutches his shoulder. "I really need a better handle on this shit."

Sprawled on her belly, Neve props herself onto her elbows. "The *hell* is your problem!?" she glares at Romer with equal parts awe and anger, then tries to slip out from under his legs.

Just as she goes to rise, Romer grabs and pulls her down, pinning her onto her back.

"Let me go!" she struggles, but he shifts his weight onto her. And then she can't even budge.

"God—you're *such* a drama queen," he chuckles.

"You think this is a joke!?"

"It's funny like a joke."

"So is a swift kick in the balls!"

Romer flinches at the sheer thought, and it's just enough for Neve to wriggle out from under him.

Covered in grass blades and tiny white petals, she rises to her feet and faces Romer, panting.

"Are you out of your mind?" Romer rises as well. His voice is stern, and all evidence of playfulness has vanished from his expression. "They will *find you*. Do you understand that? Do I need to remind you what happened at Galen's?"

Neve's shoulders slacken. He's right. But knowing something to be true does not make it any easier to accept.

"I don't care," she says with a tormented smile on her lips. "I'm a stupid girl, walking willingly into the lion's den. Are you happy? A stupid, irrational girl throwing her life away over some boy."

"Neve—" Romer takes a small step forward.

"Just let me go," she backs away. "Please? It's *my* mistake. No one will blame you for *my* mistake."

Romer's chest deflates, and through the crack in his tough exterior, she sees a vulnerability she never knew existed.

"Come here," Romer takes her arm and pulls her into a gentle embrace.

Neve rests her head onto his muscular chest, his heartbeat drowning her thoughts. His shirt is damp, its oaky fragrance making her feel lightheaded.

And then, even if for a moment, she feels peace.

From atop the green summit, Romer's gaze soars over the train tracks lining the harbor. And not too far in the distance, he fixates on the container cranes by the shipping docks.

Red, and absolutely ravishing in the sun's gleam.

The same cranes he and Dylan would stare at for hours from the roof of his workshop—drinking beer and talking about girls.

About her, he looks down at Neve, and then pulls her in even closer.

His gaze finds its way back to the cranes. To the pile of red steel he used to liken to his best friend's hair. A boy he loved like a brother. A boy he would have taken a bullet for.

Did take a bullet for. And Dylan just left him there to bleed to death, alone in the dark.

At the thought, Romer's silver scars begin to ache, his blood boiling with anger and resentment. And he stares at those cranes—at the ever-present symbol of the things he'll never be able to bury—wondering if he'll ever survive the chaos slowly killing him from within.

The color of rage. The color of war. Of love, lust, and passion. To think of all colors in the world, blood chose to be red.

CHAPTER 29

LIMBO

Neve rouses behind a clear window with the navy sky draping beyond. The night air is crisp and oxygenated, and aside from the gentle patter of raindrops and the occasional swoosh of cars in the distance, there is little else to be heard.

Neve shifts in place, and a few grass blades brush against her cheeks.

Confusion overcomes her. Is she outside?

It's definitely raining, judging by the clear bands of water running down the window pane. But then, how come she isn't getting wet?

She must still be half-dreaming, on the precipice of sleep and wakefulness. At that sweet spot, where fantasy and reality play tricks on one another.

She rubs her eyes, then follows the branches of running water upwards. But to her surprise, there seems to be no end to the window-pane. Instead, it curves and curves as Neve rolls onto her back, until she realizes she is lying beneath a water dome.

Are her eyes deceiving her?

She watches the patter of raindrops, and how the bands of running water branch out on the way down. How they cleave and coalesce, draping over the clear dome—*the invisible dome?*—like a crystalline mesh.

How?

She props herself up, and looks around.

The water dome is impeding her vision, but when she catches a glimpse of Romer sleeping behind her, it all comes rushing back: they're still on the rooftop of the Convention Center.

And Neve remembers how adamant Romer was to leave, but remained behind to keep her from doing something stupid. How they fought, no holds barred, and how it somehow helped them find their middle-ground.

Right here.

Neve glances up at the glistening mesh of water cascading around them.

He has got to see this, she thinks, then rolls onto her belly and pulls herself up to him.

She goes to nudge him awake, but hesitates at the sight of a faint glow enlivening his closed eyelids.

It's absolutely spellbinding.

Like a glacier reflecting the moonlight.

She takes another look up at the water dome, and realizes its apex is directly above Romer's head.

The glow... she looks down at him.

This is the same glow that radiated from his eyes when he exploded at her over Dylan. The same glow Neve witnessed when he was trying to pull her from Elliot's grave.

She remembers the toppled tombstones, and how each time Romer exerted himself, they inched closer and closer towards them, converging in. Even earlier today, when Neve was trying to leave, it was some invisible energy that pulled her back to Romer.

And then she recalls what Galen said, right before their session came to an abrupt end:

'In due time, those of us who indulge our minds will be able to transcend our physical limits.'

Telekinesis... She looks up at the crystalline dome, reminiscing over Galen's words, his sweet smile, and even sweeter coffee.

The thought of anything having happened to him is not only enraging, but terrifying. Because now that they've lost *The Fray Theory*, they need his guidance more than ever.

Without Galen, they're all on their own.

Neve looks back down at Romer and remembers his face in the dim light of the exhibition space—his back covered in sawdust from his fall off the ladder, and his wavy locks in disarray before he gathered them back into a half-pony.

That boy, despite his unparalleled sex-appeal, she would not have cared to see ever again. But *this* boy, sleeping right in front of her..?

He saved her life. *Twice.*

He refused to betray Dylan's trust, even in spite of his anger. And though he knew better, he still stayed behind so Neve wouldn't be alone in this.

Rough, hot-headed, honest, and kind.

He is *nothing* like Neve thought he would be, and it's starting to scare her.

She reaches up to pull a lock of his hair behind his ear, but the moment her fingertip glides against his earlobe, Romer's eyes flicker open.

And Neve finds herself incapable of looking away, utterly hypnotized by the silver magic radiating from his eyes.

And not a moment later, she is tasting his lips.

Neve's eyes snap shut as Romer grips the back of her neck, and pulls her into an even deeper kiss.

A flurry of warmth and nervous pleasure flows into her. The pressure of his lips is making her feel like she's melting into him.

A sweet ache, hot and moist.

And when Neve gasps for air, he gently slips his tongue into her mouth. The pleasure is so intense, it makes her entire body writhe.

Oh God. Oh my God. The world fades away and all that remains is euphoria. Rapture. The way their lips lock is as if they were made for each other.

She's utterly consumed by him.

Stifling a moan, Neve tries to break away, but he grabs the small of her back and pulls her even closer.

And no longer can she tell his heartbeat from her own.

With a hiss that sucks all the air from her mouth, their lips suddenly part.

Romer drops his head back down, nose crinkled, and eyes squeezed shut. And then, Neve can feel the patter of raindrops on her back.

"Are you okay?" she tries to pull off of him, but his hold of her back is firm and unyielding.

And when he opens his eyes again, he looks at her in a way she never thought he would. The way you're looked at—if you're lucky—only a handful of times in a lifetime.

His gaze drops onto Neve's lips, and with a sharp breath, he brings his head back up for another taste.

An inch shy of their mouths reuniting, Neve pulls back and licks her lips guiltily.

Romer's brows furrow as his gaze shifts between her eyes. He then lowers his head back down onto the grass, his hand sliding off the small of her back.

Holding her breath, Neve gathers herself and sits up, facing the other way.

While their lips were locked, it all made so much sense. But now when she looks around at the sodden rooftop, all she can think of is Dylan, and how she has no idea where he is.

Or how to find him.

She pulls her hair behind her ears. "Romer—"

"We don't need to talk about it."

Neve turns to face him, but he has already rolled onto his side, facing the other way.

She rummages through her mind for something to say, anything to fill the void, but nothing fits. So she turns to face her sleeping city as rain gently drizzles down, more felt than it is seen.

All of a sudden, Neve can't shake the feeling that something horrible is about to happen.

She scans the surrounding buildings, all of which are significantly taller than the Convention Center.

She and Romer may be off the streets, but they're still in full view of countless vantage points.

"You know, I'm not too sure we're safe up here."

A slight pause. "We've been safe enough," he says, his voice cold and detached.

"We could've just gotten lucky," Neve rises to her feet and rubs her arms in the chill of the night. "Just because we're off the streets, doesn't mean we have reduced visibility."

"Visibility from where?"

"From all the towers around us."

"These are all residential towers."

"What if one of the residents reports us? Thinking we're vandals, or something?"

Romer exhales a louder, huffier sigh. "Unless they want to arrest us for grazing, I think we'll be fine."

He's definitely mad.

Neve pulls her cardigan in and walks over to the edge of the roof. She gradually cranes her neck over the rim, and looks down to street level.

There are a handful of taxis parked below in front of Pacific Rim Hotel. And further down the block, a drunken couple is staggering along the sidewalk.

Nothing suspicious, as far as she can see.

"Well—" Neve backs away from the edge, "at least from up here we'd be able to see them coming. That is unless they—" she turns around to find Romer has vanished.

CHAPTER 30

THE GLITCH

Gone. There isn't a single trace of Romer. Neve looks to the rooftop's exit. Did he leave? He wouldn't. And even if he ran, he wouldn't be able to make it to the exit in the brief while Neve had her back to him.

And panic sets in.

"Romer?" Neve's wide eyes dart about the space, desperately hoping he's playing a prank on her. But there's nowhere for him to hide, even if he was.

"ROMER!?" she finds herself shouting, impervious to the consequences.

She races back up the slant to where they had just lain. To the flattened patch of grass, where it's still dry compared to the rest of the sodden rooftop.

"RO—" a sudden grip on her shoulder makes her choke on his name. And then, like flipping a switch, her surroundings shift: and she's elsewhere.

In the blink of an eye, she's gone from standing outside in the dark, to inside a light-filled room. In the span of a gasp, the fresh air has become stale.

Her eyes are stung by the brightness. Her head is spinning from the sudden shift in perspective.

Panicked, she swats the grip on her shoulder off and stumbles backwards onto the floor.

Squinting against the light, she backs away from her captor—from a man in dark clothes whose face is concealed behind a black mask. Just like the man who attacked her at Galen's.

Romer's groan gives him away.

Neve turns her head around to find him lying onto his belly, gripping the back of his neck.

The floor moans as the man in black takes a small step forward.

Neve swings her head in his direction. She then starts to back up, shielding Romer from the man who ripped them both out of space itself.

The stranger in black stops two feet shy of Neve, then suddenly swoops down.

Neve screams and recoils on instinct, but realizes the man dived down to dodge an attack from behind.

An attack from—

Neve's eyes widen, and she stares as Dylan strikes again at a speed too quick for her to even register.

The man in black easily neutralizes the attack, but Dylan launches another, and another, and another until there is a barrage of strikes and counterstrikes the likes of which Neve has never before seen—a hybrid of multiple styles of combat too advanced to even be real.

Neve stares at Dylan, struggling to recognize him. The boy battling before her has an arsenal of skills of unimaginable caliber. Tactics she would only expect of spies and assassins. Strikes so swift, they blur into the air, but powerful enough to crack a boulder.

But Dylan's opponent is no force to be reckoned with, either.

He waits for the right moment, and with one swift motion traps Dylan in a tight chokehold.

Dylan grips the man's arm, drops to his shins, and uses his weight to flip him over his shoulder. He rolls with the momentum and pins his opponent down, pulling his gun in the process. He cocks it and aims between the eyes, but suddenly drops to the floor as the man in black vanishes from right under him.

A few seconds drag by with nobody flinching. The silence stretches, swells, until it's too suffocating to stand.

Neve feels a hand on her upper back.

She swings her head around, and then unclenches when she realizes it's Romer.

They carefully rise to their feet, barely registering the details of the box they're in.

Neve looks at Dylan who is stiller than a statue.

She takes a step towards him, but the palm of his hand flies up and pins her in place.

He is staring at the floor: at the shoeprints of the man he had in his crosshairs not ten seconds ago.

"Get back—" Dylan orders, firm and commanding, at which point Romer pulls Neve back behind him.

With his eyes still glued to the shoeprints, Dylan slowly rises as well.

His eyes are unblinking. It's as if he's anticipating something. His intensity seems savage—like that of a prey *and* a predator.

He suddenly swings his arm around and begins to fire at the phantom spawned behind him at the far end of the room.

At the onslaught, Romer shoves Neve back against the wall and shields her with his body.

Neve closes her eyes and wraps her arms around Romer, her hands shielding his heart and the back of his head. And she jolts with every blaring blast of Dylan's gun, the echo of ricocheting bullets ringing in her ears.

Surviving this will be a miracle.

Standing between his enemy and the only people in the world he'd die for, Dylan fires with impeccable precision. But it's no use. His target keeps dodging his bullets by vanishing and reappearing elsewhere.

And if he keeps jumping out of harm's way, what is Dylan going to do once he has run out of bullets?

And the specter unwittingly reappears in the path of a stray bullet. His right shoulder jerks back, and his blood splatters all over the wall behind him.

Gotcha. Dylan aims at his head.

"WAIT!" the man's hand flies up, and when Dylan hesitates, he pulls off his mask.

Shocked. Relieved. Confused.

"You..." Dylan gawks at the last person on earth he'd expected to see. At the first face he saw after an eternity of agony. At the man who rescued him after five hours of suffocating in a dark coffin. The man who unearthed him from his early grave with three broken ribs and an irreparable spirit.

"I know you..." Neve's voice reaches Dylan's ears from behind. "You were at my exhibition."

What? Dylan frowns while holding the gaze of his wounded target. "I don't—" he involuntarily lowers his gun a bit. "Why are you here?"

"You know him?" Romer asks.

As though in a trance, Dylan nods microscopically. "Victor Young. He was the—" he hesitates, knowing neither Neve nor Romer knows a thing about what happened that night. "He was my drill sergeant back at the academy."

Dylan's gaze drops down to the shoeprints on the floor, and suddenly he is sick to his stomach.

Wide-eyed, he looks back up at Young.

"It was *you*," he nearly whispers. "Wasn't it?"

It's all making sense now: the clusters of trail-less shoeprints at his place... his memory loss right up to the moment he woke up at the academy's infirmary... "I never flew to New York, did I?"

"No." Young presses his mask down on his wound. "You didn't."

His response ignites the truth, and Dylan's doubts melt like candle-wax, filling the void inside him that no lie ever could.

And when he glances at Romer and sees the shock in his eyes, a part of him feels healed.

Vindicated.

"Explain this room," Dylan lifts his aim back onto Young's head, but he holds his ground, unfazed.

"You know me, Holt," Young says with unshakable conviction. "You *know* you can trust me."

"What exactly were you doing at my exhibition?" Neve's voice nears.

"The world doesn't revolve around you, princess," he replies without even looking at her.

Dylan cocks his gun.

Young's eyes narrow, his brows creasing. "Is this the thanks I get for protecting you?"

Protecting..? "What are you talking about?" Dylan asks, his wielding hand atremble.

"What do you *think* I'm talking about?"

"Say it," Dylan demands and watches Young's face darken. "I want to hear you say it."

Young closes his eyes. "Your worst nightmare."

Dylan's eyes dart over to Neve's sketchbook, and straight back to him. "Who is he?" his voice breaks. "What the *FUCK* does he want from me!?"

"Relax," Young assures. "He won't find you here."

"If you're just looking out for us—" Romer steps up, gripping Dylan's switchblade, "then why are your clothes identical to the guys that jumped us earlier?"

Dylan eyes Young's uniform.

Romer is right. The men who arrested him were wearing the exact same outfits.

Young tilts his head back, exposing his neck—a tell Dylan knows all too well: his patience is wearing thin.

"You're one of them, aren't you," Romer says, his inquiry, much more of a statement.

Young looks at him. "It's complicated."

"Simplify it for me."

He holds Romer's gaze as a condescending smile colors his stern expression. "I needed to get them off your tracks. So I infiltrated their organization."

"What organization?" Dylan asks.

Young hesitates for a moment, and then exhales a deep breath that deflates his chest. "Synchrony."

Synchrony..? The word bounces around in Dylan's skull. He isn't sure why, but it sounds like something he'd find in Alex's book: *Resonance... Synchrony...*

"If you're not with them," Romer's voice disrupts Dylan's train of thought, "then who the hell do you work for?"

Young diverts his gaze back to Dylan. "Come with me, and I'll explain everything."

Romer can't help but snicker. "How dumb do you think we are?"

"Well—you *are* rejecting my help without having the slightest clue as to what you're up against," he says. "Does that more or less answer your question?"

"Listen, asshole—" Romer takes a step forward.

"Romer—" Dylan shoots him a cautionary glance, but it's too late. All evidence of humanity has already drained from Young's face.

"On second thought—" Young drags his gaze back onto Dylan, "it might be fun to watch you be torn from limb to limb."

And with that, he vanishes into thin air.

CHAPTER 31

THE CAGE

Neve stares at the spot where Young had stood not a moment ago, as *'torn from limb to limb'* echoes in her mind. What did he mean by that? Is that the sort of thing this 'Synchrony' does to people? Or was Young referring to something else entirely?

She feels a grip on her arm and turns to Dylan as he pulls her into a firm embrace.

Neve's hands glide up his back and clasp onto his shoulders. And she nestles her chin in the hollow of his neck with eyes wide open.

Despite holding him in her arms, it still hasn't hit Neve that she's found him. That merely *minutes* ago, Dylan was a world away.

And now, the only thing between them is Neve's utter disbelief. She has *found* him...

"I was so worried," Dylan whispers in her ear.

Neve starts to well up, but she bats her eyes a few times to keep the tears from collecting. And then, through a thin veil of bitter-sweet sorrow, her focus closes in on a massive panorama spanning the entire room.

"Where are we?" Neve pulls out of Dylan's arms, her gaze glued to what reminds her of a detective's investigation wall.

"I'm guessing Young's hideout," Dylan says.

No, she thinks. *This is way more than that.*

Even with the networks of thread aside, patterns of all kinds keep jumping out at her, demanding to be deciphered—from layers of color-coded notes at the smallest scale, to giant aerial maps at the largest.

There is rhyme and reason to these walls, but not the sort that sheds light onto Young's intentions.

Is he a friend, or foe?

Are his claims fact, or fiction?

She doesn't know. The truth could fall practically anywhere along the full spectrum of possibilities.

"We need to get out of here," Romer's voice brings her back. "Like yesterday." He places his hand on a sheet of paper, and then forms a fist and pounds the same spot. "Is there like—a *door* to this place?" his gaze darts from wall to wall.

"Yeah..." Dylan responds with a bit of a lag.

"Where?" Neve asks.

"Behind the bodies."

"The *bodies*!?" Neve and Romer both exclaim.

Staring into space, Dylan nods.

"Are you alright?" Neve asks.

"I only checked the top one," Dylan looks up at the body bags. "It was one of the cops that arrested me."

"What happened?" Neve's brows crease.

"I woke up all tied up and gagged in their trunk."

"Are you serious!?" she gawks.

"How'd you get away?" Romer walks over.

"I think Young ambushed them. Shot 'em up."

"So he *did* save you?" Romer's eyes widen beneath his furrowing brows.

"I don't trust him, either," Dylan says to let Romer off the hook. "He probably thinks I don't remember, or that I didn't catch it, but right after he opened the trunk, he stuck me with a needle, and I passed out."

Needle..? Neve thinks back to the EMT and how he tried to do the exact same thing to her. "Did you see what color the drug was?" she asks.

Dylan mulls it over. "Light blue, I think?"

Neve looks to Romer with a knowing smile.

"Well, there you have it," he smiles back.

"What?" Dylan asks.

"We think we're probably dealing with some sort of crime syndicate," Romer says. "One with enough pull to influence law-enforcement, hospitals—"

"Synchrony?" Neve suggests, then turns to Dylan. "Do you think your sergeant was telling the truth?"

"I don't trust the prick," Romer says as he makes his way to the far end of the room. "Something was really off about him."

Dylan follows suit, and then the two of them start to un-stack the body bags.

Neve cringes at the sound of cold blood sloshing around inside the bags. Her mind rushes back to the man she killed in Galen's parking lot, remembering how his blood was leaking out the crack in his skull.

It takes everything she's got not to double over and throw up.

She rips her gaze away, and diverts her attention to the wall of intel. Might as well get some answers while they're still here.

Her eyes are initially drawn to a large network of red thread. A quick inspection, and she realizes it's a visual representation of Dylan's whereabouts.

No surprise there. Young has already admitted to keeping an eye out for Dylan.

So she shifts her focus onto the blue network.

This one's tricky. She doesn't recognize any of the locations marked down on this network. Except one: the Gastown gallery where she held her exhibition.

From there, she follows a short blue thread that terminates at an industrial building.

Romer's shop, she nods to herself. Where the men in black—the men from Synchrony—were waiting to grab him.

Compared to Dylan's network, Romer's is really lacking. But there *is* a rather long thread extending south, terminating at British Columbia Penitentiary.

Prison..?

Neve looks at Romer, trying her best to keep this revelation from painting him in a new light.

But she can't stop wondering about what he did.

Is *this* the secret he was keeping from her? Did he and Dylan both do something, and Romer somehow wound up with all the blame?

Suddenly, the sight of Romer handling corpses is unnerving. He just seems so unfazed by it. He almost looks like he's helping Dylan move his furniture.

Neve looks away, banishing her paranoia.

What she's seen of Romer should be enough proof of the kind of man he really is.

Before Neve takes her attention off the network, however, she notices a note pinned right next to the penitentiary. The scribbles on it look like arbitrary numbers at first, but she soon realizes they are dates corresponding to Romer's incarceration and release.

Three years... Which happen to coincide almost perfectly with Dylan's absence.

Neve backs away from the wall and stares at both networks simultaneously.

If she's right to assume that Dylan's disppearance and Romer's imprisonment are linked, then it's quite likely that Dylan's return had nothing to do with *her*.

After all, he was in New York, not the North Pole. He could have reached out to her.

If he really wanted to...

And suddenly, something else dawns on Neve—a glaring discrepancy she glossed over in the moment:

How is it that Dylan was teleported to New York without his knowledge? Wouldn't his dad have—

Holt, she remembers. Marcus Holt, the person she hates more than anyone else in the world happens to share the same blood as the boy she *loves* more than anyone else in the world?

How is that even possible!?

She stifles a bewildered laugh. It's incredible how her questions from nearly four years ago—questions she'd long abandoned—are now so serendipitously being answered.

That's why Dylan was so reluctant to introduce Neve to his father. Why he rarely ever spoke of him. And why whenever he did, he sounded like he was talking about a complete stranger.

But wait. Holt may have been a disengaged dad—*and a worldclass douche*—but what about Galen? As Dylan's godfather *and* psychiatrist, wouldn't he have been alarmed by Dylan's sudden disappearance?

Neve sinks into thought, trying to piece the puzzle together.

It makes sense that Galen would keep the theories from Dylan to shield him from the sting of the truth. It's likely that Dylan would've been even worse off if he knew his nightmares were actually happening.

But that still doesn't explain why Galen chose to confide in *her*.

And how does Young play into all this? He claims he's been watching them for their own good. But if not Synchrony, then who *does* he answer to?

Neve starts to walk along the perimeter, scanning the walls for more clues. She steps on something thin and looks down, recognizing her sketchbook almost instantly.

What is it doing *here*?

Did Young steal it from her apartment?

Bending down to grab it, she remembers her most recent drawing; her sketch of the mysterious specter that spawned at the head of Elli's grave, and then vanished into thin air.

Like Young.

But why would the man who's been plaguing her dreams want to make such a fleeting appearance?

And at a cemetery, of all places?

Neve thinks back to what Galen said about ghosts: that they are simply a glimpse of a living person in an alternate dimension—a glimpse you take through the eyes of your Proxy when you Resonate.

The more she thinks about it, the likelier it seems that he was nothing more than a vision. But that still doesn't tell her a thing about who he is, or why he's begun to infest her life.

"Everything okay?" Dylan's voice from the back of the room interrupts her train of thought.

Neve turns to him, but doesn't say a word.

Upon noticing the sketchbook in her hand, Dylan slowly rises.

He makes his way over to Neve, each step smaller than the last, until they're standing face to face.

"What?" Neve asks off the dread registered on his pale face. "What is it?"

"How do you know what he looks like?"

Neve stares for a few moments. And suddenly, her thoughts are retracing the horror Dylan revealed to her back at her apartment:

Strangled to death...

Doused in gasoline, and set on fire...

Blood jetting out a slit in his throat...

And she realizes Dylan's prophetic nighmares are not of freak accidents, but of murder.

Murder at the hands of—

Please say no. "Is this him?" she nearly whispers, terrified that her sketch is a rendition of not only *her* nightmares, but of *his* as well.

Dylan doesn't respond, but the terror in his eyes strikes to incinerate what little hope Neve had held onto. And suddenly, she's standing across him inside a burning house as cinder rains from the ceiling. As wild flames claw at their skin.

And they go up in smoke, with eyes wide open.

"Jesus—" Romer's reaction to the sketch pulls her out of her hellish nightmare.

"How do you know what he looks like?" Dylan asks again, his vocal cords tightly-strung.

Neve exhales a shaky breath. "He's the man I saw at the cemetery. Right before I started to sink."

To Sync, she thinks.

Resonance. Synchrony. Proxies.

The boys shift out of focus as Neve's gaze zigzags through the air.

If every possible world exists, then there are as many realities in which Dylan is murdered, as ones in which he isn't. So why assume that he's destined to meet his end at the hands of this Grim Reaper?

"Look—you're not alone," Romer places his hand on Dylan's shoulder, but promptly removes it before his gesture is misread as pity. "And it's not like Neve and I are *completely* useless."

"I don't want you guys involved," Dylan says.

"*Little* late for that," Romer chuckles.

"You can still get out before it's too late."

"Right," Romer crosses his arms and tilts his head back. "And *you* can't, because you're *destined* to die a horrible death at the hands of some fucker you don't even know," he nods slowly with the corners of his lips curled down. "Well... that's that," he squares his shoulders. "Let's just call it quits. That always works out for everyone," he says casually, but every single word out of his mouth is loaded with subtext.

And tainted with bitterness.

Neve looks at Dylan who's staring at Romer like a scolded child.

"Look—" she tries to break the tension, "the Fray Theory isn't about destiny. It's about choice. We all start at birth, our origin, and carve our path through life, one decision at a time—"

"The *hell* are you babbling about?" Romer frowns.

"Free will," Neve says and looks to Dylan. "What if your Proxies' deaths were all sparked by something specific? And all you have to do is avoid that same trigger in *this* dimension?"

"If the theories are true, Neve, that means there is no such thing as free will," Dylan says.

Her brows furrow. "Yes. There is. The existence of multiple dimensions means—"

"That everything is predetermined," Dylan cuts in. "I'm sorry, but free will and destiny can't coexist."

Neve feels a twinge inside her chest cavity. "No," she asserts, refusing to surrender to the same defeat. Refusing to accept the frightfully real possibility that soon, she will be burying him too.

"It's okay," Dylan shrugs.

"No... *NO*, don't give me that defeatist bullshit!"

"Neve—"

"Just because everything that *can* happen *does* happen, doesn't mean your fate is set in stone! It just means there are *so* many variations out there, that eventually *every* possibility will play out."

Dylan's lips part slightly.

"But *your* reality, in *your* dimension will always depend on *your* actions. And that's *free will*."

Dylan stares, softening a bit.

"In a universe, there's only *one* you, and *one* path for you to take," she continues with milder intensity. "Either it's predetermined, *or* you choose it one step at a time. But we don't live in a universe. We *never have.* And that means we're not stuck with an either-or scenario."

"The existence of every reality is destiny," Romer mutters to himself, "and *which* one gets to be *your* reality... that's free will."

"And how do you know one of these realities isn't already assigned to me?" Dylan challenges.

"Because you're *choosing* to stand here," she says. "*Choosing* to argue with me over being powerless. Because you're not a goddamn puppet on strings!"

"Okay—alright," he raises his hands.

Romer turns away and walks to the corner of the room. Neve takes a few moments to calm her nerves, and then looks up at Dylan who's staring soullessly at the sketchbook in her hand.

"Dylan—" she drops it to the floor. "I'm not saying you *have* to agree with me," she swallows the pill in her throat, "but I can't fight your battle without you."

"Okay," Dylan blinks a slow blink, and then nods with a somber smile.

"Okay."

CHAPTER 32

INQUIRY

Once Dylan and Romer have dragged the final body out of the way, Neve begins to carefully take off the content pasted onto the wall. Content she is unlikely to have time to read, but can't bring herself to rip off—content containing information that could very well help them out of this mess.

"Where are the handles?" Romer asks.

Neve traces along the base of the doors until she finds the gap between them. She then starts to clear her way up to where the door's handles would be.

Dylan joins in, but it soon becomes evident that these doors don't even have handles.

"The *hell*?" Romer starts massaging his shoulder.

"Hmm," Dylan leans his weight onto the doors and pushes hard, but they just shudder in place. A couple of more forceful shoves, and he withdraws and kicks the unyielding barrier.

"Probably locked from the other side," Neve says.

"Shit." Romer rests his hands on his hips, licking his lower lip. "That fucker left us here to rot."

Neve looks to Dylan. "What do you think are the odds of Young coming back?"

"Wouldn't count on it," he says. "He's not exactly stable."

Romer scoffs. "Yeah, no shit."

Dylan looks to Young's blood spatter on the wall. "And he's been shot. I highly doubt we're his priority right now." He sits down and rests his back against the wall, sinking into thought.

And silence befalls them once again.

After mulling it over, "Yeah we are," Romer nods to himself. "I mean, would you look at this place? You don't put this much effort into something and then just drop it on a whim."

"He's been *shot*," Dylan repeats.

"In the *arm*," Romer says. "It's not exactly fatal."

Neve thinks back to the night of her exhibition. To when she bumped into Young, having no idea this seemingly harmless stranger would wind up playing such a monumental role in not only *her* life, but in Dylan's and Romer's as well.

"What exactly did you mean when you said Young is not stable?" Neve sits down also, facing Dylan.

Romer walks over and leans against the adjacent wall, completing the triangle.

"He's just—*unstable*, you know? One moment he is all smiles, joking around like he's your big brother. Next thing you know, you're on the ground, praying to God he won't beat the shit out of you if you can't give him the fiftieth push-up."

"How was he not fired?" Neve frowns.

"Well, two weeks into my transfer the guy before him just upped and quit out of nowhere. They hired Young like—the next day. Which was really lucky for me because—" he pauses, looking like someone who almost just drove off a cliff. "It was good timing," he drops his head and licks his lips. "We uh—we needed someone like him to whip us into shape."

"Even if he is a bipolar psycho?" Romer asks.

"Oh, don't get me wrong, we all *hated* his guts. His drills were impossible."

"But?" Neve asks off the light in Dylan's eyes, who puffs his cheeks as he exhales through a tight smirk.

"He really *was* something else, though. Built like a rock, and *easily* twice as strong as the next guy. And twice as fast. He's like a viper when he attacks you."

"Okay, explain something to me," Neve starts, "if Young was hired *after* you started at the academy, how did he already know who you are?"

Dylan's brows sink, his enthusiasm waning.

Is it because he's been pondering the same thing?

"I mean, how did he teleport you from Vancouver to New York without you even noticing? I almost had a heart attack when he brought *me* here."

Dylan lowers his gaze, and his eyes shift ever so slightly to his right. Towards Romer, who looks away just as Neve makes eye-contact with him.

And she now feels even more confused.

"What?" she asks, looking back and forth between the two boys.

Romer runs a hand through his hair. "Look, we've got way bigger things to worry about right now."

Neve returns her focus to Dylan, who's looking at Romer with a ghost of a smile.

"Look—" she levels, "I'm just trying to understand how your sergeant plays into all of this."

"I obviously don't know, Neve."

"What do you mean, you don't know?" she frowns. "You said: *I never flew to New York, did I?* And Young said, *no, you didn't.* So my question is: how has this never come up before? One day you just woke up in New York and didn't think twice about it?"

Dylan rubs his stubble out of frustration, exhaling into his hand.

"I'm not trying to interrogate you..." she says with less sting in her voice. "I'm just trying to understand what happened."

"I was obviously dealing with a lot of shit," Dylan meets Neve's gaze with a deep frown. "And my dad thought military school would fix everything. So then

Alex—" he pauses, staring into space as though he's forgotten what he was about to say.

Neve leans in, watching as his thoughts unfold.

"Alex said he enrolled me on my behalf," he says.

"What does *that* mean?" A baffled frown contorts her face. "I'm talking about the jump from Vancouver to New York."

When Dylan doesn't respond, she takes to Romer only to find him glaring at her.

'*Drop it,*' he mouths.

CHAPTER 33

TRIGGER

I t feels like forever since anyone uttered a word. And although Neve believes pressing Dylan for answers was perfectly justified, the memory of Romer's steely glare keeps cutting her afresh. It's just not fair. They can't keep covering up the line, and then snapping at her for stepping over it. And no matter what Neve says or does, she can't seem to get through to either of them.

This is Elliot all over again.

"They're trying to turn us into weapons," Dylan breaks the silence. "We can bend the rules. Do what normal people can't."

"I think you're reaching," says Romer.

Dylan tilts his head back against the wall, staring at the ceiling. "I thought it was pity," he mutters.

"What do you mean?" Neve asks.

"Young," he clarifies. "He took special interest in me—train me outside regular hours, teach me things he wouldn't teach the other cadets..." He scoffs at his own naiveté. "I think you might be right," he tilts his head towards Neve. "He must've known about me before we even met."

"How would he?" she asks.

Dylan tightens his lips, then lowers his head back down. "I only told Ro and Alex about my dreams."

Romer raises his brows and flattens his lips.

"So that just leaves Alex," Dylan turns to Neve.

"But why would he share something like that with a random military sergeant?" Neve asks.

"Why would he share it with a girl he's just met?" Dylan squares his shoulders.

And suddenly it feels like Neve is sitting under an interrogation lamp. But Dylan *is* right. She wondered the exact same thing about Galen's intentions.

"Just to be clear, Dylan, he *only* told me about the theories," Neve finds herself defending Galen. "I even tried bringing up your nightmares, but he wouldn't have it."

"Young can teleport, right?" Romer cuts in. "Even if Galen had everything locked up in a room, who's to say Young didn't just teleport through the wall and grab whatever he needs?"

Neve and Dylan consider it. That would certainly explain how Neve's sketchbook wound up here.

"I obviously don't know Galen as well as you do," Romer says to Dylan, "but I really doubt he sold you out. I mean—you should have seen his place. It was totally ransacked."

"Who do you think Young is doing all of this for?" Neve looks about the room. "This is way too big to be a one-man operation. He must answer to somebody."

"American military?" Romer suggests.

Dylan mulls it over, then squares his shoulders. "I honestly don't know."

Even more questions with no answers.

"What do you guys think about Synchrony?" Neve asks.

Romer scoffs and crosses his arms. "I think they rake the streets for people like us, grab them when no one's watching, and then erase all traces of them."

"Do you think they want us dead?" Neve asks. "Or do you think it's like a bidding war?"

Romer squints. "Like two rival organizations that are trying to weaponize people like us?"

"Young admitted to infiltrating Synchrony," Dylan says. "Maybe it wasn't to jeopardize their operations. Maybe he was trying to take advantage of their intel in order to get to us first."

"So, you don't believe they want us dead?" Romer asks of Dylan. "Is it because they were shooting at us with darts, not bullets?"

"That doesn't mean anything," Dylan says. "It may have just been to avoid spilling blood where it's hard to clean up."

"But why *kill* us?" she asks. "Based on everything Galen said, Resonance is just the next stage in human evolution."

"Makes sense if you think about it," Dylan says. "If everyone could teleport into banks, or kill someone and disappear into thin air, there'd be anarchy. The whole system would collapse."

σ

Neve sits on an inverted crate in the corner of the room, watching Romer and Dylan repeatedly thrust themselves against the doors.

Bang, after bang, after bang, with nothing to show for it but the echo of their defeat.

Bang! "It's not working!" Neve snaps. "You're just wearing yourselves out!"

Dylan takes a few steps back and wipes the sweat from his brow. "We're not hitting you," he pants.

"It will WORK, come *ON*!" she springs to her feet. "What are you waiting for? For us to run out of air?"

"We're *not* hitting you, Neve," Dylan presses. "Just keep looking."

"These are all observational data," Neve says, "not superpower instruction manuals."

"Read that report again," Dylan suggests, "the one I showed you about Merging."

Neve strides over and holds Young's hand-written note right up to Dylan's face.

"Her Syncing is triggered by extreme duress," she paraphrases.

Dylan snatches the note out of her hand. "For you to be put under duress, you need to be exposed to *real* danger."

"*Romer*!?" Neve looks to him.

"I'm Switzerland," Romer backs up with his hands in the air.

"Look," Neve pulls up her shirt to show Dylan her stomach. Her formerly pink bruise is now purple and spanning across her entire abdomen. "You see this? I can handle it."

"What happened?" Dylan's eyes widen, emitting a soft, amber glow.

"The guy that jumped me at Galen's," she pulls her shirt back down. "He completely lost it when I fought him back and started punching me in the gut. *That's* when I started to Merge."

"Did you see his face?" Dylan's frown deepens.

"Just let it go. Okay? It's done."

"It's not done till I get my hands on him."

Neve's shoulders slacken as her intensity wanes. "He's dead, Dylan." *I crushed him to death.* "Now will you just hit me, *please*!?"

"I'll do it," Romer steps up and starts to crack his knuckles.

"You better be fucking kidding," Dylan warns.

"She's our only shot," Romer says. "She survived a crash, remember?" He forms a fist, but before he can throw it Dylan shifts in front of Neve and shoves him back against the wall.

His impact makes their metal cage quiver. And as the air soaks up the reverberations, Neve wonders if she has just triggered something she won't be able to contain.

Rustling sheets of paper fall to the floor as Romer pushes off the wall and starts to bridge the gap.

"Dylan," Neve rests her hand on his shoulder, but he doesn't even budge. "I'll be fine," she says, then jerks back as Romer's powerful punch knocks Dylan to the floor. "ROMER!"

Romer dives down and starts pounding on Dylan.

"What is the matter with you!? *STOP!*" Neve tries to pull Romer off, but he pushes her away.

Regaining her balance, Neve looks down at Dylan who's barely recoiled to shield himself from Romer's blows.

"Why aren't you fighting back!?"

"Three *YEARS!*" Romer hoists Dylan up and knees him in the gut. "Three FUCKING *YEARS!*"

Prison...

Neve's flesh starts to tighten at an unprecedented rate. Almost instantly, it feels like she's sinking into a sea of pins and needles, and she's too heavy to tread the excruciating waters.

She is at the verge of collapsing when her nervous system ceases fire, banishing all mental and sensory confusion. And then she is one with her Proxies.

Solid, and indestructible.

An ear-splitting squeak shakes up the space, and becomes worse and worse by the second. And Neve realizes that despite having surpassed the threshold of pain, her density is still rising, causing the metallic storage unit to deform under her weight.

"NEVE! THE DOORS!" Dylan shouts.

Neve snaps to attention and looks to the far end of the room. But taking a step towards it, the floor starts to fold under her foot with a deafening groan.

The entire space suddenly trembles violently, and the middle of the room dips down by a few feet.

Dylan and Romer lose their balance and slide to the center fold along with the bagged corpses.

Papers, photos and maps peel off the walls as all six planes deform, collapsing inwards. The room is crumpling like a box made of aluminum foil.

Neve is terrified. Her anxiety is exasperating her Merging. At this rate, the entire space will implode onto itself, crushing Dylan and Romer.

MOVE!

Neve explodes into a sprint towards the exit, each stomp denting the spot where her foot lands. Romer and Dylan take cover as she leaps over the entangled pile of dead and living bodies, and THRUSTS herself against the doors like a small wrecking ball.

Upon impact, whatever locking mechanism had secured the place rips off the back, and the deformed doors dislodge from their frames.

Neve's momentum propels her through the fresh air, and she plummets with an earth-shattering bang onto a cold, metal surface. An enormous dent forms where she lands, and then all she feels is the entire world atremble.

"NEVE!?" Dylan calls out from higher up.

Neve opens her eyes and looks up through heavy fog at a mountain of cargo containers stacked on top of one another.

The one Dylan is peeking out of is dark blue, and irreparably disfigured, thanks to her. The yellow one directly below is not in too good a shape either.

Neve pushes up into a heavy slouch and scans her surroundings.

She can't help but marvel at Young's genius. What a brilliant spot for him to lock up his abductees: an anonymous cargo container on a secluded industrial harbor. With his ability to jump through walls, he can come and go as he pleases without ever having to compromise the integrity of his cage.

"She alive!?" Romer's voice beckons her attention back up.

Even through the veil of sunken clouds, Neve can detect Dylan's wide grin as Romer triumphantly pats him on the back.

"That was a stupid stunt, you guys!" she yells, her irrepressible smile sweetening her tone.

"Hey—it worked!" Romer says gleefully.

Dylan gauges the drop and jumps down, landing a few feet shy of Neve.

"Well done," he reaches out with a big smile.

Neve squints at him with a tight smirk, and then takes his hand.

Dylan pulls her up, but overcompensating for her weight, she winds up slamming into him.

"Whoa, sorry—" he chuckles. "Guess you're back to normal."

Neve's gaze drops to the bruise on his lower lip, her smile vanishing. "Are you okay?"

Dylan smiles. "Let's get the hell out of here."

σ

The world below was more obscure, so they sought out the summit. They climbed the mountain of metal, and now stand atop the topmost container as the fog weaves through the gaps below.

Along the waking horizon, Vancouver is sprawled on a blanket of clouds, its glass towers soaring up to the sky like a crystal crown.

If only the three of them weren't gazing at this heavenly sight from a drifting purgatory. From atop a cargo ship so monstrously big, they can barely feel it moving.

"We're too far out," Romer says. "No way we can swim this distance back to shore."

"Think of what we'd be swimming back to," Neve says, her gaze glued to the streaks of pink breaking along the horizon.

"We need to dump those bodies," Dylan glances at the mangled container several levels below.

"I'm not doing Young's dirty work," Romer says.

"If we leave them, they're gonna rot," Dylan fires back, his patience wearing thin. "We don't know how long we're going to be stuck on this ship. We don't even know where we're headed."

Romer's gaze lingers on Dylan for a few moments, and then he looks back out at the view. "It *would* be better than being caught with them."

"Do you think Young planned this?" Neve asks.

Dylan exhales a heavy sigh. "I think it would make sense if this was his backup plan... in case we didn't trust him enough to go with him willingly."

"He hid us well, I'll give him that," Romer says.

Neve looks back out at her city, and all she sees is the landmine the three of them navigated through with sheer dumb luck.

Or *was* it luck?

They were a team of three against an unknown many. And yet somehow they managed to overcome all the obstacles without even knowing the rules?

No way.

None of this is random. It can't be. If anything, it's looking like everything that's happened, good or bad, has been instrumental to bringing the three of them to this very juncture. Almost as though someone has intentionally kept them apart, only to reunite them when the time is ripe.

But ripe for what?

She looks at the boys. At Dylan's bloody nails and Romer's bruised knuckles. At scars, and scars-in-the-making.

At a broken duo with a mending bond.

Immersed in this peaceful moment of uncertainty, she just can't bring herself to burden them with even more questions they won't be able to answer. So she stands by them and beholds her gleaming city... until it's become a spec on an endless spectrum.

CHAPTER 34

THE REAPER

The city is awakening to a gloomy morning. To dark and empty streets vanishing into ghostly fog. Today the sun's rays will not penetrate the threshold of sunken clouds. Today, all will be seen, heard, and felt through a gray filter of uncertainty.

On the green, secluded grounds of Mountain View Cemetery, a dark figure lurks within the silver mist. He's a svelte silhouette—young to the bone, but host to a weathered soul. A timeless art-piece, marred by neglect and consequence.

Beautiful, androgynous, and unimaginably lethal.

A chilled gust of wind tugs at his dangling tresses, its freshness stinging his face.

He pulls up the back of his loose-fitting charcoal sweater, reaches into the pocket of his black skinny jeans, and retrieves his pack of smokes.

He draws the last drag, and expertly throws it up to his mouth, catching it with his lips. And with the slightest flicker of his lashes, his pupils constrict to a pin-prick, and the tip of his slender cigarette ignites a passionate red.

He secures the cigarette between his long fingers and inhales the toxic fumes. His demeanor is so calm and collected, it demands to be seen.

His wild, piercing gaze slithers through the trees, searching for something, but the fog is so thick that it's impossible to see beyond fifty feet. So he closes his eyes and searches with his mind's eye, instead.

And as though he's just heard a whisper in his ear, he turns his head slightly, then sets off on a new path onto the dew-laden grass.

His brown locks brush onto his broad shoulders with each stride. And soon he finds himself standing before the mound of a newly-filled grave.

But something feels off.

All around, rectangles of fresh grass have recently been laid. But in contrast to this unnaturally ordered green quilt, the tombstones in the Reaper's vicinity are weathered. Their surfaces are grimy, and soot is caked inside their engravings.

Something big happened here, and it was quickly swept under the rug. And although he can't know for certain what this green carpet was meant to conceal, he *is* certain that it's got something to do with his vision of a tar-haired girl on her knees, wishing upon a dandelion. An anonymous girl whose pink, pillowy pout parted with awe, and whose big, brown eyes widened at the sight of him. A girl whose energy has become embedded within this very spot. Energy so dark and so irresistibly alluring, it seduced him from halfway across the world.

And now that his quest has brought him here, he is that much closer to finding her.

To demystifying her powers.

If only the fog wasn't proving so inconvenient.

In the near distance, a street light has painted the fog champagne-gold. With the faintest vibration, the Reaper vanishes and reappears atop the light-post.

From where he stands, twin rows of street lights run up the hill, punctuating the cool hues of early morning with their warm aura.

With his sights set on the summit, he Glitches from atop one light-post to another. He jumps from node to node all the way up the hill, until he has emerged from the ambiguity of the fog.

Standing atop the top-most post, he turns around and beholds a vibrant downtown slowly awakening to another ordinary day.

At the foot of this gleaming congestion, thick fog is laden like a blanket of snow. And in one spot, in particular, it is enlivened by the oscillation of pink and blue hues.

The Reaper pinpoints the tower sprouting from the colored fog, and his gaze soars all the way up to its rooftop. He gathers his focus, and in the blink of an eye, Glitches to his intended destination.

Six miles in a split-second.

He hops onto the rooftop ledge and stands at the brim. He leans forward and looks all the way down to street-level.

At his current altitude, the fog is still impeding his vision. But it's a nuisance he quickly dismisses when the remnants of a dark energy reach him from down below.

Energy not unlike what he felt at the cemetery.

He Glitches down to the heart of a barricade, a few feet shy of a wide, shallow crater.

He looks down the street at what appear to be a mangled vehicle, an idling tow truck, and multiple police vehicles.

Judging by the scarcity of onlookers, it must have been quite a while since the incident occurred—an incident which originated from the crater by his feet.

He walks down the shallow slope and stands dead center of the pit, where the girl from his vision had stood not too long ago.

But as he stands here, all he sees is an aftermath. A conclusion without a story.

And he is compelled to connect A to B.

His pupils constrict.

His irises radiate a golden gleam.

His heart starts to race, pumping an abundance of adrenaline through his system.

And then, faster than a thought, he's in Sync with thousands of his Proxies, his powerful mind linked to all the shared alternate realities.

He has become detached from time and space.

He is no longer just standing in a crater on a foggy morning. He is standing in gridlock during early rush hour. He is on a wet street with cars zooming by in the pouring rain. He is surrounded by half-a-dozen construction workers drilling into the pavement.

He is everywhere: experiencing multiple realities simultaneously.

He is every*when*: before the incident, after, and every snapshot in-between. Snapshots he intends on stitching into a cohesive whole.

A low, metallic groan shakes up the air.

The SUV starts to slide backward as though being pulled by invisible cables. In front of it, the scraped asphalt bows back down and reunites with the earth. Inch by inch, the damage to the road is being erased.

With his wild eyes aglow, he steps out of the way.

The approaching SUV passes by him, and once its front becomes flush with the crater's center, an ear-splitting screech devours the morning calm. The car uncrumples as the ripples in its snout expand like an accordion. As it stretches back to its original length, the engine and front bumper slide forward to where they used to be. Glass shards leap off the ground and swarm the windshield, snapping together like pieces of a glass puzzle—until the seams vanish, yielding a smooth and reflective surface.

The mended vehicle returns to its original spot by the sidewalk. But the Reaper's focus remains on the crater—on the spot where the mysterious girl from his vision altered her own destiny.

He begins to circle her, taking in the details of her face. Though her features are delicate, the conviction in her ruby eyes is unshakable. Simply looking at her rouses in him an excitement he has not felt in years.

He follows her line of sight upwards—up to a man suspended in the sky. To a powerful Kinetic who—in an attempt to save his own life—nearly took hers. To the panicked Kinetic screaming her name.

An insidious smile creeps onto his lips.

"Neve."

AMALGAM

With Synchrony and the Reaper on their trails, Neve, Dylan and Romer must devise an immediate survival strategy. But upon arriving at their destination, they quickly come to understand just how extensive their enemies' reach can be.

In an unexpected turn of events, escape brings them to a crossroad, and they find themselves faced with the ultimate dilemma: should they continue to evade the most powerful syndicate in the world? Or risk becoming pawns in pursuit of unimaginable power?

Letter to Readers

I am beyond grateful to have had the opportunity to share my very first novel with you! If you've enjoyed *The Fray Theory*, please take a few minutes to write a review on Goodreads and Amazon. Reviews are truly the *best* way to support a debut author, and I assure you that my Proxies and I will be forever grateful!

Have questions? Comments? Just want to say hello?

By going to *www.neloukeramati.com* and subscribing to my email list, you'll be amongst the very first to know about special promotions, be offered free ARCs of the upcoming books in the series, and be able to pose your questions and post your comments!
By subscribing, you'll also be automatically entered into my own personal giveaways where you can win autographed copies of *The Fray Theory*, and custom swag like bookmarks, postcards, and much more!

So join me on this exciting journey! And in advance, thank you so much for all your support!

Love,
Nelou

Author Bio

Nelou Keramati was born in Shiraz, the city of wine, poetry, art, and literature. At the age of twelve, her family moved to Vancouver, Canada, which she has since proudly called her home.

Following six years of studies in Biology, Cognitive Neuroscience, and Psychology, Nelou obtained her Bachelor of Arts degree in Psychology from UBC—the University of British Columbia. Four years later, upon obtaining her Masters in Architecture, she once again switched gears and embarked on the pursuit of acting, art, and writing.

She has spent the last two+ years working tirelessly on her debut novel, *The Fray Theory*, and is beyond excited to finally share it with the whole world.

Official website: www.neloukeramati.com

Follow Nelou on:
Goodreads: www.goodreads.com/neloukeramati
Amazon: www.amazon.com/author/neloukeramati
Instagram: @neloukeramati
Twitter: @neloukeramati

Made in United States
Troutdale, OR
10/02/2023